House of the Missing

House of the Missing

by Martin Llewellyn

Published by
Stork Press Ltd
170 Lymington Avenue
London
N22 6JG

www.storkpress.co.uk

First Published 2014

Copyright © Martin Llewellyn, 2014

The moral right of the author has been asserted

These characters are fictional and any resemblance to any persons living or dead is entirely coincidental

All rights reserved

No part of this publication may be reproduced, stored in or introduced into a retrieval system, or transmitted, in any form or by any means (electronic, mechanical, photocopying, recording or otherwise), without the prior written permission of both the copyright owner and the publisher of this book

Text from the song 'Blood Red Bird', recorded by Smog, words by William Callahan, is used by permission of Rough Trade Publishing Ltd. The publishers would like to thank them for their permission

Paperback 978-0-9573912-7-7
ebook 978-0-9573912-8-4

Designed by Mark Stevens. Typesetting by Thomas Bohm, User design

Printed in the UK

For my family,
near and far.

> Forest, I fear you! In my ruined heart
> your roaring wakens the same agony as in cathedrals
> when the organ moans and from the depths
> I hear that I am damned.
>
> **'Obsession' – Baudelaire**

> I was not woken by the rooster
> Nor by the crow's tough song
> But the midnight cry of a blood red bird
>
> **'Blood Red Bird' – Smog**

> In the heart of every man lies a sleeping pig.
>
> **– Proverb**

Wandering Star	1
First Dream	13
Welcome	15
Second Dream	61
Expedition	63
Hosting	81
Evening	87
Signals	95
Third Dream	115
Oleander	117
Mandragora Officinarum	131
Nocturne	139
Wandering Stars	145
Fourth Dream	151
Territory	153
Crows	171
Before the Devil	183
Empire of Trees	197
Departure	207
The Walk in the Forest	213
Last Dream	223
Ultramarine	225
Kasper	231

Wandering Star

She walks slowly through the grass and over the roots, for how long she doesn't know, among the pillars of trees, through banks of blue flowers so thick they seem like waves of the sea. They are pretty but modest. She thinks they are trying to hide themselves, their heads always drooping, only occasionally does she see their bright yellow faces. The sun still shines and it's warm enough, hot even, but of the precarious warmth, she knows this means it's either the beginning of summer or its end. She is certain that these flowers only appear in the spring; she is certain. She is pleased to have this little certainty to hang on to, arrived at with faultless, empirical logic. It is the only thing she can explain. The leaves are impossibly numerous, so that she might be any one of them. She is indistinguishable from anyone else; even to herself she is a mystery. The questions are too many to list and they keep coming, as if she were in a school room, in front of the class – a class of faceless children, as so many leaves – and a teacher asking her to finish a problem of arithmetic on the board and she knows it but... but... it makes no sense. And as soon as she has sat down she can recall the answer; now she could demonstrate any problem of algebra she wanted to, but her name, her name is an unsolvable equation – unbalanced – where everything in her life is marked with a great black X.

She carries on walking and she enjoys walking at this pace, without aim, without time, or anything interfering with her simple steps. Directionless, she stops, the air sinking in her lungs. She carries on – in the same direction? No idea – a stick in her hand she uses to swish at the plants in the undergrowth, sprouting from the base of the trees, at nettles especially, they deserve it; she considers it an act of kindness to her fellow travellers. Wherever they may be. As lost as she is. Eventually the trees begin to fade out and not crowd around her so much, and for the first time today she can see the sky, vast and endless. Apart from three clouds, far away, hovering over the horizon, dark-blue and a bit yellowy against the bright-blue of the sky, so deep and clear it looks like a liquid, as if the trees are plunging into a great ocean. The three clouds, long and thin, parallel to each other, are a little family, scratches on the belly of the sky. She notices, with something like uneasiness, how quiet it is in the clearing, a circle of trees around her suddenly seem menacing, quite different to the security, their solidity, when you're walking underneath them, alongside them and watching the squirrels dart across them, the birds singing their territories from their branches. She wonders how far she has walked in these last few hours, since waking up under the tree, a tree she didn't recognise. The leaves are like needles, soft-hard; when she stands up her skin is reddened by little attacks from so many little pins. Her black cardigan, all dusty and frayed at the end of the sleeves, is now unappealing shades of grey and brown and, try as she might to remove all the dirt, there is no getting away from the fact that it needs to be washed. Perhaps there is a stream nearby? Her dress was white but now it is a kind of grey, and strangely there are small patches of black scorch marks here and there. Her socks, too, had clearly begun life as white and now, like her hands, they're smeared with dirt, and as she feels her face there is something hard on her temple, a scab, which at her touch falls off into the lap of her skirt, and she can feel the cold sting of her blood exposed to the air. Disgusted at the scab, she flings it away where it disappears into the stretch of grass, patched with gravel and dirt, branches and pine needles. Under her fingernails there is, it seems, some solid black resin that will never move, and she feels this is very bad, for some reason, but can't directly think why. There is nothing she can do about it now anyway, until she comes across a river, or it begins to rain. Then she will have to sit under a tree until it passes.

Picking some handfuls of grass, she rubs the little blades between her palms, which don't really help, and she succeeds only in adding some green stains to the black ones. She also rubs some on her shoes; black originally, they are now covered in the same dust and dirt as the rest of her; the laces don't have long left, she thinks. But laces are really the least of her problems. There is a dry rushing and a cracking noise and she looks around, her head darting to look all around her. She sees a squirrel almost directly in front of her. It is rust coloured, apart from its chest, which is a lighter cream colour. Holding an acorn, it stands on its hind legs and is looking at her so intently she thinks for a second it is going to start speaking and ask her what she's doing here in such a dirty state. It holds her in its gaze, its eyes two black bulbs in its head, and she notices for the first time how ugly squirrels are: big, ugly teeth and big blank eyes... Then it is gone, bounding across the floor of leaves like a dolphin's fin breaking the waves, and it disappears up a tree.

The squirrels continue their noise around her and she thinks how they always seem busy and never stop working, carrying their acorns around. What must it be like to eat an acorn? What must it be like to eat? She immediately wishes she hadn't thought this as it seems to trigger a contraction in her stomach, and she begins to worry that she might never meet someone to ask for food. This, in turn, sets off another wave, as she notices her pace quickening involuntarily. What...

what if she doesn't meet someone? Why has she been thinking that she will? Has she been deliberately trying not to think about meeting someone only to try and hide the possibility... and she can't hear it in her head or on her tongue, and the mere thought of the trees, this forest, lasting forever, slows her down, discouraged, and only seems to increase the squeezing of the walls round her hollow belly. The anxiety wells up in her mouth and she starts humming to fight against it, and it works. Almost miraculously she feels better. A melody, which she doesn't remember but knows somehow. She hopes it is like finding a path in among these trees – one which will lead her out to people, a town even. She finds herself thinking of stories where people like her, girls with dirty fingernails, no doubt, are lost in the woods, have strayed from their path – although she never had one to begin with – and end up being eaten by wolves or tricked and fattened up by witches.

The colours are growing deeper, more vivid somehow. The green in the leaves is starting to glow, as if they were illuminated from inside. And she falls into a trance of watching her feet move one in front of the other repetitively, hypnotically, crunching over the floor of the forest, twigs, pine cones, leaves, over the exposed intestines of roots.

Then, as she looks up, she sees there is a tree which has suffered some terrible fate. It appears to be carved from bone – it is white, split in two down its trunk. One part still struggles to look upwards; the other has lain down on the ground, full of cracks she sees as she clambers up on it, hands outstretched for balance. There are depressions and holes full of mud, and moss patchworks the surface where disgusting insects that make her shudder with their grotesque excess of limbs scuttle, dart suddenly across; they don't know where they are going either. She walks up the trunk to the deep hole in the middle and peers down into the trunk's evacuated core to see... blackness. It's deep and she wonders how far down into the earth it goes.

She quickly leaves the tree behind. A sudden feeling. A quick impulse. She runs, trying to outpace herself and to reach something, something other than trees. Perhaps she hopes this burst of energy will reveal something to her, where she's heading. But nothing, nothing and nothing but trees, and then the undergrowth starts to bite and jut out at her, impeding her and her energy seeps out from her through her shoes, through her hard breaths into the still, hot air; it's still so warm, as if the sun, so far away in the sky, has crept closer to the earth to come closer to the flowers who yearn for it. She stops for a second, determining which way looks the most promising, but now she grows frustrated with the trees; where before they seemed comforting, protecting sentinels leading her somewhere, now... now they have changed, they infuriatingly look skyward, ignoring her, the small and lonely girl nothing but a momentary, confused whisper, a breeze brushing past their tough, wrinkled hides. She does not know which is the more annoying – the endless journey or the lack of revelation. She tries harder and harder to think about her name, and then thinks about someone else calling her, but her mind still stays a white page, a blank map; only the faintest lines seem to emerge from the blinding whiteness, coalescing to form the outline of her own clothes and become knotted up in the black marks on them.

Waking up under the tree is the first thing she remembers. Maybe, she thinks, it has always been this way. She has always lived like this under the trees. One day at a time. Or maybe she has been abandoned. But she still cannot think about or remember her family. A foundling found by no one. Only the trees are here. Soon, though, they begin to thin out a bit; there is more of the sky to see, becoming a deeper blue, the trees greener too, as if they have all started glowing to rebel against the night, before the darkness extinguishes all colours.

She carries on walking, reluctant to leave behind the cheery-sounding splashing of the stream, but eventually it fades as the trees move in and muffle all the sound again. The ground becomes steep. She begins to run, but it's so steep that at one point she's scared by her own velocity as her legs reach the limit of their span, their speed, and just one false step will mean her tumbling headfirst down the slope.

Once at the foot of the bank, she hears flapping and the harsh croaks of crows; she sees two of them waltzing between branches, shaking them and angrily slamming into leaves and twigs as if they are about to kill each other. The trees begin to fade away again, she notices, showing more of the sky, which has become an even darker blue, even grey, and has bits of yellow cloud smeared across it.

Hovering and floating above the trees, some black shadows are moving. Smoke. She looks intently at this disintegrating blackness; she's stopped walking. She sees some white flashes and then dark red flashes, and she looks again at the smoke to see the blackness and looks around, confused, to see where these other colours come from. She feels nervous and cold now at the sight of that black smoke. *It is familiar.* The scorched patches on her clothes were made by smoke like that, she thinks, touching them, putting her fingers through the small holes, accidentally ripping one of them, making it bigger. The column of smoke drifts lazily upwards, dispersing. It is not even a column, she thinks, more like patches of cloud that soon join the real clouds in the turquoise sky. It is becoming dark quickly. The night is eager to take over, and despite her uneasiness about the strange familiarity of the smoke, she starts walking more quickly towards it; it is at least something to do, something of an adventure. She is disappointed with her memory. She had thought it would make everything clear, answer all the questions with answers so simple she would wonder how she could ever have forgotten them. Instead it makes everything uncertain and makes her worry; everything is even more unfamiliar and unsettling now than it had been before. The light visible through the trees no longer leads into a distance but fades quickly into the darkness and shadows cast by the trees; under the trees they even blot out the sky, the sky itself losing its way in the darkness. Because the light has become cloudy and the trees conspire to ally themselves with the darkness, she thinks she has missed the source of the smoke, walked past it or simply walked in the wrong direction. She can think of nothing better to do than carry on walking this way; this way seems no worse or better than any of the other ways she could have chosen. The noises – birds crashing through branches or the sudden rush of leaves and crack of a twig – seem closer now as if the creatures are beginning to take an interest in her, beginning to follow her. Through the trees there is a light – an orange glow, quickly there, and now it's gone – so she increases her speed, to keep herself from feeling the dead touch of the cold over her, and her speed allows her to distract herself from the uneasy feeling first unfurled when she saw the smoke. More than that, she is afraid of losing sight of where the light has come from and is already, with a sense of unease that is becoming the dominant condition of her new state, worried she has missed or otherwise lost the firelight. It appears again, a flickering orange blue this time, but only for a few seconds before it is extinguished by the cold blue mud of darkness, of shadows swelling from everywhere, like the tentacles of some unspeakable leviathan from a deep ocean; a monster formed by nothing but rum and rumour.

The trees have become fewer and fall back as she passes through them like a breeze, a little moving silhouette, a woodland creature in its new habitat. The light, even when allowed into a clearing, is failing; further over by the far line of trees – a black wall – there is a large shape, a house? Too small. She walks over to it unsteadily; the satisfaction of having found it evaporates quickly in the cold blue-grey light, lost. It is not a house, hut, barn; nothing is recognisable in this light. Shadows smother all clarity and objects throw out shadows as a disguise. Nothing is what it seems; everything wants to be nothing.

It is a plane but not a normal plane. It has crashed. Her heart shrinks – even this pilot was lost. She walks closer to the plane and then stops. There is someone in the plane. Looking at her. But they are not *seeing* her. Her hands jut upwards to her mouth and she starts holding her breath. For a while. Then exhales. She will not wake him; he will not hear. His head is shaped oddly and then she wonders, what if there are others, and her legs become shaky and she steps back to survey everything around her and make sure none of his co-pilots or navigators are crawling around the wreckage. She has waited forever – in a way it has been forever, she thinks – to meet someone, and now she wants nothing more than to remain alone, separate from this dead person – he died lost. She thinks about turning away, running, far past the clearing, until the morning and she feels the sun's gold breath on her face. And then she thinks, her hands falling down from her face, keeping her mouth warm until the sun comes back, how this would be leaving the dead man. An act of betrayal. After all, she is the only person who knows about him now. He is something of a friend to her, or at least he won't do her any harm. Despite his unpleasant face – she can only look at it for a second at a time – there is still a glint in one of his eyes and he seems to be looking at her, always in her direction. He looks like a soldier as he has some shiny buttons on his shoulders. His uniform – but she is drawn back to his face, horribly red even in the coolness of this light – his uniform is the same colour as this light, almost. His skin is red and black, and for the first time she notices the smell, and then something crackles blue and orange; the fire, the broken machine, sending out its distress signal. There is a smell too, of burning, sickly and oily. And she's the one who responded to it, except now she's annoyed with the pilot; why couldn't he have stayed alive – then they could have become friends and found a way out of the forest together. He seems to be smiling at her, his teeth visible as if he is pleased to have ended up this way. She steps back, uncertain where to look, as if she has intruded upon his private communion with death.

His plane is strange, painted strangely as if it is attempting to hide; black and dark-blue shapes blur its edges against the dark-green grass and dark-blue light. It is like it is pretending to be a fish, a drowned fish. One of its wings is broken, there is only half a wing – the one that is closest to her; the plane is leaning on it like an overbalancing old man would lean on his walking stick. The other part of it is lost somewhere. She looks around for it but can't see it. She walks around the plane, the dead pilot giving his silent permission; he is content to sit still. She looks up at the wing; the shredded metal and wood has entrenched itself in the grass, churning some of it up further back. There is a big black cross painted on the back of the plane, its corners growing into sharp points at each of its four extremes, a symbol of something beyond this forest, beyond these trees. It reminds her of the black marks on her clothes.

She wanders around the back of the plane, its tail in the air. The plane and the man inside both look exposed and cold, and as she walks back round to see the pilot from the other side, his skin looks different – blue and cold – and his smile has changed and his teeth have bitten through the skin of his cheek. His face is black and bloody, and she knows he's still looking at her, and it becomes too much to bear. The shiny parts of his uniform and the dirty straw colour of his hair are not reassuring and seem to have come from a museum – they don't seem real. Only his black, bright eyes and bloodied face seem real – too real – and she can't hold it and breaks away from his gaze, self-conscious, as anyone would be being stared at incessantly; she starts to run, any thought of betrayal as far away as the land from where the pilot started his journey. She runs in the opposite direction the plane came from and plunges back into the sheltering blackness of the trees, chilled suddenly, and she feels it; her skin chills at the horror of the thought that she is running in the direction, not away from the pilot's destination, but instead running towards his land.

It is not somewhere she wants to be. There would be no one there she would want to meet; she can't explain why but that doesn't make it any less true. And she has chosen this direction, and there is nothing to do now but stick to it, and the most important thing is to put as much distance between her and the dead pilot as quickly as possible. The thoughts snap out at her, as do the tree branches, that he has begun to stir, to shift slowly from his cockpit and stumble, crawl after her, blind but following her smell, her heat left lingering in the still night air, left behind on brushed-against leaves, burnishing the green leaf tips pink; a path for him to follow.

Then she stops. Breathless. The scorching agony in her lungs has sunk to her stomach and she sinks down, legs folding underneath her, to stop from feeling sick. She looks up at the trees, smiles and laughs suddenly, finding the reason for all this running ridiculous; her childish fear about the pilot was just that, the imagination of a child. Standing up, she feels better, proud at not being a child anymore – he, the pilot, he was old, he was a man, a soldier! He didn't make it out of this forest and he had a plane, maps, compass, chart. She was not dead – tired and hungry, but not dead, and she would not die alone, lost in this forest. Looking around, the darkness is not terrifying but it is... boring, not much to see.

She ambles along, hungry, tired. She wishes she hadn't thought of those things, because if she hadn't they might not have become true and they were now undeniable. She tries to think which of the two she was the more – tired... no, not really, the sprint away from the crashed plane had woken her up, but hungry, yes.

There's no getting away from that – all the running in the world would do no good. It is deeper than this forest, darker, more overwhelming than the night. It is silent too; it's not darkness but silence – that darkness within noise – suspended between these trees. That's what scares her now and she hums again, loudly, tunelessly, the image of the pilot's grinning, bloody teeth and black eyes coming closer to her mind, and she stumbles on, tired, so that even her legs feel like they are made of wood; they want to stay close to the earth, fall to the forest floor and sleep. Her head, too, feels heavy, and her neck has lost all its stiff uprightness; her head rolls around as if it is filled with water, though it is filled with liquid – blood – she thinks, thoughts of blood. How much blood is in a head, a body? How many bottles would she fill? And this colour bleeds its trail back to the pilot and she squeezes her eyes tight and stops walking and squeezes them tighter to keep him out. She opens them.

She leans against a tree and slides down to its roots. In the grey night light, the moon distant and pale, tired too, she sees a bird. It is called...? It is tired too, sleeping, its head laid against its breast, its wings folded against its side, and she is glad to have found someone else as sleepy as she is. Its feathers look so smooth, as if they are made of silk, and she wants to reach out and let her hand fall down its wings, but she is afraid she might wake it and then it would fly away and leave her alone. And her hand, almost against her will – that has fallen asleep too – reaches out and feels the surface of the feathers, trembling, and she withdraws it again. Quickly. It's cold. And it makes her feel cold, and she pulls her cardigan round her and her knees up. But she stays and she realises the bird's eyes are closed, and her tiredness before seems like a light yawn and a slow hum to the weight that comes over her now. She feels as if she is petrifying with tiredness – maybe that is how the bird feels. She looks at it and lies down on the cold grass, and she doesn't mind what happens to her in sleep; if she turns to wood that is fine, and even if the pilot treads his way through the bushes and over the roots of the trees to kiss her or eat her that is fine, because she will be as wood. Her tiredness is so heavy she feels she will turn black. Black, like trees, their leaves; the bird, the cold bird.

First Dream

I am on a ship, a small boat maybe. The water around is very dark so I don't think I am on a river. I think I am sailing across a vast ocean, an ocean so big people speak different languages on either shore; they don't even recognise each other when they land. I think we will be landing soon, and then all of a sudden there are planes overhead and I'm scared; black underbellies, and there's nowhere to hide on my boat, but my boat is disguised. There are several of them and they are making a giant 'V' in the sky and they soon disappear over the horizon. It is dark like the water and I try and peer into the depths but the water has a cold fur like it is the deep, dark roots of fire and then, unable to look anymore at the water, I look up and see stars, so many stars, and they are whirling around the sky, they are dancing. I hope I never land.

Welcome

The noise of the planes comes back. An explosion obliterates all sight and sound and she's awake in a bed. She jumps up and out, the room small and dark, and sees her shoes and clothes in a pile by the foot of the bed on a wooden trunk. Her breathing short and sharp, she bundles the clothes over herself, making her shiver slightly. She looks towards the window and realises there are shutters blocking out the light, and she opens the window, pulling the handle with a formless word of effort and pushes the shutter. She's blinded by the brilliant light from the sun. Scrambling to pull the shutter closed again, she feels the sun-roasted air, alive and thick, unlike the cold atmosphere in this room – whose room is it? She sinks back onto the bed, the weight of seeing too much. Why could she not remember what had happened last night, where did she fall asleep? She thinks it was a tree – a bird, fallen from its branch, bough broken – but she is certain she did not fall asleep here, here in this room. She feels the tears come from nowhere and her face, nose, eyes – *her skin* – becoming fluid, dripping; was this to be the rest of her life, this pattern of waking up somewhere different every morning with no memory of how she got there, how her life is being lived, in tears. At least, she thinks, she can remember yesterday, although it is hazy through her fatigue. She feels embarrassed, rubbing her face dry again – need to see clearly in this new room – dampening the sleeves of her cardigan. She looks around, realising now how quiet it is; she stands up and sees that it's quite plain, dark; it feels a bit damp, though this could just be the effect from the inferno outside. She looks at the wall behind her, the bed by the window, a little space, and sees someone looking at her. What feels like acid flashes up her veins and nervous system into her brain and bursts into her heart, before she sees it is herself. In a mirror. She assumes it is herself, who is she? That's her, standing there; foolishly a quick turnaround to check it is her and no other. It's as if she is meeting her brother or sister for the first time; there is a definite likeness but a strange unfamiliarity.

The other girl is thin, dirty but not short. How old is she? Fourteen? Fifteen? Sixteen? She can see the full extent to which her clothes have accumulated dirt and grass, a twig still hanging from the hem of her filthy white skirt. As if she is the Princess of the Forest. Instantly, in the mirror, they seem to have a different aspect; does she like these clothes? She certainly wishes she could be cleaner. And the dirt on her face – her face – is hers. She finds she cannot look at her face for long; those eyes are lost and empty, desperate; does she have to be so obvious in everything? A chorus of voices fall on her and they are whispering they're embarrassed and frustrated by this new girl, slightly contemptuous. The girl knows that she feels ashamed, yet refrains from forming the word in her mind in the presence of this other girl – this girl who has come from nowhere to suddenly impose her face, her body, her filthy clothes on her.

I was here first.

Once all the hard work has been done, here she is, wanting food, wanting a warm bath, wanting attention. And what is most infuriating is that the other girl simply stands there, looking through her, as if looking back in time. She doesn't have any answers. If anything, she has made her feel more alone, more helpless and more lost. She tears herself away from the girl's frame, too clear and too close to the other objects behind her: some books on shelves, a jug resting on a small white flower of lace. The low dark beams cut into the space of the room like low-hanging branches. Is she a prisoner here, like her mute twin in the glass, or can she leave any time she wants? She moves over to the door and sees there's no key in the lock and she opens the door which makes such a creaking noise that she realises there was no real need for a key given this door is as effective as any sentry. The floor creaks whenever she moves and she cannot mute her presence; on this side of the mirror every movement is accompanied by a noise. Even her own breathing seems to have the force of a hurricane. Her own heart thumps with such vigour and force she thinks it is a wonder the whole house does not reverberate to its rhythm.

The door opens smoothly and her breath whirls tightly trapped in her lungs as she's too something – anything, everything – to breathe, expecting… pilots? There is nothing but a dark corridor, doors either side. Light towards the end where the wall gives way to stairs, stairs down. She rushes down to avoid any grasping strangers from the doors, where she exhales, too noisily. There are voices downstairs: a woman's voice, talking fluidly, talking a lot, but about what she doesn't know, can't understand. Even the words in this place are strange to her. She hovers at the top of the stairs, uncertain whether to descend or not, waiting until she's spotted, but there is no end it seems to the woman's chatter, and then… she's spotted. The talking stops.

The woman, older, her hair, blonde, tied back under a headscarf, has lines scored into her face and her eyes are deep-blue and staring at her. She is smiling and says something in a way that seems directed to her but also to a man sitting at the table. They look friendly enough and the woman starts to beckon her down the stairs and points to a chair at the table. She then turns back to the stove and occupies herself in preparing some food and coffee. The girl hovers, still uncertain; walking down the stairs takes all her concentration – she feels she must make a good impression – and the man looks at her and says something like 'Rose godsz, dee-y-ed,' gesturing again to the chair, and so she sits down quickly. She wonders whether she has suffered some strange trauma in the night that has made her mute, mute and simple, unable to understand people anymore; she must be like an animal to them. Was that to be her fate, to be kept as their house animal?

She decides to speak to see if her language has changed.

'Hello. I'm very pleased to meet you,' she states, perhaps too boldly to the man, and extends her hand.

His gesture of lifting his coffee to his mouth freezes, and his eyes fix on her over the rim of his steaming mug. He puts it down and takes her hand and says: '*Prodz aszj shour beig ish warsm.*'

She feels relieved that at least she makes sense, and she gratefully drinks the hot coffee the woman puts down loudly with some grey – what, oats? She says thank you and the woman looks at her, lifting the briefest of smiles. What has happened during the night? What strange reversal has occurred where she's now even a stranger to language – how far has she wandered? He says something in a rough tone of voice, in their mysterious language, too quickly for her to gather any words from his mouth; haltingly, the strange way their mouths move as if clearing something from within their mouth, between their teeth. She grunts in response, or what sounds like a wordless exhalation; perhaps it is a word in this curious language, there is no way of knowing.

Neither the man nor the woman seem to want to carry on talking and seem more content to drink their coffee and potter by the stove respectively, and this casual disregard reassures her and she does likewise, settles back in her chair and churns the bowl of oats. She tries to be equally casual in her eating, but her hunger awakens at this first nudge and despite herself she's unable to stop herself wolfing it all down, scraping every last bit into her spoon, and, almost as soon as she's finished, feeling sick.

The man is looking at her, smiling, and, despite herself, she smiles back as it's the first time someone's smiled at her since possibly the first time in her life. For all she knows. Mortified, she feels herself blush under his gaze, this handsome man. He puts down his mug and puts his fingers to his mouth and then a bird starts singing. She looks around, her eyes swoon in their orbits, and then she laughs embarrassed at her own stupidity, her hands rushing to her mouth and she feels herself blush. The song is replicated by his mouth and his fingers somehow. It sounds just like the birds she heard yesterday, accompanying her first walk, her first day in this world. He must have walked in the forest a lot. Maybe that's how he ended up here, maybe everyone here was lost, here in this house of the missing.

The man sees something darken her face. Her hands fall from her mouth and look to the door, anxious to know where she has come from and where she is. Just like anyone, he chuckles to himself, especially these days. This inner laugh brings both the eyes of the girl to him as well as the beginning of another earful from his wife. He decides to ignore his wife by placidly agreeing to everything she says, sounding noises of acknowledgement every so often.

He stretches his hand out to the girl.

'Pleased to meet you,' he says.

She looks blank, remains mute. Eyes wide open.

He pushes his finger into the shirt of his chest; 'Jan', his name, she thinks, that must be his name.

'Jan,' she repeats.

'Good,' he replies, giving her a quick burst of birdsong as a reward. 'We speak French too in this part of the forest.'

Then the woman slams a wooden bowl down hard on the table, making the table shake and seemingly silencing even the birds outside.

'You haven't been listening to me? Have you?' He starts to protest and she ignores him, carrying on.

'What are we going to do with her?'

He says: 'Ach,' and looks at the girl, his face mock-terrified.

Even the girl understands this means he can't be bothered with these questions. His wife understands all too well and because this is a real problem and inconvenience – rather than his unwillingness to get down to the town and sell some furniture or animal carcasses – becomes more and more angry, determined to make him react.

'How should I know?'

'You seem to like her, treating her as if she were a dumb animal, impressing her with your stupid bird noises.'

The girl can tell by the tone that she is the subject of their discussion and it's unfavourable. She knows what to do and then, looking towards the door, sees the forest is inviting her back, the trees flicking their branches at her, beckoning her.

'She's not a pet for you.'

The sun is waiting for her. The birds will start their song again when she emerges; obviously, this is where this woman wants her to be. Out of her house.

'We don't have enough food for another one.'

Her fate is being decided, hanging in the balance, like a fruit sinking under its own weight of inexorable ripening from a branch; it is only a matter of time. To fall or to be caught. Now she has to decide when the best time to leave will be; it shouldn't be too soon as that would be impolite.

'What are you talking about? There is plenty for everyone. There is more than we can eat sometimes. It will just mean more work for you – as if you don't already give it all to the boy.'

She looks at him, talking almost absent-mindedly, only looking at her once he has finished talking to check she has been listening. She is fixed still in anger, her arms folded across her chest, underneath her breasts. Her eyes black and narrow, dark and angry. There is a bark of a word which drags her back from the unknown world beyond the door. The woman is looking at her, demandingly, and holding out some carrots. The man, whom she looks to for some guidance, motions her to go receive her vegetable-preparing duty.

The woman shouts: 'You! She should make herself useful. She looks like she'll be more use than our one anyway,' while her new kitchen-hand dutifully washes the carrots in a bowl beside the stove.

The man gets up from where he's sitting and walks over to the woman and holds her, despite her protests that she has to finish cleaning.

'Let me go, can't you see I'm busy?'

'She has to stay here, where else will she go? She can't go back outside, can she?'

His wife shakes herself free and looks at the child, still peeling.

'She has to stay. You know that as well as I do. It's not a coincidence I found her, nothing is coincidence these days.'

'Yes and maybe one day you will tell me, your wife, where exactly you go? You think I don't know? Why don't you tell me where you go? Birdwatching? You can hunt what we need in ten minutes but you are off for a day and a night. You think you own these woods, that you're their master, but you're nothing. You'll come to your end in those trees and I won't be able to mourn you.'

He takes an apple from the table and walks towards the door, moving towards the guns that rest, black and rigid, beside the door.

'If you don't want her here then you carry her out into the forest when she's asleep and you leave her there.'

He walks out the door, watched intently by the girl. The woman shouts something at him, that word again, his name – *Jan!* She has rushed to the door.

She carries on, desperate to please this woman who, she understands, holds her fate in her hands. And she wants very much to stay now. For a while at least. She can slot into this household if only the woman will let her – even if it is to be their servant.

As the morning progresses, the woman hands her more vegetables, more mimed instructions – never-ending chores. The woman spends the morning preparing food, cleaning the kitchen. Then when the girl's hands are raw with cold water and the peel of potatoes and some other vegetables she doesn't know the name of, never having seen them before, she is handed a cloth and commanded, through mime, to clean the stove and table. She has worked very hard, and on the stool in the corner of the kitchen, where she sits, vegetable knife gripped tight, she can see the door to the outside, through which the man had passed this morning. Her affection for him has only grown now that she has tried to recall the previous night, vexed, that the first night in this new life should be as mysterious and unknown as her previous existence. He had carried her here. Rescued her. Strange, she thinks, the forest had been empty but for dead pilots during the day but apparently teemed with Samaritan hunters at night.

She is impatient for him to return. The pressing anxiety she tries hard to disregard, but which tightens within her all the more, expresses itself in the trap-tight grip on her knife. That woman, so far, has not turned on her but she might. She doesn't want her here. After this cleaning task was completed, she would be shown the cellar that also needed cleaning and the door would slam shut behind her and she would be left alone to rot, soon too weak to fend off the rats gnawing her flesh. Or she would be shown the interior of the oven to clean – 'that's right girl, the grease all the way at the back' – that hot hungry maw, yearning for little lost girls to transform into tasty pies. Or to clean out the pigs, pigs too, which had developed a remembering for young flesh. Shoved into the mud she would be crushed by the bloated sow, then to be gashed open by the boar's hard, curved tusks. Looking at the table, so very clean it seems to her, she couldn't help giggle at her own nonsense – was she going to turn the very furniture of this house into a starving predator? A misplaced sense of her own importance, that everything here would be impatiently gasping for her to satiate its own endless needs.

The woman comes back and, inspecting her work, seems impressed in her own way.

Her level of expectation in the efforts of others is low. In general, she is ready to be disappointed, so that anything that exceeds these devalued standards she doesn't quite know how to react to; the corresponding depth of her expectations of others is also further depressed by the height of the sense of her own – unrecognised – efforts. Yet, here, in the little shabby foreign girl, is someone who apparently possesses a work ethic of sorts. She could test it. She would push it.

'Good.' Exaggerated nodding for the foreigner. Though no smiling yet. Now. What could she be sent to do? Eva has not been expecting this surplus of labour otherwise she would have been more prepared, made a list. She speaks LOUDLY – S-L-O-W-L-Y – and mimes, in her way, which consists mainly of 'shoo-ing' motions:

'Go outside now – go check on the hens.'

The girl has no idea what she is saying. In fact, for a second she is stunned with worry that maybe the woman wants to get rid of her. Yet she realises the words and the strange movements are more complex. She thinks of going outside and trying to guess then what she wants, but considers she would be angry if she came back in empty-handed, if, indeed, she is being asked to collect something. All she can think of to do is respond in an equally exaggerated manner – what? Instantly she realises she has been too brusque in her gesticulations; the shrug of the shoulder has been too much, the eyebrows raised too far.

'Impudent child,' is the response. 'You must be a deaf-mute, then, girl.' She grabs her roughly by the hand – picks up a small basket with the other – and leads her out to the small chicken coop. She points at the eggs, even picking one up, and fervently hopes the foreign girl – the maid, the guest? They would deal with that later – would understand. She is already sorting the chores in her head by the difficulty involved in explaining them to someone who doesn't speak their language. Possibly a deaf-mute. Possibly just stupid. Then she looks at the girl, in her dirty clothes, scuffed shoes and the uncomplaining zeal in sending the hens flying to retrieve their eggs, and she later remembers it was the clothes more than the girl's placid compliance that made her regret that last thought. She leaves the girl to gather the eggs and place them in the basket bedded with straw and walks back to the house and tries hard to think about having this girl around. They only have a boy. It would make a change. It would redress the balance with the man and the son she has always lived with in this house. And, the boy, where is he? Now there is someone whose idleness he did not inherit from her.

It is a few hours later; she and the girl sit down for lunch. A few hours after that he comes in. He creeps in the kitchen door, avoiding the front door, knowing his mother had wanted him in the house today, had things for him to do today. Eva hears the noises of welcome and then her son's graceless entry, banging into the doorframe. His movements have been awkward for several months now as if he were still a stranger to his gangly limbs, as if he were still figuring them out. He has been making the most of it these last few years, with the school closed down. His father's reluctance to have him along hunting and in the workshop means she has had to find ways to occupy him. She has to keep him close to home. But every day she thanks God he is still alive. So many boys his age are dead and gone or had gone and were now surely dead. Out here they are reasonably safe. Even the village has been largely unaffected. A few notices nailed to the door of the village hall announced the new regime. A new, foreign flag over the door of the police station. Formalising the conquest. A few convoys passing through every now and again. That was all; it wasn't much but still she had seen the mothers in the early days, in the square, with their husbands trying to calm them down. Their wails sounded inhuman, unnatural even, as if they had been possessed by devils. And she was scared by them, even if she had known their boys, if her own son had played with them, she was terrified by them, as if they themselves had become tainted and she felt ashamed. She could not look them in the eye – barely look at them at all. Just get on with it and ignore them, their now meaningless existence, their slow movements emptied of purpose, their faces emptied of love. She prayed for them but could not talk to them as Jan could with their husbands and she felt ashamed. She shakes her thoughts from her head as a dog shakes itself free of water. She sees him climbing exaggeratedly on the stairs – he still doesn't realise it is impossible to not be heard on the stairs – until he senses her eyes on him. He looks slowly round as if a rapid turn of the head would make too much noise. She looks at him, motioning with her finger to follow her to the kitchen. She tells him not to waste the day sleeping or playing with his father's guns out alone in the forest. She tells him there was someone else who – because his father had already made the decision – would be living with them.

'Go and see to her.'

She is there, still, in the coop. She has decided she hates chickens. Stupid sounds, lizard eyes and grotesque bubble bodies. She never realised, or, never would have thought, that in such proximity chickens could have such a stink about them. She has placed her own modest pyramid of eggs in the basket, but she doesn't know how long she is supposed to stay out here. The incessant cackling, the feathers that dart around her head, tickling her ears and nose, the mess – she's had enough. She climbs out of the coop, her hair everywhere, straw and feathers attached to her so that she feels like a poor attempt at a scarecrow, and then she sees him looking at her. Standing, eating an apple. The chickens seem to have noticed too and become equally self-conscious as they are quiet now, waiting. She cradles some eggs in the fold of her skirt, a feather still attached to her ear as if seeking a new home; he ate his bright-red apple languidly, noisily. The apple's juice sparks around his mouth, some flesh trickles across his lips and moistens his chin. She cannot tell how old he is but knows he is much younger than the man she met this morning. How old? Maybe a year or so older than her; maybe the same age, but he is taller than she is. He has a black cap, black waistcoat and black trousers and boots on, but his shirt is white. His clothes are quite clean in relation to hers. His skin is lighter than that of his parents – resembling his father more than his mother – but still seems thicker, browner than hers. It is as if the skin camouflages his real age, like a tree, the rough bark guarding the number of rings within. Her own state is no better, she remembers, looking down at herself, embarrassed at her own clothes; dirty they had been to begin with and now she is covered in the filth of poultry. She wishes he would stop looking at her or say something.

'So you were lost?' He had been told she is a stranger who doesn't understand their language. Nonetheless, he asks her anyway. To see what she will do.

She freezes. It's even more of a shock to hear this boy use her language and she's taken into his eyes, the mouth that has spoken to her, and her elbows unbend and her skirt slips and the dozen or so eggs plummet to earth exploding at her feet. She stands unbelieving for a second and there is nothing she can do. She hears him laugh, snort even on his red apple, but can't look at him. She feels the blood blushing her face. He walks over. Staring at the eggs.

'Mother won't be happy. About what you did.'

Staring downwards, some of the guts of the eggs have splattered her shoes, further discolouring the shoes that were once black.

'Then I'll say it was your fault.'

'She won't understand you. She doesn't speak French. Not really.'

'Why do you? Both of you can?' Then, forgetting about the eggs, she knows this boy can tell her everything about this new place.

'Can you tell me where I am?'

He replies quickly in the foreign language. A word that sounds made-up. Polska?

'Where's that?'

'Poland.'

She asks him a stream of questions, tumbling over one another, like children desperate to escape the classroom at the end of the day. She learns the names of her new guardians and she knows what year it is and then she comes to know about the war. The war that is consuming the world. The war that must have spat out the lost pilot, back there, as the bone in fish flesh is spat back out onto the plate. He was a German pilot. The final name she learns is his: Kasper. He talks quickly, Polish words filling in the gaps in the tide of French washing over her and that she listens to as if it is scripture. She looks from her shoes to his face and back again, trying to rub the drying egg paste from her shoes in the dust. She listens to his school French, surprisingly comprehensive. He waves his arms around a lot, his ungainly limbs, awkward yet endlessly moving as if the sun would stop shining, stop generating its heat, if he stopped, as if he would drop dead. She listens, bored now, by his litany of details confirming that the pilot must have been German. How he would have despatched him, if he had still been alive. He was a good shot and could break a rabbit's neck in one movement; how different could an animal be from a man? He looks up at her, the apple, long devoured, still grasped tight in his hand, rusted brown. And she realises she can smell the apple, smelling dark and brown, thick and rich. She doesn't know – doesn't care – and shrugs her shoulders. And she doesn't believe him anyway. He doesn't know how to shoot. If he did, he would have joined the army.

She moves to place the eggs carefully in the basket and then grasps it securely in front of her. Now there is something between them. She feels a little safer.

So she asks him: 'Why aren't you fighting in the war? Fighting the Germans?'

'There's no war anymore, not in Poland anyway. Everyone who's fought against the Germans has lost. It's because they've got the best tanks. I'm going to join the Resistance though. They use...' He falters at describing himself as a child, as anything less than a man, in front of this new, lost girl. This new, pretty, girl; different to all the other girls in the village with her tanned skin, dark-brown hair and brown eyes. Even though she is a mess and looks a bit strange. And looks at you strangely, intently. She is pretty. Is that why he can't stop talking, can't stop throwing his arms around, even standing on the tree stump that marks the centre of the backyard, his father having cut it down long ago to use its wood.

'They can't use adults for certain things though. That's why they need me.'

'What can you do?'

'Carry guns, explosives, food. Anything. Messages. They won't suspect me and I can run really fast.'

There is a shout from the house and she looks, almost desperately at him, wanting him to stay and talk to her. He starts to walk away, without hesitation. He stops momentarily to fling his apple away. A great arc of a movement as if the apple core were something cursed he cannot allow to be close to him. She watches him skip, stumble and drag his feet into the dark door of the house.

She's dizzy; the hens have started their stupid squawk and cackle again. She has to slow down her breathing, her mind intoxicated with new names – *Poland. Kasper.* Her tongue is waiting to say them and she says them out loud, one after the other. These words are her only anchors now, in this voyage without a beginning and who knows what destination? Is it here? How would she ever know? She doesn't know what to do, whether to go in or stay out here. This is the first time she has looked at the trees today and how different they look from yesterday; how tame and still they are. Yesterday, they were like waves against her, always moving, shifting, unsettling but exciting. They always revealed something new – a new path. A place to sleep, watched over. She gathers up the eggs, the few remaining, hoping that they would be enough to please the woman of this house. Before stepping back in, she looks back at the trees, rendered matte-green in the unsparing midday sun; simple, like old men standing about in a town square, talking quietly. Nothing to do but watch her enter the house. The eggs she carries in the basket, treading as if walking between sleeping guard dogs.

Once inside the cool kitchen she sees that the woman is in the middle of talking to him – to Kasper – slowly, impatiently. And the woman turns round to see her and she freezes in the beam of her gaze and feels ashamed of the amount of eggs she has in her lap. Eva doesn't look at her for long, she is too angry and incensed by the pathetic sum of eggs the girl has managed to accumulate. She turns away and brusquely motions to her to place the basket on the kitchen table. Once Kasper has gone, she motions again at her to sit down at the table. The girl does so. She looks at the woman, unsmiling, wondering how long she will be imprisoned by her commands, and she wishes Kasper or the other older man could have been here as they did not think her their servant, mutely motioning her about the kitchen and yard. She has her head slumped between her fists on the table, waiting for another order, a new chore. The woman pushes her elbows off the table, waving her finger in her face, and before she can respond there's some soup and bread and some thin slices of pink meat set down in front of her.

She is hungry enough to forget about everything else and starts on the soup, which tastes of beetroot, and she is glad it is not too hot. And then she feels happy and warm and cannot tell if it is the soup or the fact that Kasper has stumbled back into the kitchen and is now sitting down noisily and gracelessly at the table. He half-shouts something, his head half-turned to her, and the woman comes back with Kasper's lunch, smacking his cap off of his head, accompanied by a verbal admonishment. Kasper either doesn't care or is expecting this and has long grown accustomed to it and then he starts eating as awkwardly and gracelessly as he does everything else, a sheen over his skin. She can smell his smell, the sweat and the beetroot soup. It's not an unpleasant smell, she thinks, better than those horrible chickens anyway. Kasper eats noisily, drops spattering. She is fascinated by his eating, as if he is an animal that has learned to imitate human behaviour. He finishes eating long before she does and stares at her meat so intensely she feels compelled to offer him some, followed by some of her bread.

The woman sits down finally too, after bustling about at some tasks the girl cannot figure out. Her presence quietens Kasper, and she eats more slowly, more carefully. She feels the woman's big blue-grey, or green, eyes on her and is surprised how someone's gaze can unnerve her so, and how different it feels to either the man or Kasper's gaze. She can't think how or explain why.

The threadbare red and gold tablecloth has to be cleaned outside; that task falls to her, and Kasper does the washing up. The woman goes upstairs. She is soon finished and, not for the first time that day, doesn't know what to do with herself. She sits at the table, arms outstretched and head laid down on her shoulder, looking at the house sideways, flicking some crumbs around. She feels suddenly lethargic and unwilling, maybe, to let Kasper out of her sight in case he starts talking again. It is as if he has found part of her in the forest too – brought all her words back in a chest, like pirate gold. He doesn't seem to notice or care that her gaze is following him. She wants to talk to him or to have him just start talking, about this place, this old house, anything, but he is kept busy with the bucket and soap and high piles of dishes and pots. Then the woman comes down into the kitchen again and starts talking to Kasper and seems to be telling him to hurry or finish or something. She has sat up now, to not appear indolent, as much as one can while sitting down. Her eyes are nervously trained on the woman now instead of lazily trailing after Kasper's awkward gestures and moves. Then the woman looks at her and she feels her face freeze and her heartbeat rise up, and the woman motions to her and her face has a different look on it and she can't work it out, but she no longer feels nervous and goes up unhesitatingly to her and takes her outstretched hand. It feels rough and dry, like a leaf, but also strong like a tree trunk, firm, warm; it leads her up the stairs. She breathes in the woman's smell – so different from her own, and Kasper's. There is something artificial about her scent.

They go past the door she appeared from and down towards the end of the dark corridor, dark even when the sun is at its most radiant outside, illuminating everything. She feels this is a secret place, the darkness an unspoken word, a mute vow. This part of the house is the woman's domain and no one else's, not even the sun's. What is she going to reveal to her, this woman, what is she going to show her that she can't say herself? She can't help herself, and she takes back her hand towards her and says: 'Where are we going?'

The woman isn't angry. She smiles and shows her the door. The woman has let go of her hand and taken the handle. Easing it downwards she opens it and the light spills out, as if she is keeping a room of fire inside. Her eyes adjust and the hand pulls her forwards again, the light channelled through a large window overlooking a large bed. The beams seem high and fragile, distant. The woman leaves her hand and she turns away to the mirror: a great fan of silver, spreading like a peacock's tail over the dresser. The girl looks at it, surprised to see something so elegant and thin, spindly, in this room of rough-hewn wood and creaky, worn floorboards. This room seems to change the woman. Where below she was stern and commanding, here she seems lighter, happier even. She disappears into another room from where the girl hears water running. She comes back with a cloth and points at the chair, saying something encouraging. Once sat down, a little apprehensively, the woman – somewhat roughly – puts the cloth to her face. It is breathtakingly cold and she gasps and the woman responds with a sympathetic noise. She looks again at the dresser, and the cold water seems to have momentarily sharpened her vision as she sees it isn't bare but covered in little things. There are some photographs, blurry at this distance, so she leans in, takes a few steps to bring them into focus. They are pictures of the woman – Eva. The real Eva has disappeared back into the other bathroom. In the photos she looks as if she's disguised as someone else.

Younger, her hair is given its own existence, instead of being viciously scraped back over her scalp, underneath her headscarf; one or two strands keep her face upright, or so it made it appear at any rate. Her clothes, also, looked as if she were planning to be on the cover of a magazine. She was smiling but smiling coyly, as if she didn't want to and was only doing it as a favour to the person taking the photos. She was sitting in a city somewhere and it was bright.

The real her comes back and the girl stumbles back into the chair and she knows she's been looking at the photos, and possibly all the other trinkets on the dresser. One she now moves to pick up: the hairbrush, which is extremely stiff and makes the girl and the woman wonder whether her hair has ever been brushed before. She looks distastefully at all the objects gathered up, looking so incongruous deep within the trees that they almost may as well have been pieces in a museum, relics of a long-forgotten, long-lost civilisation. The girl wonders if the woman really doesn't like those things to remind her that they represent some other version of herself. Which one was the real one? Did it make her sad to see these reminders of when her skin was still soft, her hair styled and fine, her clothes... how completely different she was now. There is a bottle on the dresser, small and delicate, crafted from glass so it looked like a glass hummingbird, or another little, delicate airborne animal. Deep within its glass body, as if it were its heart, there is a little chamber of golden liquid. When was the last time she had put some on herself? What did it smell like? Of the city, of her hair? Of when she was young? Those days lost forever. The girl almost dares not breathe, her induction into the world of adults makes her feel ever more like a child, and when the woman looks at her, what does she see? Was she sad because she reminded her of her own days as a girl? Or angry, envious – of the girl she had always wanted but not like this. Not fallen like fruit onto her doorstep. Not a girl who might have been any of those girls from the city, this girl she could not understand and whom she couldn't talk to like her own daughter.

She sits back, admiring her handiwork; the girl's appearance a little more pleasing and a little less savage, but what was to be done with her clothes? Those strange clothes, they could tell her more about the girl than the girl herself could. As her husband would say, the girl was like a piece of wood, a knot inside another knot, impossible to saw through, impossible to use.

Eva realises the girl has been sitting there, still and silent, and she tries to smile but it comes out strangely. This foreign-looking girl from the woods, she's never seen the likes of her before. Not for years has she seen foreign girls and that was in another place, another world. One that now feels like she dreamed it – were it not for the few relics of that lost world she had managed to salvage. It all happened so quickly. Their country collapsed in an instant. They could not bring much, fleeing before the invasion. Biting at their heels as they fled to the *dacha*.

She can feel the girl looking at her, and her thoughts must have risen to the surface, discolouring her face. The girl looks disconcerted and wary and so Eva tries to forget about the past and she tries to smile again and tells the girl: 'You look much better' hoping that the meaning would shine through the sounds.

'Let's go downstairs and prepare supper.' She stands up and holds out her hand to guide the girl out of the bedroom. To her surprise, she takes it. And she, not a little awkwardly, has to close the door and gently pull her through the door after her, her eyes never leaving her, into the dark corridor. She wonders if her son or husband would notice any difference.

It is her second surprise of the day that both of them remark on it. Her husband doesn't say anything but she can read the look that registers the change. And the boy says she looks much prettier, to which the girl gives a pouty look, not missing a step as she carries some beetroot to the table. But then, after the girl's appearance, nothing could surprise her again; she looks at her and still finds it hard to take her in as a physical presence – like the table, like the house, her son, the trees outside. In these strange times she knows she should be more used to surprises and should count herself lucky that it was only a little foreign French-speaking girl who had come to her door.

The girl who couldn't stop thinking about the hidden woman inside Eva and seeing her photographs and objects from another time and place and how she is lucky to have them; even if they make her sad, she is lucky to have them. They were little fragments of memory, manifest, as much a part of her as her hardened hands, the rough cloth covering her. It covered an inner self, buried, and all the more precious for not being visible, for being unknown. There was a moment of resentment, of envy: why should Eva be so blessed? Laying three plates. Why couldn't she have a bag with her? Nestling with her memories, like the stems of pollen in a flower; some photos, a pendant of her mother or grandmother, some letters, something, anything.

A noise at the door rouses her from this obscure reverie and she's so happy to see the door opening, with a slam, roughly, an inelegant signal of the arrival of the man who passes into the house. She smiles involuntarily at him and almost feels like curtseying and instead just stands there foolishly, stripped bare by inaction. He smiles at her, throws something at the startled Kasper, which he juggles for a few seconds before catching it by its tail out in front of him – a wild bird.

Kasper, proud of himself to have shown such dexterity, holds the bird aloft, his words in French directed to her: 'Look, look!'

Over Kasper's rather simple statements, the father shouts something at his wife, using a word the girl knows means 'French'.

She snaps back into her movements and lays the cutlery where it seems appropriate. And, not having something thrust into her hanging arms immediately, she saunters over to the door, too warm still to shut, and looks out, out of the house and into the forest. She sees the trees, at a distance, still there – high, dark columns – and feels, not afraid, but something. A feeling as unsettling, as disorienting, as seeing that crashed plane for the first time. Yet she remembers this was the first time she considered the trees this way; now she's in the house – she belonged indoors – the trees are angry; do they consider her theirs? Then the wind starts up and lifts the trees' branches, gesturing to her, and she wrenches her eyes from them and the unpleasant whistling noise they are making, hissing even, saying they can wait.

She would have to come back some time. *They would wait.*

She turns away and sees the father, Jan, cleaning his boots. Kasper is somewhere else and Eva places some plates stacked with food – beetroot, cabbage, bacon – onto the table, gesturing her to take her place at the table, in the kitchen in this house.

The girl knows she has entered the palace of endless food; if she were to begin marking up novel experiences in her new life then this meal certainly would be the first time she has eaten so much she feels sick. And she cannot even finish off the last survivors on her plate; despite the possibility that this may cause offence, she nonetheless thinks that the prospect of being sick would, on balance, cause greater concern. She realises this potentially unprecedented gluttony was compensation for enduring conversation that she did not understand and, because of which, coupled with the feeling of nausea, has cast her into a glum mood by the end of the meal. Despite Kasper throwing the occasional common word at her and despite having been given a role and then a place at the table, everything nominally contrived to make her integral to her new surroundings, the dislocation was just too great. She is as removed from them as the food they eat, nakedly inferior, as familiar as the furniture but just as far beneath them, as if they would ever start to converse with the chairs they sat on.

She waits until Eva, inevitably, gestures at her and Kasper to clear away the meal. The father also rises, asking Eva a question in the process. Kasper takes an interest in this question, though his observations about the war and his ambitions to find a place in it went largely ignored by his parents. Kasper looks at her and she does her best to ignore him but looks at the father, reassured as ever by his ambling around to the other room. Strange that man being a hunter, in his slow, almost shuffling movements. Looking at Kasper, she tries to think of him at that age. Were there any photos of him?

Kasper shouts something, in that uneven voice of his, which would have been deep if not for the syllables of light, childish excitement that betray him: 'They're going to baptise you.' Smiling, he disappears outside and brings back in, almost immediately, a bucket and begins the laborious process of washing up. Water gets everywhere. She has to convey all the dirty objects on the table to him and wishes she didn't have to.

'You know they were talking about you, at dinner. If you keep eating like you do you won't be that thin for much longer.'

She looks at him. 'You're lying – they never said any such thing. You're the one who eats like a pig.' Vindicated by the indisputable empiricism of this observation, she does as best she can to ignore him until:

'Well, once they've fattened you up, then they'll serve you up with sour cream...'

A plate falls. Eva looks in. Before the plate has even finished shattering and, reverting back to what seems her normal mode of behaviour, she shouts something in a harsh sequence of 'ch', 'jush' and 'kzsh' sounds, and Kasper, protesting, points at her, but soon falls silent. The man comes in, Eva following a few seconds later, telling Kasper to do something.

She sees the man, more alive, swift and purposeful, and she watches him, still, until Kasper tells her to sit too. The man sits down. Eva, by the enormous black kettle, shouts requests for tea, which Kasper relays to everyone and then tells the girl that they are flicking through a diary of Holy days, observances and prayers with some selected psalms also, such as the eleventh:

> There is nothing a good man can do
> when everything falls apart

Kasper duly translates these in an overly sarcastic, bored tone of voice so that his father rebukes him with a swipe of his enormous hand round his head, scuffing his hair. Jan gets into his stride and therefore – possibly forgetting the original purpose of the gathering – reads out some more. Another cuff for Kasper, this time to remind him of his interpreting duty.

He obliges, with more sad songs about being abandoned.

'Don't they sound like our songs?' Jan asks happily, proud that Poland's own songs resemble those from Judea.

Strange he should be so happy about things that are so sad, she thinks, once Kasper has given her the gist of these questions to no one. Eva, concentrating on some sewing, starts humming a song she had heard her mother hum. It was about suffering terribly and how this means God loved her all the more, all the more did she love God.

'Now. Let's see,' Jan put forth, trying his best to sound official. Trying to look over his spectacles. Eva continues humming.

'Now,' he repeats.

She stops humming, looks up and then continues sewing. 'We're listening.'

Kasper imitates his father's authoritative demeanour. And does it without smiling, his hands folded on the table in front of him, fingers interlaced.

The girl can't help smiling. Until she feels his father looking at her.

'Today is the 20th – I believe that to be correct.' He waits for a grunt from him and a sigh of assent from her. She, however, is transfixed. As if the book he is holding were not merely a catalogue of names and portmanteau identities but a Holy and divinely inspired book that would reveal her life, and recount it all, beginning with her birth. Ending with her heart beating at this table, in a foreign country.

'Well.'

Silence.

Kasper looks up without looking round, clownishly, but she couldn't laugh this time.

'Well, what is it?' Eva asks, without looking up.

'Well. We can't call the girl Bernard.'

'Indeed,' his wife confirms. 'Ask her to choose her name.'

Kasper tells her she is to be called Bernard, and the nameless girl pales, thinking of the big dogs in Switzerland. She does not want to share the same name as a dog, if at all possible.

Eva tells Kasper off, takes the book from her husband and hands it to her. She understands, as the mother looks at her. Her blonde hair, despite its rough appearance in daylight, now in candlelight, shimmers and glistens. And it makes her think of the church. And the Bible; the psalms she has recognised, even with Kasper's translation. She looks at the names, all of them familiar. Her heart starts to beat frantically with the thought that her own might be in this list, the first layer of the unknown taken away. The first stone taken away in a wall concealing a long-lost garden. She can hear Kasper asking questions but can do no more than create a sound in her mouth in response. She can barely continue looking and then sees the name Madeleine. Mary Magdalene. But in the silence, with all of them looking at her. She says it out loud, without any further reflection; the first word her new parents have understood: *Madeleine.*

Kasper repeats: 'Magdalena.' Kasper tells her his parents think it is a beautiful name, and Eva says it suits her, and Jan says it won't be long until her birthday – only two months now. And then Eva stands up, returns and takes the new Madeleine's hand and drops a pendant into it, small and gold on a fine gold chain. Kasper tells her she is being given something to protect her, and Eva crosses herself in a gesture Madeleine recognises. She looks at the pendant. Within is the blithely sacred face of Mary, the virgin in blue and white, a burning heart, rays of golden light transecting it in her chest between her breasts. Madeleine looks at Eva and sees her smiling at her, her hair like gold light.

Jan has risen to get some wine, much to Kasper's delight, and Eva pours Madeleine a half-measure. Wine. It tastes like leaves and trees. She thinks it would be nice if it wasn't for that other dry, dirt taste that sours her breath and leaves its acid aftertaste in her mouth. But she has another sip and then another and she has finished her glass. She finds Kasper hilarious as he tells her that his parents are already drunk, and Jan takes him under his arm, and, standing up – seemingly even more enormous than usual, too big for the house! – takes Kasper in his arms, violently protesting, swinging arms and legs as Eva, perhaps also unwound by the wine, laughs, her hands held together. She says something to her which she can't understand, much as she wants to. And then feels as sleepy as she has ever been in her life, her life as she can remember it as such. She has spent much of her new life in the arms of the man from the woods. His arms could well be made of trees, she thinks, as the candles blur and their light forms long spears that pierce the corners of her vision. Is it he that makes her feel so warm?

Or the wine? She becomes aware of Eva following below, beneath them, and does she try and reach out for her? She can't remember.

Eva has candles in one hand, laid by the bedside table. Where have Jan and Kasper gone? She is put into the – cold – bed. Watching the candles sink into themselves, too tired to stay upright, too tired.

Eva looks at her clothes she has laid out. Those scorch marks. What has the child – the Madeleine girl – seen? To have left such marks on her clothes? She asks her husband but he's too sleepy for wine and kisses her in response, pulls her down onto him on the bed.

'The door is still open...!'

She insists, but she knows he doesn't know; only the girl, and she has chosen to forget rather than remember. How lucky she is. What kind of chance brought her here, to her house filled with light, filled with love. She kisses her husband and they sink into bed together and she hopes – prays – they will stay lucky. He is distracting; where does he find the energy?

'Go shut the door...'

And she hopes that the girl – Madeleine – will not prove to be unlucky.

The next morning begins with an explosion. Bright light and heat. All around and all at once. Then a voice. A name. *Madeleine*. She opens her eyes wide. Her memory unglues itself from the walls of her head and begins to flow again: *my name*.

She sees Eva standing there, having drawn the curtains, the sun so bright and already disgorging such a heat; it's as if it's hanging from the eaves just outside the window. Eva smiles – her frame lit by a halo of light – and she reaches an arm down, also fringed with fire, and rubs her hair. Her head hurts, it feels heavy and as if it's coated with something. She fumbles to take the hand and allows herself to be half-dragged from bed, yawning widely. On the edge of the bed she's embarrassed to be so slow and exhausted, but Eva seems unperturbed, even expecting this slow start to the day. They amble slowly to the bathroom. She washes her face and hair in a chipped enamel bowl. She sees her face in pale reflection in the water. And she looks at the chipped surface: the small patches of dark and rough alloyed metal exposed beneath the smooth, white enamel. She runs her finger over the differing textures. If it weren't for the damage the bowl has suffered, its basic nature would still be hidden. Once she has finished Eva brings in her clothes and a box. Madeleine, in an over-large nightshirt, flecked darkly by water, sees they are going to try and clean and patch up her clothes.

They start to trade words as they each take a needle and thread, though there's nothing much they can do with some of the holes in her cardigan. She's handed her own skirt and some thread and begins to sew up some of the smaller holes. It's easy, she must have done it before. Or maybe she just has a knack for it, but she wants to know whether this is the first time she has stitched clothes back together or not. She looks over at Eva who notices her looking and gestures with her head – not stopping the motions her hands are carrying out – to continue. So she does. Until everything is repaired.

It was pleasant, the unthinking motion of the needle and the folds of fabric slowly meeting each other, and it suited the heavy and numb sensation in her head. It was like the feeling of heaviness draining away was imitated by the motion of the tears in the fabric gradually disappearing; little white lines were all that were left.

When they have finished, Eva again gestures to her to leave the clothes and follow her to a chest of drawers. She takes out a dress, red, almost pink it had faded so much. Madeleine changes and flinches at the feel of the thin yet heavy fabric dragging on her shoulders. Eva says something, looking at her in the hope she understands, and Madeleine thinks she is asking whether she likes the dress and looks back at her clothes, secure in the knowledge that having just spent hours repairing them they wouldn't be thrown out, and she speaks – her voice a little heavier and cracked in places – asking about her clothes. She never imagined she would feel so perturbed by not wearing her own clothes, clothes she had never thought twice about before in their short time together, but they were the only signs that she had existed before the trees and the forest claimed her.

Eva gives her back her shoes and then turns her back to her again, hunched over the drawers, trailing out a cut of fabric Madeleine couldn't figure out. Where would it go, she was already covered? She watches Eva spin it and fold and then, with one arm – bringing her close to her belly curving out and her breasts resting on her chest – places it on her head. Her black hair is covered by the white fabric so lightly she hardly feels it, as if it has been cut from a patch of cloud.

After resting her hand on her shoulder, she turns and collects Eva's clothes and they proceed through the house picking up more and more piles of clothes, rough and heavy from the odour of Jan; she recognises his smell, and Kasper's sourer tang, almost of fruit. And of Eva's clothes, though she carries them, she can detect her fragrances above the other two, of cooking fat and raw water but also something else. But it's his smell – the smell of wood, of trees – that she realises she has smelled before. It was the first thing she had smelled, in her boat, except there wasn't the smell of water; it was the smell of blood.

The clothes all bundled up in her arms, she follows Eva out the door and into the dark corridor, the sound of her steps virtually the only guide to her movements. Then down the stairs, gingerly and slowly, one at a time.

After a few steps the light comes and she can see the banister and into the kitchen, which seems to be a room of light; the now familiar objects around her – the table, the stove, the gun rack – all seem pale and faded. Eva's sharp words hit her at the same time as the door, and she is pushed back but eventually shoves her way out into the heat of the day. She follows her round the back of the house near some trees and soon hears the sound of water trickling across and over all the other sounds: the birds, their own steps over the twigs and stones and the occasional fleeting noises of animals somewhere else.

There is a wide wooden tub by the little stream. Eva signals to her to leave the clothes on the bank and fill the tub using the bucket – a bucket much heavier when full of water than when it was empty. It is as if it's fighting her and, disobediently, spews and sloshes as much water as it can onto her new outfit before grudgingly disgorging it out into the tub. The water feels refreshingly cold in the heat, droplets cutting through the syrupy air like diamonds. Soon, though, it has chilled her fingers as she passes garment after garment to Eva. She shows her how to rinse and rub them in the quick-running water of the stream. They are then scrubbed viciously against the washboard, and Eva piles up several at a time before they both go to hang them up on the lines strung across a patch of ground at the back of the house, heavy and dripping their wet weight onto the grass.

She looks at Eva's fingers, raw and white; how cold and numb they must be, much more than hers, which are now tingling with coldness. She bunches her fists and rubs them down the sides of her new red dress; the damp parts, deeper red, are like the black patches on her old dress, on her old cardigan.

They tramp back to the stream, the tub and the coldness, lingering slightly to be warmed by the sun, which, ferociously imperious, nearing its zenith, can't warm the bones of their fingers.

Eva, walking behind her, reaches out and straightens and tightens her headscarf. She rubs her head, slowly, affectionately, and when Madeleine turns round, Eva smiles sadly, as if the smile can't shift the weight of sadness, too heavy, too set.

Kasper appears before them from between the trees, as if he were made of the same matter as the air itself; Eva resumes her typical posture, her voice the same timbre, and barks some syllables with few vowels at Kasper, before he glances curiously at Madeleine and her new red dress, patched with water.

As they are rinsing and scrubbing the clothes, Kasper comes back with two glasses of cold water. He gives one to Eva, who sips quickly before resuming her fierce punishment of the clothes.

Kasper asks: 'Are you enjoying your day? Aren't you glad I came to give you some water?'

'Yes, I suppose so.'

She drinks the water, gulping, drinking more and more, drinking it all down – she could never have enough. She was glad indeed that he'd brought it to her.

'You can get me some more if you want.' Though she didn't want any more now, as it chilled her insides, sitting heavy and expansively in her stomach. She walks away to haul some more clothes to hang on the line and Kasper too, disappears. She doesn't know where to. She doesn't see him again till lunch.

As she and Eva sit down to some cold meat, cheese, blackberries and blueberries, stuffing it into their mouths with the deserved justification of those who have laboured hard and have little time for social graces, Kasper sits down with them and eats in the same manner, although that was the normal way for him to eat. It had been the same last night, she remembers. She winces at the thought of the state of her head this morning and reaches for some more water.

After lunch, Eva asks them to do the dishes; Madeleine is now recognising the words for washing, drying, laundry, for most words related to domestic chores. Once they have finished, after Kasper complaining first that she was going too slowly, then that she was too fast, she asks him how they were supposed to know the time to be back to help prepare the dinner. Kasper gives the impression he had been expecting this question, and, without saying anything, puts his hand into his pocket and slowly, deliberately slowly, until the impatience shows on her face, draws out a watch.

'It's silver,' he says.

She looks at its bone-white face, Roman numerals gripping the edge.

'It also tells the date.'

And she also sees the tiny picture of the sun in one aperture. He drops it into her hand, telling her she can only look at it and to be careful.

She asks: 'Where did you get it?'

'My father was given it. By someone in the village. It was a reward for saving a child from drowning.'

'Your father is very brave,' she says, thinking about the night she didn't remember, when he carried her in his arms to this house.

'Yes, but I'm going to be as brave as him.' Kasper corrected himself: 'Well, really I already am, I can kill an animal or an enemy soldier just like he can.'

'Did he fight in the war? Against the Germans?' She is wandering around the house as she says this, seeking to stay out of Eva's orbit in case she is pulled back in and commanded to cook or clean or sweep or something else; she almost shudders at the thought of facing the hens again. It's noon or thereabouts and the heat is expanding into every space and pressing down against them. She looks to see him behind her with his hands in his pockets, seemingly the heat suppressing even his energy as well. Even the chickens seem quiet, now she thinks about it.

'Do you want to go for a walk?'

'Where to?'

'I don't know. Anywhere. Into the forest.'

'There's nothing there. Do you want to go hunting?'

'No. It'll be less hot there.' She starts to walk towards the trees, across the tract of dirt and stumps, and she can hear him shuffling along behind her, slowly. She can't walk quickly either, the dust feels like sand in this heat but she feels cool at least in her new clothes. The summer air is like honey, slow and thick and difficult to pass through. Clouds of small insects seem to materialise from nowhere and she waves them away impatiently. But she slows until they are level before moving beneath the trees. She sees behind his shoulder a small outhouse she'd never noticed before and asks him: 'What's in there?'

'That's my father's house. That's where he makes his things.' He doesn't seem roused by the question, not even looking back and ambling into the forest. She has stopped, however, piqued.

'What things?'

'Things out of wood.'

'What things out of wood?'

'Whatever they ask him to. Beds, gun parts, cupboards, dolls.'

Madeleine has trouble imagining him with his big arms and hands fashioning something as small and fragile as a doll. Kasper says something. She remembers from nowhere being carried up the stairs to bed last night. She feels Kasper looking at her.

'What?'

'I help him sometimes. When the war's over he wants me to become his apprentice, but I prefer hunting.'

Then, as if reminded of all the animals waiting to be slaughtered, he walks on into the trees. She breaks her stare at the house and turns to the trees and follows him in, past the first tree and into the almost immediate smell of pine. The air is cool and the light is forbidding, falling in occasional shafts between the branches. The noises of birds and animals become more apparent as they listen and she feels happy to be among the trees. But she is also glad Kasper is here. It is difficult to think of him hunting anything; too clumsy, too noisy, you heard him from the other side of the house. He seems to want to announce his presence rather than conceal it. He has a stick in his hand, like she did yesterday, and swishes and jabs at invisible things. She picks up a stick too but keeps it to herself for fear of waking up the trees or attracting the attention of any more lost pilots.

'You know, I've seen a soldier,' she says before she had even realised she'd said it.

Kasper's reaction was so quick she stops, startled. He looks at her like never before: 'No you haven't. Where?'

She carries on, enjoying his full attention and playing with it as she wishes.

'I don't know. Here, in the forest.'

'Was he one of them? Did you kill him?'

'He was dead.' And, despite Kasper's envy, she wishes she'd never started this because the pilot now lived in her mind. Even if he was the enemy, she was his only witness and she realises she wishes he hadn't been dead and she has a feeling she'd never expected – the guilt that she could have helped him – and that maybe, somehow, he wasn't dead and had been trying to call to her to help him. But... but she knew he was dead. She realises she's been walking on, her stick swiping the air as if it was a magic wand to try and wipe him from her memory or bring him back to life. If only it was possible to resurrect people you loved. People you knew didn't deserve to die. Kasper is saying something but she isn't paying attention.

'You've never seen a soldier,' Kasper reiterates. How could she have seen one and he not? Why would she lie? She is so strange. Maybe all foreign girls are like this.

'Where was he then? Where was the plane?'

'I've lost my memory, remember?'

Kasper is frustrated by this, unsatisfactory as a response but indisputable as a fact. Unless.

'Well maybe you have.'

She responds, her stick waving suspended, holding it up high.

'Yes, I have.' As she watches him move on ahead of her, she feels all alone and the forest suddenly seems to have become quiet as if waiting for her answer. Why has he suddenly turned and convinced the birds and the trees? She has lost her ability to move, to look around, even to look up. She feels she has to deny his accusation.

But what she says is true: 'I don't remember anything. Why would anyone wish away their memories? No mother, father, nothing.' Her angry words spiral like bees from their hive, on the attack, thick and fast. She sees him walk on, past the roots of trees, thick like musculature, furred with moss.

She asks: 'Where are you going?'

He carries on walking for a bit, then stops. He looks round to see her looking at him.

'I'm going back,' she says and slowly turns round.

Kasper shrugs and walks, following her and past her, walking quickly, forcing her to keep pace with his long strides. Walking quicker than she was used to, she is soon breathing heavily, plunging into this unfamiliar territory. Soon the trees relent and fall back and she can see the outhouse and slows down, as if caught by its magnetic field. Kasper continues onwards and she can no longer see him. Alone, she walks towards the smaller house, as if it is in the middle of a maze; the trees are more numerous here than around the main house, trying to keep it hidden. She walks closer and closer, her heart beating louder and louder. It is made of wood, the same dark vertical flats as the other house but this wood seems darker. There is only one window, dark as well, as if it were made from metal rather than glass. Shiny and black, it, too, refuses to give away anything that might be hidden within – reflecting the trees, blackly, black trees against a grey sky. Madeleine strains to get close to it but the coldness and the blackness of the trees suddenly make her recoil, as if something has pushed her; she doesn't feel it is her own volition, nor even a defensive reflex, but she starts backwards, still transfixed by the black window until she's sufficiently far enough away to look away and start towards the big house. Closer to the big house, she starts to run, again, as if against her will. Happy though, to be dragged or pulled towards it, like a rock in space towards a planet, this house is reassuring. Its rough wood scratched by the rain and snow; its ivy tracing lines all over the walls. She looks at its thick, heart-shaped leaves, hanging towards the earth, holding the house tight in its thin green grip.

She wonders where he has got to. She goes through the front door to be enveloped by the sweltering atmosphere of the kitchen and Eva's form, more discernible after a few seconds, moving through the clouds of steam and the heat that seems to have warped and blurred the air itself. Madeleine hears the shout of recognition and her name, and Eva emerges from the cloud of vapours – red-faced and red-tempered – 'here!'

A bowl of potatoes is given to her to get on with. She walks through the cloud of steam to sit down at the table and looks through the white, cloudy air at the backdoor, which is open although it seems to have no effect in making the kitchen more bearable. Eva, wiping her forehead on her sleeve, motions that Madeleine can leave and sit in the backyard and seems to bark something – guessing – about Kasper helping. She takes the bowl and knife and leaves the room of steam. She comes into the backyard, the sun high and bright, as if she were leaving the house of shade and coming into the House of the Sun. Her own forehead is moist from the humid, hot kitchen.

She sits down at a rough table that is uneven and whose surface is split open; the surface is smooth but the interior surfaces of the lesions are rough, beneath the surface. She places the bowl on the table, adjusting herself, letting herself cool down on the wicker chair. It is quiet out here and even the sounds coming from the kitchen, as if there were an army of cooks in there rather than just one woman, are muted by the steam. Soft, white, almost transparent wisp, trail up over the doorframe and up the wall before dissipating into the air. She starts peeling, taking in the garden, if that isn't misleading, as she is sitting in a large stretch of dust. The vegetable patches, which she can see part of, are on the other side of the house. Further on, towards the trees, the sheets lay hanging across the lines where she and Eva had hoisted them this morning. And beyond the sheets she can see a figure moving and almost immediately knows it's Kasper.

There is nothing else so awkward in the forest. It makes her smile to think of him in the army, the secret Resistance, hiding and planting bombs and how terrible he would be at it. And then she loses her smile, sad all of a sudden at the thought of him being exposed to danger and guilty at how she could ever have seen something funny in it. She looks in his direction again but he has vanished. She starts her chore, trying not to think about anything, least of all Kasper; instead, listening intently to the heavy silence that seems to have been squeezed from above in-between everything like glowing, molten steel into a mould.

She duly delivers the bowl to her new guardian, who seems pleased, or, at least, not visibly displeased. Madeleine is then shown the stew that needs supervision and stirring. At least she notices the steam has diminished a little.

Later, Eva, after having gone upstairs for a short while, comes back down the noisy stairs – as if it hurt them to be stepped upon – with two large baskets and beckons her to join her outside. They were to take down, fold, and bring in the sheets. As Madeleine walks out, behind Eva, she can see – past the sides of Eva's sturdy back – the cool sky, less blue and more grey, the trees blackened a little at their tips, the air much cooler too, and Kasper sitting on a stump, eating an apple and polishing a gun. Madeleine is fixed intently on the long rifle resting against his leg so much so that she stumbles over a bucket and then Eva shouts something, quick and rough. Kasper languidly shoots something back at her, repeating a phrase over and over, three times. She makes out a word like 'devil', not the French exactly, but similar: 'diabeł'.

She absent-mindedly tries repeating it but Eva spins round and says – in French – 'What?'

Madeleine starts, without thinking, to speak in French, her eyes wide and the words evaporating into nothingness, her throat contracting. Eva gestures quickly and sharply to the sheets, and Madeleine, her head low as if obeying her queen, scurries towards the sheets, mostly still but swaying languidly a little in the slight breeze, and runs into their midst, blotting out her view of Kasper and his mother.

The sheets smell fresh and cool, white and smooth. She walks between them and she feels as if she is moving about in a palace. A palace would have finer walls than linen, of course, silks and satins, velvets, so its august occupants would not feel the wind or the cold. She walks on through, not remembering this many sheets having been washed this morning. As if she were in a maze, enclosed, she looks up to see the blue expanse of sky. She lays down her basket and begins to pull down one of the sheets; she can't reach the top – where it is held by a slim stretch of rope – and the sheet soon collapses on top of her, heavy in a bundle, as if it wanted to swallow her and make her disappear. It is warm and even a little stiff and she has trouble fighting it off, and then she has to fold it awkwardly and unsatisfactorily and then to put it in the basket, squashed and stained in places. Madeleine is looking at it when she hears the strange-sounding vowels being flattened by the consonants of their language, struggling as she did with the sheets – as if it were some monster risen from the sea to try and drag her back in or else a ghost that has stepped out of a haunted house to make her its bride – both these dramatic scenarios interrupted by her words coming closer and closer, until she can recognise Eva's face appear behind some sheets, effortlessly flung aside; there is no question who won the struggle in that case. The harsh-sounding words become even more harsh-sounding and staccato, and Eva looks down at the sheet squashed into the basket like it is concealing something, a baby from a hospital, guns into a prison. Eva majestically takes control of the sheet again and hauls it out but doesn't motion Madeleine to follow her and uses a word she remembers often being flung dismissively at Kasper and so she did as it bade as well. It seems and feels like it was thrown in her face – a renewed attack – as she retreats, and their fingers crawl towards their respective corners. The sheet billows out between them like a sail suddenly caught full in the belly by the wind. Another harsh-sleepy word from Eva and the sheet flaps again like the slow beat of an enormous bird's wing and then they fold it over, walking towards each other like the shy partners in a dance coming to an end too soon. They repeat this routine as many times as there are sheets left. Madeleine feels she has forgotten how many there were.

When they finish, they are standing in the bare garden again. She sees Kasper has gone; she is following Eva again like a duckling in a stream, into the house, up the stairs and into the main bedchamber. The corridors are lightless and oppressive and she can't tell where walls and ceilings join, of the definite edges and size of things. The bedroom is somewhat lighter and she is relieved when Eva commands her to put down the basket. Madeleine looks around the room; it smells adult somehow but she doesn't know why, it is just different. It's warmer than her room. Pictures in silver frames stand in front of the dresser where her toilet had been performed this morning. Some small pictures in wooden frames hang on the walls, blazingly golden; Madeleine can make out angels and halos. Bright-red cloths cover the trunks, and a few baskets like the one she has just been carrying are here and there at the foot of the giant bed. Opposite the dresser is a table, like the dresser, more slender and elegant than the bed, and the wardrobe she catches sight of over her shoulder. As she turns to stare at it face on, it towers above her as if she were meeting a giant, her head only coming to his knees.

There's a noise behind her and Eva comes up to hold her, spits on her finger and roughly cleans something from her cheek, hard as if she were fervently rubbing a brass for good fortune and does not realise that the cheeks of girls are softer, and it isn't necessary to rub quite so hard. She sweeps back a strand of brown hair that has fallen down and holds her chin, looking down from a slightly lower height than the wardrobe and Madeleine looks at Eva. Eva is looking at her with such a strange look she can't bear it and looks away, becoming nervous, and then Eva with her rough and cold hand strokes her cheeks that have blossomed red and hot and makes a sound Madeleine correctly interprets as a dismissal.

She leaves quickly and goes downstairs, through the kitchen, into the backyard to see if Kasper has come back but there is no one there, just the odd sound from the hen coop. She rubs her cheek, still warm, and looks around. This expanse of time is unexpected so she is unprepared and has no immediate idea of how to fill it. Looking at the trees ahead of her, in the late afternoon sun, they seem neutral, as unassuming as the open door behind her, the axe leaning against the doorframe, the hen coop. They are neither welcoming nor menacing. There is nothing forbidding about them, as she ambles towards them, not like the outhouse she and Kasper saw that morning. She stops when she thinks about the house – the smaller house would be more accurate, she considers. As she nears the house she can't remember why she has the impression that it's somehow forbidding. She steps closer and closer until she is almost at the door, and she is aware of her own breathing and how her mouth has dried and her palms have become a little fluid. The eaves cast a dark pall over the walls and windows, and looking into the windows she can't see anything. The windows are dusty and cobwebbed, and inside is dark; vague outlines of large objects, like furniture, become clear, but slowly the fears she had felt yesterday start to seep back into her mind. What is this place for? Why does it make her nervous? Kasper hasn't seemed overly disturbed by it and he is the last person who would imprison and kill wanderers for food. Except, maybe, if he was really hungry. But it'd more likely be him who ended up being eaten.

And with a start she jumps back from the window and stumbles back from the house, over the tree roots and twigs. That thought, the fear: it isn't Kasper, it is his mother, it is Eva who still makes her nervous. Her welcome has been ambivalent. She never smiled, but then she has given her new clothes, washed her, tended to her. Walking slowly back to the house, looking up to the trees and the high, blue sky beyond their peaks, she realises it isn't her; she had dressed her in this new dress, washed the dirt from her face.

It is the pilot. It is the forest.

She quickens her pace and she hears her name being called and she follows it, running, quicker and quicker, towards the house, following the sound of her name.

On the stove and in the pots of boiling water she sees potatoes or what look like potatoes but are actually something else. More spongy, more uniform in shape. *Pierogi*. Eva, never hesitating to mobilise someone else's hesitation, tells her to drain the things in the pot and set them on the table. Small fragments of brown meat that are bacon, and some sour cream, are set alongside; the smaller fragments drowned in – and the meat swimming in – the burgundy-red beetroot soup that sloshes in the deep lap of the bowl.

They sit down in silence after Madeleine has ferried the three substantial bowls to the expansive brown table. Kasper joins her and Eva. She has not seen him since this morning, sitting in the garden, with the rifle beside him. Madeleine remembers how insouciant he was, eating his apple as if it were completely normal. To eat an apple before shooting. Shooting what? What has he been doing? He is more quiet than normal. And when he looks up, brown juices all over his chin as if he has burst a brown fruit between his teeth, looking directly into her eyes, she freezes. She has been gazing at him, oblivious to his noisy, splashing eating and gazing at his green eyes – resting lazily on the food in the bowl – and his dirty brown skin. She flushes red; her face gauchely falls down towards her own bowl of potatoes and dumplings, the steam rising to envelop her in a cloud of sympathetic disguise; it only serves to open her pores and flush her skin an even more vivid hue of crimson.

Eva has taken no notice and is eating silently, until she asks Madeleine if she wants salt. Madeleine does not understand and only when repeated does the girl look up.

This girl is a strange one, flustered and blushing even when sitting eating at the table, not being talked to. Perhaps they are all like this where she comes from. The west. French women: she remembers them from the city. This girl is not like any of them. As the girl fumbles with the pepper pot, she thinks she may well be mentally damaged. Those scorch marks and dark patches on her skin and clothes have also burned and scarred her brain; the wounds are inside as well, unseen. This softens her attitude towards her somewhat. She could not help her heritage, and as for being touched by the devil, that is only a theory and not in evidence continuously. She is still useful.

Then Eva looks over at Kasper, nearly nose deep in the gravy, and it strikes her. How can it not have crossed her mind before: two young children under the same roof? She much prefers this line of thought to the previous one; what mother does not think her male child – their own deeply submerged alter-ego – irresistible. No matter she would never let her dear boy be trapped by this girl, a possible simpleton – the thought creases the corner of her mouth slightly but she goes back to her food and finds it tastes better.

After they have finished, Kasper disappears and Eva wearily stands up, gesturing for Madeleine to join her at the stove. Madeleine collects all the peelings, all the detritus, everything sodden and cold and damp. She puts it into a bowl and, following Eva's directions that jolt through her arms, finds the patch in the vegetable plot onto which she dumps everything. It is cool outside, refreshing after the heavy meal. She thinks of Jan and where he could be, out there in the cool air and dark space between the trees. What if he is rescuing another girl? What if she were to have a pretend sister, as she was their pretend daughter? She clenches the empty, dirty bowl tighter and wishes he does not; she hopes he is killing. Killing Germans or Russians or whoever fault this war is. If none of these things, then finding their supper for tomorrow night. Why has he missed this evening's meal? *What if he were dead?*

At this most morbid thought her name shoots through the air, startling her; the bowl slips from her grip, and she hastily recovers it and dashes inside. Eva doesn't seem worried, but then how could she tell – how would she even know? She walks back inside and Eva doesn't seem to pick up that the girl has been thinking about her husband. The more she tries not to think about it the more awkward around Eva she becomes.

Wiping down the table and placing the bowls in the sink, she paces around the stove as Eva scrubs and rinses, and when Eva does look up and asks her, she scatters the metal and wooden spoons and knives and forks. Eva stops, more surprised than Madeleine. She looks at Madeleine, her brows folding, and she can't be angry at the girl's clumsiness, she is too tired. She waves Madeleine away, carries on washing the dishes, in the colder and dirtier water. Madeleine backs away slowly, not sure if she has been dismissed or not, but she guesses that if she hasn't then she will be called back. Her pace increases as she approaches the stairs and slows as she doesn't want to make too much noise on them. She falls into bed; it's a bed for her own cleanliness, her smell, her new fragrance, which is unfamiliar but which she has the feeling has always been there. Her skin, for the first time, is soft and smooth. She can barely stop from rubbing her fingers along her arms, the inside of her elbows and her hair – how soft. She has never thought it could be this soft. She thought it was like leaves for the trees, rough and spiky – tough. It is the first night she has not collapsed and sunk into sleep freighted by exhaustion, and all of a sudden she feels apprehensive that it will be her last night here, now that she's content and happy. Her heart starts to thud and her stomach, full of food, begins to churn, and she involuntarily exclaims '*No*' to the house, to these strangers and their strange language – to anyone who is there and who might listen – to keep her and not to abandon her.

She does not want to wake up again, burned and bruised, under a tree with no memory of how her skin was, with only the smell of smoke and not her own smell. And she decides, as tears well up and she gets out of bed, she decides she will not fall asleep. She would be ready for anyone who thinks they will get the better of her, move her without her permission. They had better be ready for a fight – she would rather die than leave. She lights the candle and, momentarily, shrinks back into bed as she sees the darkness – huge and thick, opening its black maw agape – all around outside the bright sphere of candlelight. It seems different in the house, an uninvited guest; it belongs outside, not inside, where it is held back by the moon and the stars. She thinks suddenly whether monsters are afraid of the moon and the stars. Are they afraid of people? Of the darkness?

Is it because they are lost?

Maybe it is because they have been abandoned and they don't know where they belong. But she does not belong here – where does she belong then? She wants to know but not now, not right now; tomorrow she will find out more. For tonight she is tired, very full with their hot heavy food, but still a bit chilly. Instead of patrolling her room, she will stay awake under the covers, be a bit warmer but no less vigilant. Sitting up, she's alert, looking at the darkness in the room, or what she had earlier considered to be darkness, and it is not really, neither the silvery water the moon shone through nor the solid blackness that even the trees could hide and fade back into sometimes. It is the anaemic offspring of the darkness of the world, fading under her look, so she could discern objects – the jug, wardrobe, discarded clothes, window frame – some in their entirety and some where the darkness still bled into their edges. Madeleine loses herself in that void between darkness and complete dark; deciding she could keep watch just as well if she were on her side and looking at the candle as her partner in this sentinel night. She would start to think about a way back home out of the forest tomorrow, but for tonight she will stay awake, the candlelight bathing her face and her own sweet smell bathing her body, and they nestle up against her as she falls asleep in the warm and sweet-smelling sheets.

Second Dream

I am on a small boat, maybe. There is just room enough for me and some provisions. The water around is very dark so I don't think I am on a river; I think I am sailing across a vast ocean. I am throwing some small pebbles into the water. I pull my blanket closer over me. I lean over the side to watch them hit the water but the motion makes me feel dizzy and the salt smell seems to be everywhere, even in my nose, even in my mouth. I look up and see stars, so many stars, and they are whirling around the sky, they are dancing, but then the dizziness returns and I cough up the blood that gushes into my mouth. There is a lot so it runs up through my nose as well, and the horrible smell makes me retch. And I accidentally bite my tongue but it is hard and loose. I take it from between my gums and examine the object in my finger and it is my tooth. All my precious white teeth. There is a pile on my lap and it is the teeth that have been sinking into the blue marine depths, snaking a bloody trail. I fall back and the stars slowly grow dim.

Expedition

The next morning she is startled awake to the sound of her new name – in the same way as each of the previous days – by Eva. Her name rustles softly as her sheets – *Madeleine, Madeleine*. Eva leaves – her tasks never-ending.

This is the second day, or third, or is it even the fourth? She has been feeling progressively less heavy-headed in the mornings since her horrible hangover a few days ago. Her eyes open as soon as Eva touches her and her energy flows into her as if her own body were more prepared and had been better at adjusting to this new life than she has, than the girl-before-Madeleine was. Her red dress is draped over the chair. She thinks it suits her better than the chair, as if the chair were pretending to be her, and then she looks at her belly in the mirror and how this food from Dolnoslaskie, they said, has made her big, bigger even than a few days ago.

Maybe the girl in the mirror is lying. Sticking it out to pretend; a malicious convex pose. And she stares hard at the stomach and her chest, which isn't aching today, she realises. But as she dresses she can't not look at the other girl's face – into her eyes. Once washed and dressed and ready, she leaves the room – her room – with exuberant haste to get away from that mirror. The mirror has reminded her of her last thoughts last night, before falling asleep. How foolish she was to have been afraid of the dark. To want to be back in the forest again.

Walking downstairs, her energy transforms into a hummed melody. She can't see Eva anywhere. She ambles out into the backyard where still no one can be seen, and as she turns to go back inside there is someone standing almost directly in front of her – Kasper – she is close to him, as close as they've ever been. His awkward noises at having startled her make him seem as perturbed as she had been. Limbs flailing to dramatise his questions:

'Were you scared? Did you think I was a soldier?'

Madeleine refuses to answer and walks back in, his name now associated with dirty skin, spots here and there, tufts of stubble, a strange smell – his breath. Since the incident at dinner she has been wary of Kasper. She can't be certain of whether Eva has noticed her acting strangely or not; she must keep her distance from him. He doesn't seem to notice or pay her any more or less attention than before. He was still flitting about the edges of her awareness, never directly in front of her – outside, in the trees, somewhere else. She wants to wait until his vague enthusiasm dies down; she knows he is still hovering behind her.

And then he bounds in front of her, to the stove.

'Do you want some tea? I'll make us some tea. Tea's good. Do you like tea?'

'Yes, thank you.' She wonders whether the one response would cover the rapid camera-quick firing of questions. She sits down at the table and watches someone else work. To sit on the chair and do nothing. It has been a while since she has done that. Her time alone in the forest seems ages ago now, another life, if that expression makes sense.

Kasper shocks her out of her thoughts by dropping a cup on the table so she has to scramble to save it from plummeting to its death on the floor.

'So, you were in the city? Were you born there?'

She tries to say the words casually as if a response was optional; any reply would be of only limited interest.

'What?' He doesn't hear as he can only hear the noise of the cups, spoons and the kettle starting to wail steam. Kasper grabs the kettle, burns his hand, finds a cloth, lifts the kettle, its alarm ceasing rapidly, as if it has been warning them it might explode. She moves towards the cupboard where the samovar is kept and places it down with two glasses, and also a small pot for the sugar as Kasper liberally drowns his tea in sugar, despite having been repeatedly told about its ever-increasing scarcity. Kasper doesn't notice the teapot and pours the hot water in, all the while as if he were in a race, as if Madeleine was holding a watch. She likes him being here as he dissolves the sadness she has felt but hasn't been able to place since waking up this morning, like the sun burning away the morning mist. Kasper tells her that they had moved to the city before the war, when he was younger, about ten years ago. There they had lived in an apartment smaller than this house.

'Why did you leave?'

Kasper remains silent, and she isn't sure if she should repeat the question or not.

'The war. The Germans. They used to argue about it a lot. We had to leave at night. They were... they wanted us for the army. Father didn't want us to join. He said the war was already lost for us. We had to survive from now on, so we came here to the *dacha*, in the *las*.'

'Do you like it here, in the forest?'

He looks at her, blankly.

Shrugging: 'Yes. Yes, I will meet some partisans soon. They live in the forest. I practise with my gun all the time. My mother doesn't understand, she thinks I should stay home and help her. That's why it's good you're here.'

She sips her tea, bitter and black.

'Do you want to see my gun? Do you know how to shoot?'

She looks up, unsure what to say although there was only one answer. She shrugs too: 'No.'

'I will teach you. That way you can pretend to be the Germans and I can be the partisans. It's boring pretending trees and animals are soldiers.'

'Why do I have to be the Germans?'

'Well, you be the Russians then.'

'I don't want to.' Two hands cupping the warm glass.

Kasper continues to slurp his tea. She considers though, perhaps, it would be better to be in the forest with him than spending another day by the stove, hot and moist. She could still feel the sweat in the more obscure parts of her body, nestled in the folds of her dress.

'Is it difficult to shoot a gun?'

'Maybe for girls. It's easy for me but I can show you.'

They left the glasses. Kasper is even more jittery than normal once the glass of sugar starts to circulate and becomes absorbed into his skin and hair. She feels as though she's doing something she shouldn't. She's thinking about what's making her sad; is it the mirror? She thinks of Eva and Jan and, as Kasper reaches the gun rack, picks one rifle and then another one, and wishes he were here. To feel safer. To go out in the forest with a gun, she somehow feels more uncertain and fearful. To go back out into the forest with Kasper, armed, feels like a contravention; it is an act against the forest. The forest will turn against them. Kasper keeps hold of the rifles; she keeps thinking they are tree branches: one resting on his shoulder, the other one in his hand. She has added the word gun to her fast-expanding Polish lexicon.

As they wander deeper in, she can't shake her thoughts from last night. Are her parents wandering too? Would they recognise her, her hair swept back, hidden under the scarf? The forest is darker today, darker than she remembers. How would she recognise them? The forest is quieter too, the birds are gone, the squirrels and every other animal. They are hiding from them, from their guns. What is he going to shoot? Will they meet another pilot? Maybe soldiers who are alive?

She stops, unable to hide the tremor in her voice, 'Where are we going?'

He continues walking, just turning his head. 'To shoot.'

She wants to be sure, what if they meet strangers? Would he shoot them? What if they were lost? Her parents?

'Stop!'

He does so, looking at her strangely, as if he knew some strange behaviour was coming and, now she is acting as the strange little girl he knew, he is relieved to be able to deal with it and get on with shooting.

'What?'

And she stands, her arms rigid by her sides and with her fists clenched, she can't express what it is, not to herself in her own head, much less to a foreign boy, in the middle of these quiet, dark trees.

'Tell me where we're going.'

He doesn't understand and shrugs his shoulders. This is the time he doesn't understand. She feels like she is a petulant impression of Eva, reduced to savage gestures and curt monosyllabic expressions of frustration.

'Where?'

'Here.'

But he keeps walking and there is nothing she can do but walk with him. For something to say she asks him questions about Polish. With his head always looking straight ahead he teaches her the correct pronunciation of 'My Name is Madeleine.' To say, 'I don't know how old I am.' To say, 'I am lost.' To say, 'Gun.'

I shoot/you shoot/he-she-it shoots.

We are lost/you are lost/they are lost.

Kasper says: 'You're not lost. You're free. I wish I was free. I have to stay at home when I could be out fighting Germans, fighting for Poland. Fighting for Europe. I could be a partisan, living free in the woods. Just free, with my gun.'

'You do live in the woods. Anyway, I don't feel free. I don't know. I don't mind waking up in the house every morning.' Looking around the trees, shining brightly in the sun, the leaves illuminated by the golden light and the sharp murmur of bird song, she realises she does feel free in the forest. But this freedom does not feel like she might expect it to.

They have come to a clearing. A little way away from them is a fallen log. Kasper gives her a gun, looking up at her when she doesn't take it. She is looking at the gun instead.

'Take it,' he says. 'It won't hurt you. Unless you put it to your head.' He snorts, thickly, snottily.

He proffers it to her again and she takes it, slowly, gingerly, as if it were the leash of a fierce dog. It is lighter than she thought it would be. The black metal parts glint and almost shimmer like black water. She then holds it with two hands and this immediately puts her more at ease; it is she who controls the gun. She watches him walk over to the fallen log, several metres away, and place some objects on top, delicately, as if decorating a mantelpiece. Madeleine still has the gun in her hands when Kasper comes back to her, uncertain of where to rest it, not wanting to draw any mockery from Kasper. He had rested some small square wooden panels, daubed with rough circles of red paint, on the log. As small as birds.

Walking back towards her he suddenly cracks open the rifle and takes two bullets and lets them slide down into its long mouth, as if feeding his child. Then he snaps it back with a loud echoing clicking sound, as if setting a trap, as if breaking its neck. Her heart is beating fast as he comes to her and, smiling, rapidly puts the gun to his shoulder and moves imperceptibly to unleash the loudest sound she has ever heard.

The forest splits apart. The birds who were all sleeping erupt from their nest beds and fly into the air, shouting and screaming at having been disturbed. Kasper laughs at the same time. Madeleine jumps, and in the depths of the reverberating noise and bright yellow light illuminating the air around them, she sees some small part of the fallen tree jolt and a few splinters fly apart.

He says something short and bitter sounding in Polish, before turning to her to state the obvious: 'Missed. Now your turn.'

There is a bitter, moist smell in the air, and she wonders if it is the smoke. He says it's the cordite. She doesn't ask what that is. Madeleine turns to face the little targets on the log – first step. Then she tries to imitate Kasper as closely as possible, putting the rifle to her shoulder – step two. Madeleine looks to Kasper, asking without saying. Kasper obligingly nods. Her finger, damply, is warming the trigger, making it greasy, and she looks down the tube, squinting one eye then the other one as the wooden blocks become blurred and indistinct from the log and the background. She closes her eyes and squeezes the trigger back.

There's a hollow click and a stifled laughter beside her. She looks at him, shaking his head, bringing out a small box from his bag: 'Forgot this.'

He presents her, between forefinger and thumb, with a metal cylinder, small and mutely golden. She takes it and sees that her gun is different to Kasper's, more slender. Kasper shows her how to insert the bullet into the chamber, pull back the lever and then lock it into place in the chamber in a series of satisfying one-two-three solid snapping sounds. Then he lifts it to her shoulder, clumsily, and it hits her collarbone and she sharply pulls back.

'Leave it – I can do this myself.'

It is heavy to steady and doesn't fit against her shoulder. The hard wood sits awkwardly against her bones and against her right breast, and she hesitates and looks at the log and the shapes. Her vision slips out of focus and the objects become translucent veils, doubled, tripled, overlapping and confused. She pulls the trigger. The rifle slams back and she staggers backwards, not letting go of it as she holds it in the air as if it were a rope that would save her from falling. The loud cracking sound was the rifle exploding in her hands or her collarbone breaking, or both. She stands, her legs shaking, her heart panicking, frozen in a posture of shock, and slowly she manages to drag her eyes over to look at Kasper, who is staring fixedly at the tree. She follows his gaze to see one of the three wooden panels has been neatly pierced by the bullet in the top right corner. Her shoulder is throbbing and her hands are now slick with sweat, unsure whether she is supposed to be happy for hitting the target or disappointed for not having struck at its red centre.

Kasper immediately lifts up his gun and shoots at the targets, again hitting the fallen tree. His gun is much louder than hers. Then he hastily empties out two more cartridges from the bag and stuffs them into the barrels before snapping it shut again. The first one explodes without seemingly hitting anything and the second, let off barely a second later, hits the corner of the target, causing it to pirouette off the log and jump off somewhere behind the tree, as if attempting to hide from the bullets being fired at it. The echo of the shots is still drifting among the trees when he turns to her to say something in Polish, then something inarticulate, but which might have meant 'lucky'. Madeleine doesn't really hear him whatever he has said.

I shoot.

And as her heart slowly returns to normal coming to beat its ordinary rhythm, the gun feels lighter in her hands, her hands feel light, *she* is lighter. This is how *he* hunted. And looking down at the long, menacing barrel, it is a line. As she looks around the trees, they are still: the gun is the line she has drawn between herself and the forest. Anything – any lost pilot – could try and come and find her now. She would be ready. She is ready. This is real freedom.

Kasper isn't smiling anymore, and she looks up at the sky; it has turned cloudy, white, like the bark of some of the beech and ash trees. Kasper is walking to pick up the wooden targets.

Kasper shoots. Madeleine shoots.
We hunt.

'Let's go,' Kasper says.

She has the gun and as she looks closely at it, following Kasper into the forest, the dark, varnished wood feels cool in her hand. The gun makes no difference; the trees are too quiet, too patient. The forest is still greater than her. The only silence is their path through the forest, the stones and twigs, the nervous breaths from their lungs.

'Look for nests,' Kasper instructs her. 'They're easiest to shoot when feeding their babies. Then we can try to shoot them when they're flying.'

Madeleine walks along beside Kasper, his head constantly searching and looking, so enthusiastically she wonders if he is just pretending. She can't think of his father acting this way, wherever he is.

'When do you think the war will end?' She has to repeat the question a few times and her hunting companion is still resolutely looking at the trees. 'When all the soldiers and armies have killed each other?'

'No. There will always be fresh recruits. New regiments.'

Madeleine thinks about a war with no end, and she's glad she never knew the pilot. She is perturbed at the frequency he keeps coming into her mind. It feels intrusive, unsettling, like seeing maggots in a bowl of milk. Kasper still walks along looking up at the trees. The sky is still white and the forest is still quiet.

'Why did it start?'

'The Germans started it. They invaded us. They need more land. Or maybe they've gone mad. Like the Russians. We weren't ready but we'll defeat them both and destroy them. Look. Up there.'

She swings her head around with absolutely no idea of where Kasper is looking. He shoots into the trees and she follows the line of his gun and the shattering of some leaves and branches high up in a beech tree. Some birds chatter and flap around but none come tumbling to the ground. She looks at Kasper who looks impassively at his gun, his expression controlled, as if this is the outcome he was expecting or there was something that unexpectedly went wrong with the gun as he pulls levers and empties cartridges with more fuss than he did before.

'All the invaders will die. Like your pilot.'

She thinks his insinuation is strange and replies: 'He wasn't my pilot. He was lost. He was all alone.' And she wishes she hadn't said the last part because the pilot was her discovery and the only person who knows what happened to him. And even if he was a German, an invader, she still does not wish him dead. She would have tried to save him. Why should he have had to die?

'It was the monster that got him.'

'What?'

'*Potwór.*' He says some other things in Polish, indicating his impatience and reminding Madeleine of Eva. And he gestures, again like Eva might, walking away from her, gesturing that they leave. The gesture is in the direction of home but she has no orientation.

'The monster.' As if it is common knowledge so he will not elucidate. It is something she should know. They eventually hear the sound of the stream; they are nearly home. *The monster.* As if it is the password to enter the forest. She tries to ask some more questions about it but he is unresponsive. She begins to look forward to getting back to the house so she can be away from Kasper. Thinking about what has happened, she thinks it's unfair. The way he's suddenly become so taciturn, she might as well be talking to a tree. She can't help smiling to herself as she pictures knocking on his head and producing the same dull, hollow sound as knocking on a tree. For the first time she is looking forward to seeing Eva and can even understand how she is always impatient and exasperated if all Polish men are like this. But not all. All Polish boys.

She starts to recognise the scenery, the pattern of the trees; they are familiar now. They welcome her and she is home. The dull brown colour through the cracked and broken pine twigs is her home. The smoky smell in the kitchen. The cold, high bed and dark, somewhat damp bedroom is hers. The mirror is hers but the girl on the other side is not. She forgets she is carrying the gun and, bored, starts to rock it on its worn leather strap. The metal feels cold now. She grabs it, as if reacting to an ambush, and aims it at trees, at the clouds beginning to break up, and then the flare of the sun through some disintegrating clouds. The muzzle of the gun disappears in the face of that faraway great explosion in the sky and an arc of light falls to glint more brightly than she would have thought possible, blinding her. Through the streams of her eyes she sees him looking at her, though he may as well be a tree for all his movement. She stands rubbing her eyes and Kasper's looking at her to see what she does next.

She takes the gun, swings it up to her shoulder where it still doesn't feel comfortable, and points directly at him: '*Me regarde pas comme ça.*'

She watches him go as expressively as possible, demonstrating that she's gone insane, that the gun has turned her into somebody else. And watching him slouch away makes her heart sink, and she drops the rifle from its alert position. She doesn't want the gun anymore, but she does; it is hard to give up. That's why men become soldiers: it makes them powerful; nobody argues with them. Why don't women? Why doesn't Eva? She thinks of all these women – women in kitchens, stressed and straining, breaking chickens' necks; these women would be the more ferocious warriors. This war will last forever. She sits on a stump and lets the rifle fall near her. There will always be soldiers. Everyone thinks they can win with a gun in their hands. She sits listening to the quiet forest and looking at the empty sky. No birds and no planes. The sun has started to shine even though it's getting darker; the breeze scatters cold air around rather than dispelling the hot air. She likes handling the rifle: its wooden parts are warm and smooth, its black metal bits cold and grooved. She lowers the rifle and ambles back to the house, looking for Kasper. Would he be lying in wait? An ambush from the staircase, a raid from the backyard? She wishes he would, almost. Kasper could point and aim his gun at her. She deserves it. She doesn't know why she did it.

Jan walks through the trees, his rifle strapped on his back, the strap on his shoulder. Eva had asked him for the umpteenth time to go into the village and ask about Madeleine. Someone must know something. Girls do not wander around forests, especially in the middle of a war, she had said. Walking up to the police station – a small hut, annexed to the town hall – he has thought of a million reasons not to come here, but the one reason he should come here is more persuasive. What anyone in a small town would know about a girl who is most likely from the other side of Europe is beyond him, but it's been a while since he's been to the town. Entering the room he realises he has not been here since they tried to ask him questions about Tereza. And when they see him, the way they freeze suggests to Jan that they have not forgotten either. Their uniforms are of the old regime, threadbare and shabby, the leather of their belts and straps worn and cracked. They bear the red patches of the new regime on their arms and chests. The junior officer at the desk in front of him, the corporal, looks alarmed and looks back to the captain who is more assured and folds his arms returning Jan's gaze unflinchingly.

'Well what brings the ambassador here, I wonder?' the captain asks. He lights a cigarette and walks to the desk, his subordinate giving way to take up a position behind him.

Jan knows this will not be helpful, but his promise to Eva demands it: 'I've come to report a missing girl.'

'A missing girl?' the officer repeats back to Jan.

'Yes, has anyone here reported someone missing? She's about sixteen years old, about so tall' – indicating with his hand – 'and she has no memory of where she's come from.'

'She's not blonde is she?'

Jan shakes his head.

'Pity, we could have sent her off to Germany. The commissioner would no doubt have profited from it. And maybe I could be moved from this piss-hole of a town.'

'Now you do know?' Jan said.

'Yes, we know someone's missing. Everyone knows someone who's missing. This whole country is missing. Just what do you expect me to do about it ambassador?'

'Nothing could be expected of you, captain. Not before and not now.'

'If I may make a suggestion: you are aware that that monster's been seen out in the woods again. You could bring us its head. Or the head of that witch. As for the girl, I suggest you enjoy her. She will no doubt make a refreshing change from your wife.' The captain exhales and rubs out his cigarette in the dented brass ashtray. Jan takes his wrist and holds his hand to the desk, and the captain looks up at Jan, desperately, unable to move his hand.

'What are—'

Jan embeds his hunting knife into the captain's hand, slicing easily between the thin bones and through the meat until he feels its point slowly sink into the solid surface of the desk. The captain's scream sounds far away to Jan, but he savours the man's quivering before swiftly withdrawing the knife. The captain instantly falls to the floor, wrapped around his bleeding hand. The other officer does not know what to do and stands looking at the squealing, bleeding officer on the floor.

'Attend to your captain, corporal. Injury procedures.' Jan walks out, the corporal nearly having saluted him. The dark-red bloodstain he sees on the desk underneath the captain's hand seems to be the image of a bird of prey.

Madeleine rests the long-necked gun by the door and wanders into the kitchen; Eva is not around. She pours some water from the jug into a scratched and chipped glass. The whole kitchen feels cold, so she wanders into the dining room, where they have only eaten once, and sees that the table has been set. She doesn't remember the table and its setting being this ornate; the glasses glisten in the dim light, like the light glints in an animal's eyes. The cutlery shines like coins on a riverbed or the sandy, murky depths of a well. The tablecloth is a deep-red as if it has been washed and rinsed in a bucket of blood. There are two broad golden bowls in the centre. Towards either end of the table are some squat golden candlesticks holding two pale-yellow candles, which are nearly both burned down to their base. The kitchen is brighter, at least, and now she notices there is a steaming samovar on the table and boiling pots on the stove, and she realises the kitchen is warm. The bright light somehow darkens the interior at the same time.

Eva comes from behind her, making Madeleine jump. She doesn't know how long she's been there. She says something as she gestures at the table in the other room. She rubs her face and doesn't look Madeleine in the eye. Her breathing is staccato, deep. Madeleine wonders whether she has been crying and thinks about how long it's been since she saw him. Maybe he's left, maybe he's gone. And something like a sudden panic comes into her heart, thudding against it, thinking quickly whether she can stay here with only Eva and Kasper. Then she dismisses this as silly or at least as unknowable; why would Jan do that? But something else she doesn't like grips her in turn; what if he brings back someone else; what if he's looking for a way to get rid of her so a new girl can come take her place? Is she crying because she took a last-minute liking to her but it's too late because she's not good enough, doesn't understand Polish – because she threatened to shoot their son today.

'I'm sorry!' she shouts at Eva.

Eva stops, suddenly. Madeleine is surprised more than anything; she doesn't realise she has this much power or presence in her voice. Eva looks at her, looks back at the pots and, after checking the rest of the stove, takes her hand, brushing away the tears that have formed at the corners of her deep brown eyes.

She says something as she leads them out the back door.

'Let's go. It's Sunday, we need some flowers for the table.'

Madeleine, beginning to feel foolish, is eager to achieve whatever Eva wants with a minimum of discussion; she wants to be pure, invisible efficiency. Eva is still talking though, saying four, five, six or seven words, single words repeatedly. They have to find seven stags to bring home and eat? To wring the necks of seven chickens? (She would happily agree to that.) A prayer? Days of the week? Which day is it today? All the words are thick and impenetrable, consonants softened and molten. They sound like vowels sinking and colliding with each other, like corpses sliding slowly downwards, into the aquamarine fields; white shadows jettisoned from the black hulk of a sinking ship. Madeleine is perturbed by this image that seems to come from nowhere into her mind. Just outside the door of the kitchen Eva pauses and disappears back inside. She returns with two shawls: thick and black and with a musty smell.

They wander out of the back door into the cool twilight. She senses the sun sinking by the second. She is unnerved by Eva walking slowly, slowly, looking at the ground. She has never seen her move so slowly, sapped of speed. The sky is pale-blue, but dark at the same time, lit by the retreating sun as if the world is sinking deep into the ocean, leaving the sun far above. She follows Eva, who skirts the trees, and Madeleine realises she has never come this way before. They mingle with some trees before reaching a clearing; they could almost be fields but for the lack of any crops. They do grow flowers though, and as Eva stoops to pick them, one hand grasping the two edges of the shawl, she hears her talking. She moves closer but the words remain strange to her even at a closer distance. They both have bunches of honeysuckle, lilies, bluebells and some Madeleine can't identify.

'God is strange, he's strange to me. Even after all this time. I don't know if he hears me. I try to do the right thing, to live righteously, but I never know if he is pleased or not. I try to be pious and good and amend for my boy's lack and religious shortcomings. Even Jan, since we've come here, since he lives here, he no longer hears. No longer...'

Madeleine continues to pick, measuring the expansiveness of Eva's bouquet to judge her own.

Eva looks at her and says: 'It's as if I'm confessing to a priest.' The confession that ended in the promise of repentance, of the absolution of venial sins by uttering the names of Mary and the saints. She thinks but does not say the following thought, that she might as well be talking to Him himself for all the response she gets from the girl. Madeleine. The whore's name. The poor women, the lost women. Pity them and help them. Helping them will dissolve the pity.

I have helped this girl as your son helped her namesake. Am I not deserving? It has been a long time since she has been to church, been in the closer presence of God, or at least in the company of those who claim to make sense of his absence. Out here in the field of flowers, in the forest, it is difficult sometimes.

Sometimes, I feel I am worthy, you sent me this girl to help me. She is your lost child, am I not doing right by her?

Eva looks down to see she has gathered a copious bundle of flowers, too many for the vases she has, too many more counting Madeleine's contribution. The girl is still picking. She moves over to her, says her name: 'Madeleine, let's go home.'

And Madeleine shows she understands what she says now and they progress through the flowers that remain in the fields back to the house, brighter in the darkness than when they left.

Hosting

Madeleine takes charge of the wealth of flowers they had amassed and sets to cleaning them of earth over a bucket, then cutting the stems, arranging the different colours. She's frustrated by her inability to pick out more than individual words from Eva's speeches to herself in the fields. Eva comes to give her a vase, cut in ornate patterns depicting foliage curling around the rim and forming three slender ridges down the sides before fanning out again in a thick bulb of glass. Madeleine finds it hard to lift and to transport it to the dark, expansive dining table. The smell of the flowers strays throughout the dining room and kitchen, mingling with the steaming stew and vegetables, creating a pleasant-not-pleasant heavy odour that seems to prowl around beneath them like a domestic animal. Eva has found some more vessels to deal with the rest of the flowers, and as Madeleine is arranging some more in a not particularly suitable glass, she almost drops the glass she is holding at an angle to slip more flowers into its mouth.

The noise of the door is too loud and quick for it to be Kasper. Her heart and stomach are jittery and it takes a moment for the adrenaline to dissolve away into her system, the solid bones, the taut muscles; these keep her steady and nearly elegant. He comes in through the door, his boots falling loudly and heavily on the solid dark floorboards. She looks at his dirty face and his big dirty hands and she sees around his arms a mass of brown-grey fur hanging over one arm and an indistinct smudge of blue-grey feathers over the other one.

He is very close to his wife, and she looks down at his arms as he proffers them both to her, very close so the fur and feathers are almost touching her breasts. His face disappears, from Madeleine's perspective, behind his wife's head as he leans in to whisper something in her ear. She is still looking down and nods. She gestures to the arm covered in fur, the arm which holds two dead rabbits. He leaves his wife and she notices that Kasper has come in and seems excited by his father's possessions. He walks up and his father turns round to him and holds up the two rabbits that were bigger than she imagined they would be; he held them by their ears and they dangled down, long, thin and inert. She is transfixed and only looks at Jan when they swing through space suddenly and quickly. Startled, she watches one double somersault into Kasper's arms. He fumbles but holds on to it. And then Jan motions to her; she thinks she might have to catch one too but he just signals with the rabbit, as if the rabbit is in agreement with him, to stand by the table and prepare it. Kasper knows what to do; he has done this before. The rabbit lands heavily on the table, a soft thud, like fruit falling from a tree. She looks at it; one of its eyes is slightly open, looking at nothing. And she sees its fore paws hanging as if it is too weak to keep them straight. Jan and Kasper are talking excitedly. Jan motions and says something to her she doesn't understand, but she is pleased not to have to look at the rabbit any longer. She sees he is pointing to a bucket in the far corner of the kitchen and she goes to fetch it, brings it back and positions it under the edge of the table. Kasper has brought a rough board and two knives, laying them down on the table. Jan is in the process of taking off his big overcoat and boots, noisily flinging them by the door. Eva has bought some more candles and sets them by the rabbit. Kasper looks at her, pleased to be able to show her what he is about to do. She notices her heart is beating faster, her stomach enduring acidic storms. She keeps telling herself there is nothing to be afraid of, but it doesn't help. Thinking about what could have been scaring her made it worse, though she realises at some point that it is nothing to do with the rabbit and the blood. She would soon see it was not disappointing Kasper or his father.

It was Sunday, and the word she had heard was *Niedziela*, which Kasper repeats to her when she asks him, as if it were his least favourite thing. Sundays were marked by the other heavy and sour odour of oil lamps that Eva lit for the occasion. Jan gestures to Madeleine to leave it by the rabbit. Kasper hovers about, as awkwardly and unaffectedly as usual. His earlier skirmish with Madeleine seems to have been forgotten as he explains with low relish how they will have to rip out the heart and lungs of the *królik*. His father will already have cleared the rabbit of its piss by rubbing downwards on its bladder. Now they will have to gut the entrails once the rabbit is finished cooling. Madeleine is still transfixed by the rabbit so she doesn't hear Jan's order to Kasper to finish the preparation. Kasper roughly pushes her arm and she makes an exaggerated vowel sound of complaint. He responds by brandishing a short knife awkwardly and passing Madeleine one, at which she flinches and automatically responds in a harsher tone of voice than she intended. If Kasper notices the tone, he doesn't say anything. Jan comes back, munching on something, and tells Kasper to proceed. Kasper, with a swift purpose of movement that shocks Madeleine almost as much as where his hand ultimately ends up, seems to punch the rabbit so hard his hand disappears into its body. Strung up, like the crucifixion of the animal kingdom, the rabbit's paws are tied up to the wooden frame, its back paws limp and, beginning to stiffen, hanging straight, unnaturally straight. In the rabbit's body, Kasper pulls at its stomach and his hand looks dark in the low oil lamplight as if he has just plunged his fingers into a jar full of ink. He throws what looks like an inedible part of a vegetable but which is the dark, leaking rag of its stomach into a sack by the table. Kasper – looking like a doctor on a surgical ward for rabbits – with his one bloody fist, motions for Madeleine to come forward as a junior assistant for her training. He tells her to puncture the diaphragm. She closes her eyes, barely able to see any detail of the rabbit's ragged interior anyway in the soft lamplight, and hears a small kind of popping sound, a small resistance on the point of her knife. She looks at Jan who's looking back at her, leaning back on the table, keeping a commentary for Eva, who appears to be laughing.

Kasper's anatomical French comes back to him as he instructs: 'Now, grab the heart and lungs.'

She is not as surprised by what he says as his manner: unaffected, like a doctor, she thinks, for the second time. But why should this be abnormal? They need to eat, she needs to eat – I/you/he-she-it – this is her contribution to Jan's efforts, undertaken alone in the forest. This doesn't make it any easier though, to move her hands towards the rabbit's cold and dark hollow body, from which rivulets of blood are trickling after the removal of the diaphragm. She continues to conjugate all the Polish verbs she knows and it distracts her somewhat after the task at hand. She slowly pushes into its cavity, more disgusted by the discovery the rabbit is cold rather than warm, and feels around the moist and small organs. She pulls on them slightly but they don't budge. Kasper shouts 'pull' as she looks at them both, Jan's face red and smiling as he lights his pipe. And in trying to get a better grip she squeezes the lungs and feels a sludging wetness start to snail down her fist and wrist.

'Pull,' says Kasper, starting to snortle unhelpfully. And she gasps as she wrenches the heart and lungs free; the rabbit's useless neck jolts in reflex at the final operation. She looks at the dark-red, almost black, indefinable objects in her fingers, like crushed fruit, but not juicy like fruit, not sweet-smelling, not soft. Kasper tells her to throw them away and she flings them into the sack as Jan congratulates her and ruffles her hair. He undoes the rabbit from its frame and fixes the other one up, but Eva, mercifully, takes her away and washes her hands in the basin, leaving the second rabbit to the more indifferent, practised minds of the father and son. Eva washes Madeleine's hands clean, and brushes her head, rearranging her hair. The smell of the innards remains on her fingers and even the heavy, thick fragrance of the flowers can't cover it up. Then Eva takes over and takes the silver bowl that has caught the rabbits' blood as well as the rabbits and throws them on the board to cut them up. Kasper pushes into her, laughing, telling her to help him. They have to fill jugs with water, put vegetables into bowls, place bread on the table.

When they reach the darkness he says to her: 'Have you forgotten about the monster?'

'What monster?' she replies, trying to be blasé.

The potwór.

'You remember. The monster. It knows where you live.'

'Then it knows where you live too. Though why would it want you?' She was pleased with this remark.

'I know how to kill monsters. It likes girls and you're not from this forest.'

I'm more part of the forest than you are. All you do is shoot guns in it – I used to live there.

Taking the silence for apprehension, he continues: 'It prefers girls. Foreign girls.'

He's interrupted by Eva shouting at him, or them both, she can't tell, but Kasper plods off. She comes back into the kitchen and immediately sees Jan sitting down on a chair, oil, metal parts and rags spread about him, cleaning the gun resting against his inner thigh. The bloody, meaty smell of the roasting rabbits adds to the hothouse of smells, and she wonders how many smells can coexist in the same space before they all collapse in a strong wind that will blow through the house, or whether her nose will start to bleed. She starts and sees Jan looking at her, draining what looks like a glass of beer.

'*Ça va, ma pouce?*' he asks.

This unexpected French fills her face with blood in embarrassment. She smiles and giggles, hating herself for not being able to formulate words in response. His accent is so heavy and deep it's hard to understand him. He stands up and walks towards her and ruffles up her hair again and mock pushes her into the dining room, telling his son to hurry up.

Evening

Jan pulls a chair out for Madeleine, the upholstery on the seat dark, a bit greasy and a little shabby. Eva appears before Kasper bearing the steaming carcass of the rabbit and Madeleine finds she can't stop looking at it, the meat so recently red and raw now sweet-smelling and black-brown. Kasper clumsily and splashily pours water into everyone's mug while Eva, having brought the oil lamp to the middle of the large table, starts to say grace. Madeleine listens to the hushed words in a language she has only made a few guesses at. She looks at the glass and bowls glowing in the light of the lamp, the surfaces gleam and shadow according to the flickering of the flame in its glass case, like a trapped spirit or genie. Eva finishes talking and Kasper starts eating. Jan slaps his arm with a violence that shocks Madeleine and talks quickly to him, while Kasper grumbles and serves the vegetables, potatoes and rabbit onto Madeleine's plate. She says 'thank you' in Polish, which makes Eva look up.

'We'll have to watch what we say about her then,' Jan says in French.

Eva replies in Polish: 'You can translate, you're so fond of French.'

Kasper lowers his eyes and Madeleine notices his discomfort and the shortness of Eva's tone. She studies the relatively clean cutlery, heavy in her hands as if they are weapons that can only be used with skills taught by extensive training. The rabbit is delicious but she still feels strange to have to be eating it; she would make a poor hunter. She thinks she will have to commemorate these rabbits, maybe say a prayer; God will listen – rabbits are God's creatures. Maybe she will light a candle for them when she goes to bed.

Eva is scolding Jan again. 'Instead of getting some thread or shoes you got beer.'

'Beer is very difficult to get hold of – I didn't want to miss this opportunity.'

She points at Kasper, stabbing the air in front of her with her fork. 'And this one, useless enough, he'll get the wrong idea from you, behaving in this way. Fine example. Fine mess you all make of everything.'

'Who?' asks Kasper, genuinely curious.

'Our kind,' Jan exhales, sipping his beer, and pouring some into his glass, his smouldering pipe in his other hand. 'Enjoy this while you can before you marry.'

'The world will be destroyed by men before he will have a chance to propose. And who will take him? Good for nothing.'

They finish eating in silence; Madeleine didn't realise how hungry she was until she started eating.

Then Jan rises to fetch the bottle of wine or essence of wine; Eva tells Kasper to fetch some more water.

Wine. Water. Words she knows now: *come, go.*

Sunday.

Hunt.

Forest.

Rabbit.

Lost.

The verb endings are complicated, especially to differentiate by sound.

Eva says her name more loudly and Madeleine jumps. She jumps up and takes some of the plates into the kitchen. Jan and Kasper remain seated talking and Jan refills his pipe.

She comes back in to see Kasper animated again, although this means mistranslating things his parents have said to unsettle Madeleine. But she is more resistant to it now she realises all of them have a basic understanding of French. Jan is leafing through the shiny, reflective black book that is the Bible, and once Eva has settled with some water, Kasper tells her it is from Exodus, chapters 11 to 14, when Moses announces the death of the first-born sons and of the Israelites' flight from Egypt. Madeleine has some more wine in her elegant Sunday wine glass and manages to take only very small sips and it doesn't taste as bitter this way. The wine looks deep-red in the dim, golden light, like the rabbits' blood. It looks precious, like the juice in Eva's perfume bottles, pressed from rubies. The whole glass looks like a jewel, shining like flames on buried treasure.

Before Jan starts reading, Eva says another short prayer and this time clasps her hands. Madeleine sees a metallic ring on Eva's finger, gold but almost white. There are no rings on Jan's fingers. Jan taps his pipe while she is praying. Madeleine wonders what she can be saying, as she's almost whispering. It's strange the familiar biblical words in their language, as if they've been distorted – Moses, Egypt, God. She thinks how the Israelites' God let them be taken captive in the first place, and didn't the Egyptians have a God? How cruel that they had no defence against all their sons dying on the same night. No warning. No time to say goodbye.

The flowers look dark in the dim light; they need the daylight to make them seem alive, like sunlight shining through stained-glass windows. They begin to reassert their fragrance after the meat has been cleared away and the smell of roasting fat has begun to dissipate. The smoke from the pipe drifts across the table, blue and thick as if it's incense in a church, wrapping itself in and over the equally heavy smell of the flowers.

When they all stand up, her head feels heavy as if all the scents of the day have seeped into her head and liquefied there, congealing like the rabbits' fat on the plates. She stays at the table with Kasper, while Eva disappears into the kitchen, Madeleine seemingly being excused her duties for the Sunday evening.

Kasper sits hunched; he seems to be tired too, his arms on the table, his head sunk on his arms. Madeleine realises she's never explored this room and moves slowly and sleepily over to the corner, by the far window, the deep-blue light as if it is the glass that's stained sapphire blue, or, she thinks, like a porthole in a submarine, fathoms deep under the surface of the ocean. There are a few books standing lonely on the shelves: two more Bibles, one hymn book and an encyclopaedia. One of the Bibles is in French, and Madeleine realises, happy now, as if she has instantly decoded the secrets of a lost civilisation, that the pages she flicks through are all familiar – the Garden of Eden, the Flood, the Gospel according to Mark, the visions of St John the Divine, the rivers that surrounded Eden, the work of Ruth, the awful horror Jesus spoke of before the Last Supper and the White Rider who signals the end of life and of a new life. She reads short passages from these books, the words not all familiar enough so she gets bored quickly. Bored and then sleepy and cold. The house is quiet, the odd creak – where has everyone gone?

There are shadows moving vigorously from the kitchen, and as she moves through the door to see, she bumps into Eva coming the other way with the lamp in her hand.

She says: 'Good night,' and puts her hand on Madeleine's head. Smiling, she swirls around elegantly, more so than Madeleine has ever seen her, and takes the lamp upstairs.

Madeleine decides to take the Bible with her to bed, to be a little warmer even though she knows she will now not be able to read more than a few pages, but she feels compelled nonetheless. Madeleine reads the Book of Ruth again and the descriptions of such an all-consuming friendship leave her feeling empty and sad, staring at the window, the glass appearing dark and opaque rather than translucent. She reads Ruth's talk to Naomi:

> Where you go I will go;
> Where you lodge I will lodge;
> Your people shall be my people,
> And your God my God.
> Where you die I will die – there will I be buried.

A few minutes later Madeleine blows out the candles and is unready for the complete darkness that immediately fills the room. Eventually it ebbs away once the light flows in from the windows, from which she keeps the shutters open.

She sees lines of light seeping from under the doors of both Kasper's and his parents' rooms. She still bumps into the table and banister, blaming the wine. She undresses and slides, shivering and quickly, under the many heavy covers. The bed is a hard coldness and seems to take forever to warm up. She looks at the halo of candlelight and eventually blows it out, leaving the phosphorus smell she hates drifting in the darkness.

It seems only minutes later that she wakes up and it's still dark. She knows she has to wake up, and in the early morning cold she slips into her red dress. She knows she has to go out into the woods. Eva isn't awake yet and there's no sound, but she has to go and she creeps downstairs and breathes more freely once she's outside. Yet she's surprised and also unsettled at how dark it remains outside and how noisy it is. All the birds are singing although it doesn't sound as it usually sounds. The sweet and light songs and refrains sound instead choked and garbled as if the birds have become forgetful or drunk or insane, if it's possible for birds to become drunk or insane. She looks at some flapping in the lower branches and sees the birds have become grotesquely fat and swollen and she peers closer at them and sees they're not the usual birds but chickens.

The night sky is as bright as when there's a full moon, except she can't see the moon tonight, the moon has replaced the sun. She can't see it, obscured by the trees. The chickens are visible in the lower branches. And as she walks – gingerly now – under the trees, and their stark branches stretch out black against the moonlit sky, she hears a soft thump behind her and then a delirious cackling. One of the chickens has fallen down, fallen like over-ripe fruit and then screams off into the night, running – however the locomotion of chickens may be described – and making un-chicken-like sounds, more like the pressured exhalations of steam engines.

She can see it suddenly become brighter as she passes through a clearing, but the moon is still invisible and she can't see any stars either. A sharp, short movement makes her jump: the trees are moving. Running. Then she looks closer – it isn't the trees. One of the trees is blasted white by the bright moonlight and she sees its shadows suddenly jolt and writhe behind it like dark lightning, and then she sees that its shadows start to move and spasm, then fall still again in the moonlight. The moonlight vanishes all at once as if the moon has become screened by deep clouds. Madeleine moves towards the trees, resting her head on its soft bark. It feels comforting against her forehead and she rubs her hands over the bark, unlike any she's ever felt before; in waves, her hands follow the grain of the bark in one direction and go against it in the other. She looks at the bark to see it's soft and prickly; it's composed of hairs – this tree has grown a beard. This tree is furred and soft as are the other trees behind it that she can see. She moves to run her palm over another one; these trees must be male. She continues to run her hand over their soft sharpness.

Her heart is thumping in her chest and her hands and armpits are moist and hot and she wants to run but is mesmerised by the bearded trees. But she hears a sound, soft and faint – a voice! Someone is lost among these horrible dead trees. She can't see anything but is relieved it isn't a chicken garbling from one of the tree branches. Then she almost steps on it but can see in the darkness, by the black and twisted roots of one pale tree, a small bird. Small and red and black. The bird is lying at the roots of the tree, its wings broken and shattered, its black feathers clotted with blood, crying out two drawn-out vowels, recognisable in any language – '*Ma-ma...*' She sees its throat constricting and swallowing, unable to say anything else. Its throat is gargled thickly with blood and its small face is dark and shines like dew on flowers. What is he doing here? The trees look on down, silently, trapped in their own agony of inertia. She breaks away, running for some reason, and tears are coming from her eyes, blurring her vision, but the bird's voice seems to keep up with her and as she whips past the soft trees and the soft ground it becomes harder and harder to maintain her speed, and soon it is as if she is wading through water up to her waist. And now she can hear what it is that the bird has started to cry – '*Ma-deleine...*'

She thinks she hears something else; can it really be a talking bird?

'Help me!'

Or is it the tree? The tree grabs her and lacerates her chest.

She gasps and reaches out, jolting in her bed, reaching out to clutch the pillow and the sheets. Breathing deeply. She is in her bed, crying, and her sheets are around her knees and her nightshirt is sodden with her own sweat. She pulls up the sheets and pulls up her knees to her chin. Then she quickly reaches over to light the candles, thankful she brought some matches up to her room. The soft light starts to expand, like a golden exhalation, and she feels more scared, the darkness made visible by the light, by what she might see in the room – *by the tree roots*. But it's quiet and the shadows are still and sway slowly in time with the thin plume of the candle's flame. She realises the nightmare is over, its dark, horrible spell is broken and she is safe – safe enough. She wipes her face and eventually settles back down into bed. She cannot bear to extinguish the candles and be in darkness again and so she pulls the thin sheet over her head and the candle glows pale gold through the sheet as if it is dawn. It seems quiet under the sheet, quiet and warm, and Madeleine begins to feels sleepy.

Signals

The next morning Madeleine wakes up to the warm sheet covering her mouth and cheek, making them slightly moist. Before she can remember that there was something unpleasant on her mind, she remembers the bird under the tree and buries her face in the warm pillow. She wrenches her eyes tightly shut so that formless planes of purple and orange light appear and dissolve under her eyelids and are replaced by clouds in the sky, and she remembers it was only a dream. She can understand why she might have a nightmare. All she has been through – the wandering, the pilot, the new house, the strange land, strangers hiding from the war. Everything has turned out fine, she reflects, dressing and studying herself in the mirror, defiantly staring at the girl, pulling on her dress, her face wet with cold water. It was only a bad dream. Things could be much worse. Yet, there's something in the face of the other girl, the girl whose name is not Madeleine; the other nameless girl who does remember and makes Madeleine pull away from the mirror and feel perturbed and must check now whether this isn't a nightmare too.

She pulls a sheet from the bed and throws it over the mirror. She opens the door and steps, quickly, into the hallway and onto the landing, and she can hear Eva's voice. For the first time she feels immensely relieved to hear her stressed voice and exasperated tone. She goes back into her room and looks at the covered mirror and it makes her more uneasy. She can't see the other girl and she doesn't know what the other girl is doing. Angry with herself for being so irrational and surrendering to her paranoid fears, she wrenches the sheet from the mirror and angrily accuses the girl who's equally angry at having been covered. Madeleine stays fixed by the accusing gaze of the girl, the girl who knows what happened to them, the one who must remember why she ended up in these dark forests. The one who knows why Madeleine suffered the nightmare. And the one who stays silent. Did she suffer nightmares before? What could her dreams have been like with a full memory? Are these the same nightmares…? Madeleine breaks away, she has to leave, she has to speak to someone, be with someone else. She walks towards Kasper's room. As she approaches, she knows how strange and impolite this is and she hesitates, but she still feels uneasy and perturbed by her nightmare.

She thinks that some time in Kasper's company can't be as bad as this, and he wouldn't send her out to the chickens. The chickens from the nightmare flash up in her mind like a great wave breaking catastrophically over the sails of a ship and propels her to knock against his door.

He opens quickly with the weary expression of being all too used to seeing only one person at his door – someone with a list of chores. He visibly pales when he sees Madeleine and this gives her the edge. She advances into the room, brushing past him, and he draws back, the door fanning open to reveal his chamber. It is as disordered as she expects but gives more the impression of an adult's room than that of an adolescent, the strange smell, which is not pleasant but not unpleasant either, aside. It's dusty too, some small, dirty glasses by the unmade bed. The curtains are half drawn leaving the tranche of sunlight to illuminate the dust like the beam of a searchlight.

'What are you doing here?' Kasper asks.

'You don't mind do you? I just wanted to see your room? I didn't have anything else to do? Did you just wake up?'

Kasper splutters a denial.

There is a radio on the large desk; it, too is disordered and in pieces, as though having recently suffered a small explosion. There is a large map, several maps, scattered around on the desk and on the floor. She swans around his room, feeling liberated by his awkwardness and, having taken him by surprise, she relishes her pretence at playing the queen paying an impromptu regal visit to one of her simple woodland subjects. She asks him about various objects and he stammers incomprehensible responses, although he starts to recover his poise when she asks about the radio.

'I'm repairing it. It's very old, made in Gdansk before the war. I want to find out how to eavesdrop on German military communications.'

'You wouldn't be able to do that,' Madeleine scoffs.

'Yes I could, I used to listen to ship communications and locate their position and course. I even heard when they sank.'

'Really?'

'Do you know what CQD means?'

'No, what does it mean?' She thinks that even for Polish the absence of all vowels is a little much.

'It's a distress signal in code.'

'Not SOS?'

'They are both used. CQD is older but I heard ships use it when nobody answers their SOS.'

Madeleine feels gloomy by the talk of sinking ships, even though any conversation that did not revolve around birds was welcome. But, still, she will change the subject.

'What are you doing today? Do you want to go... shooting?'

'We're not supposed to go into the woods too much.'

'Why not?' Madeleine asks, picking up some maps of Europe and one of the eastern United States. Both deliver a shock to Madeleine, showing her in intricate detail that the world is out there. She may have forgotten it but it is still there – it has not stopped existing. There was Kasper's tight, inelegant scribble in some of the remote parts of the map, looking itself like a code. Unbreakable by being unreadable.

'But of course I go wherever I want...' Kasper continues, to justify and exaggerate his freedom. Madeleine, with the map of Eastern Europe in her hand, is entranced by it, not listening to Kasper. She looks closer at the lines and names, black, red and blue. The names in Polish render everything unfamiliar, so that it may as well be a map of some alien planet. She unfolds it, following thick and thin pencil lines that Kasper, presumably, had drawn emanating from Prussia like the legs of a spider into Poland and through Czechoslovakia to meet lines from the Soviet Union. The map ended, seemingly arbitrarily, somewhere to the west of Potsdam. There were no names she could see further west. Although the Polish would have effaced the familiarity of any of the names, the shape of things might have synchronised with something in her head.

'... I know every part of the woods, so I know all the hiding places the partisans use to hide from the Germans and the Russians.' Kasper was looking through the window, a general addressing his army of trees, the emperor gazing over the myriad green peoples and banners of his empire.

'Where are we?'

Kasper was interrupted. 'What? What are you talking about?'

'Where on this map?'

He strode over to where Madeleine had perched on the edge of the bed, the map laid flat on her lap. The spot was circled, in the middle of woods that reached as far as Leipzig and as far as Kiev. The nearest city is Wrocław.

'Have you ever been there?'

'Yes, a long time ago before the war. It was very muddy. Small. The village is closer. They're strange, though, in that village.'

Madeleine smiled, involuntarily, that Kasper would describe others as strange.

'I don't think I've ever seen the sea.' Madeleine says in a tone that surprises her in its sadness, as if the illusion of fulfilling a long-held ambition was finally slipping away. 'Why don't we go?'

'Where?'

'To the village? Is it far from the sea?'

'We'd need a car,' Kasper scoffs, barely able to articulate his response to the French girl's ignorance. 'It will take weeks, even when there is no war.'

Madeleine sat on the bed, her hands holding the edge of the mattress either side, becoming more desperate to shake the unease. It might be left to her, to seek Eva and lose herself and her unpleasant feeling in the mindlessness of household chores and domestic obedience. This was the last option.

'Let's go hunting then.'

Kasper, shuffling papers and maps, perks up, like a little animal alert to something on the wind.

'Where?'

'Anywhere.'

'For what?'

'Well, where does Jan go?'

Kasper looks down, away. Mumbles something and begins to pack up his bag, filled with some sketches, a canteen and a knife.

They decide to see if they can find any Germans or Russians to attack or partisans to assist. The first mission is to evade the eyes of Eva to avoid being recruited for chores. Kasper is expert in the evasive arts, however; the skills of rural combat and stealthy evasion begin at home. They swing a leg over the lower windowsill, Kasper going first and gripping onto the ivy that covers that part of the house. Madeleine doesn't object but her heart seems to push a nervousness down to her legs, which are unsteady, and her hands, slightly moist, grip the ivy in a tight, white embrace. The dress slides up her thighs and she suffers from a further unsteadying in her legs and arms in an attack of modesty, hoping Kasper doesn't look up. But then she hears the heavy thump of his boots thudding onto the earth. The ivy is dirty and she can see their path down the ivy has disturbed all kinds of insects, some crawling over her fingers, some flying away or flying by her face. The ivy has a strong smell of fresh leaves and wood. She hears Kasper saying something, and she guesses by his tone it might translate into 'hurry', and as she lands, more heavily than she thought she would, Kasper is running, bent over, into the trees and waving for her to escape the house and potential capture.

Eva never fails to hear the thumps and bangs, and sometimes even the oaths that sound through the north-west dining room wall. As she watches first her son disappear into the forest, running in his usual silly way, she sees the girl follow him. She finds she doesn't have the inclination to shout at them to return. There is not much for them to do in the house in any case, and she feels Madeleine, if allowed ample time in Kasper's company, will become irritated and bored with him and return, ready and willing to help under her own free will, instead of running around the forest like an animal. Or a soldier. She remembers that she could have done with thread from the village and had missed her chance to send the children.

She herself had not been back to the village since the beginning of the occupation. She stood, clutching Jan's hand as discreetly as possible, watching the German column travel through the village. Numberless men, grey-green, mostly *Feldwebel*, marching straight, looking dead ahead or down at the ground. The ground they had conquered. They had dirty faces most of them. They looked tired. This was only one battalion of one division of several armies – how many? – pushing through the forest to the Ukrainian and Russian fronts. Another battalion, she was told by Jan, was mechanised, and they heard it before they saw the half-tracks, one containing an officer with gold around his shoulders and a cap with a skull at its centre. His vehicle stationed itself in front of the church. The crowd gathered round but kept their distance and retreated as ordinances were nailed to the doors – no Jews here though. They live in the cities. Then they saw the noise that had been created. It shook the earth and penetrated into their stomachs and Eva felt as though she might be sick as the monstrous *Panzer* tanks rolled past bearing their perverted crosses; some had men on their backs, sunlight flashing blinding white from their binoculars or other flecks of metal on their shoulders or from their guns, reflecting the sun blackly. These men looked more relaxed, contented even, as if they were not going to war but were going on holiday. How could anyone stand against them? Eva saw trees – even the bigger, thicker ones – crippled at their base and pushed over as if they were reeds under the feet of children. A slow, agonising cracking sound as if the tanks were eating them. For the one time in her life she felt an unbalancing in her usual antipathy towards the Russian betrayers and invaders and would not have wished these machines on anyone as they had destroyed Polish horses and whole districts of Krakow and Lublin. Then Jan said even though the tanks were big, Russia was bigger; they would be swallowed up in the emptiness of Ukraine before they even saw the roofs of Moscow. They were only metal; metal can rust and break. Then it would end, somewhere in the Russian hinterland. Everything that has a beginning has an end. Apart from God, she crossed herself quickly. Don't fight – just let them through, then it will end.

Why is this happening now, when her boy is young? Helpless. She pressed him close to her, and held Jan's hand, both of them unusually quiet. They walked back home, and through a break in the trees Eva could see the sky turning red, the sun setting in the north – a fiery glow fringing the dark-blue twilight in a vivid blood-orange light.

She knew her mother would have taken the partition and invasion as the sign of the end of days, and she knew, though she never said it, she was grateful for her husband's more relaxed views on the Church's teachings. Her mother had once called him a heretic, a heathen, but then she did hold the view that even the local priest was neither as devout nor as faithful as he could be. Her frequent chastisements on matters of ecclesiastical procedure were an enduring embarrassment for Eva. Everything, from a blocked sink to a thunderstorm to a neighbour's impoliteness, was attributable either to the ordeals sent by the ministrations of God or the machinations of the Antichrist. From Jan's wanderings, he had reassured her that this area was relatively clear of Germans, and their auxiliaries kept to the towns and there were none in the village. They were all in the black troop trains heading for Belarus and Ukraine, their gun turrets aimed at the sky and the stars. And he had even seen the black trains coming the other way, slicing through the dark night, packed with the starving and white corpses of Russian prisoners, their cages exposed to the night – a transport of ghosts – heading to hell. It was an image that had haunted her for days and kept Kasper confined to the house, scrubbing every surface to a brilliance never attained since.

She watches them leave; Madeleine is a good worker, easy to please. It flutters over her mind, like the wings of a crow, that the girl is some gypsy thief. Her real name is one of the guttural, horrible names they use for one another. But she is genuinely foreign, French, something haughty in her manner, no matter how deferential she is. She cannot hide it like the women in

Krakow. Watching the space in the trees in which the children have disappeared, she finds she has been fixed on the spot, rubbing her pendant that sits on her breastbone, the metal now warm, slightly moist. She crosses herself, praying, her reverie of the German invasion into the forest had unsettled her from nothing. *If God loses you in your passage across this earth, may the saints find you and keep you. Keep you close and never let you go. St Christopher and St Nicholas will watch over you.*

Looking up at the trees, the sun, as she was used to, hidden by the netting of the trees, the rays shooting down as they penetrate and transect the flesh of clouds, the forest illuminated by columns of gold, Madeleine thinks of birds.

'When birds die do they fall down from the trees?' she asks without thinking and instantly wishes she hadn't.

'What?' Kasper doesn't even deign to look round. 'I suppose so.' But as he says this, he desperately tries to think of when he had actually seen a bird drop down dead from a tree.

They have reached the creek that Kasper told her feeds the well for the village.

'How deep is the forest?' Madeleine asks.

'How deep? You mean how big?'

'Yes. How big?'

They hear some noises. Madeleine looks at Kasper, who shows no expression but keeps his gun on his shoulder, and then, as it is clear that whoever it is is heading in their direction, he gestures to Madeleine to follow him behind the tree.

'Is it the monster?'

'No, never comes in daylight.'

The loud voices precede the appearance of a gang of children, one of whom, the tallest, is a boy dressed like Kasper, and, Madeleine notices, is carrying a gun. There are two girls talking between themselves at the rear of the group. Kasper, without warning, walks out to meet them. Madeleine follows in his footsteps, coyly observing the children. The leader seems to be called Tadeusz; no one else is introduced and no one asks who Madeleine is, although none of them can take their eyes from her. She feels herself blushing under their scrutiny. Kasper, by way of explanation, ventures to say she is French. He and Tadeusz then discuss the Germans and the war; the village is quiet, no partisan or German activity.

'We're out hunting too,' Kasper exclaims. 'I'm going to capture the monster and show it to her.'

It is hard to say who the children seem more frightened by; they all shout what they know about the monster at them; Kasper can only translate about half.

Medium-height boy, signs of facial hair, light-brown hair: 'It only eats girls.'

Smaller of the two girls, freckles, blonde hair, blue eyes: 'It only eats boys.'

The tallest boy, who also seems to be the oldest: 'It hunts you down by following the scent of your blood.'

The larger of the girls, black hair and blue eyes, says while looking directly at Madeleine: 'Its mother is a witch.'

Another boy, carrying a rifle: 'It has yellow eyes and sharp black teeth.'

Then they set about arguing about the precise physical description.

'Let's have a competition to see who can hunt it down,' Kasper proffers, a challenge to the other group.

'It sleeps during the day, everyone knows that. It only hunts by night.'

'You be the Germans and we'll be the partisans, and we have to defend the house by the creek there and you have to take it from us.'

Madeleine doesn't know if Kasper hasn't heard or is deliberately ignoring the other boy.

'Why do we have to be the Germans? Why can't you be?' The other boy doesn't seem to mind.

They eventually agree to settle it, as seems appropriate, through marksmanship. Madeleine, figuring it out from their motions as much as anything, wonders why Kasper would have agreed to this competition, having witnessed his shooting skills before. She thinks for a second he might even delegate the honour to her. But he doesn't. As they walk to a suitable scene for the contest, she sees that he is down-faced and introverted, studying the leaves on the dark forest floor.

She tells him: 'I know you'll win.'

No response, so she returns to looking at the others, chirping and chattering excitedly ahead of them, the boys taking turns to look down the long barrel of the rifle.

Tadeusz will shoot first. She sees the girls are dressed much like she is, although their dresses and skirts are a little shorter. Madeleine doesn't know how this decision has been reached; there has been no coin toss, and she looks at Kasper to see if he will demand one.

Tadeusz shoots first and shatters the bottle that has been placed on the log. The boys cheer and the girls are clapping, shouting. Then Kasper checks his gun, aims, fires and misses, unspectacularly chipping the log.

'Best two out of three.'

To no avail: Kasper is German and Madeleine finds herself conscripted into the *Wehrmacht*.

'You have to defend the tree and the bottle, we'll attack you,' their enemies shout, disappearing into the trees. They sit down, in silence, and wait, their backs to the tree. Madeleine begins to feel hungry. She'd been so set on leaving the house she'd forgotten to suggest they have breakfast. It was mid-afternoon now.

'What shall we do?'

'We're playing the game,' Kasper replies.

'Let's play something else, this one's boring.'

'They're not very good partisans. I would have won by now.'

Madeleine says: 'Close your eyes as tightly as you can. What do you see?'

'Nothing. Darkness.'

'Close your eyes tighter. Like this.'

He scrunches his eyes, his head tilting downwards with the effort, and she places her hand over his eyes to darken the darkness he would see.

'Do you know about space? If you look up into space it is the same as if you are looking back in time. The stars are old and we see them when they were young.'

'Is that what you see?'

Kasper still sees nothing. Then formless shapes appear and seem to move towards him in the darkness. Then...

'I see stars. Millions and thousands of stars. Like in the real sky. Lots and lots of stars. Spinning. Falling. Is that what you can see?' he asks.

Madeleine looks at him then. As if she were holding her breath to dive under water, she crunches her eyes shut. Kasper realises only when she exhales, gushing like the fountain from a whale's spine, that she has been holding her breath to burn the images brighter behind her eyes, to burnish them with fire, as if she were breathing onto smouldering paper.

'Do you see stars?' Kasper asks.

'No,' Madeleine says, 'I see trees.'

'It's like we're watching darkness.' He shakes his head to be free of her hand and she lets go. He stands up and lurches around, his arms out, zombie-like, to try and find her and grab hold of her. And she yelps, springs up like a squirrel and darts several steps away, the dust clouding up; she issues a challenge through the miasma.

'Come find me. Bet you can't. You're too slow.'

He stumbles around, the dust whirling around him, eyes crumpled closed vainly trying to follow the sounds of her taunts.

'Don't walk into a tree or you will see stars.'

She watches him stumble dizzily away into the trees and she almost screams. Her hands move up to her mouth to keep in the noises gushing up from within. Then they hear a gun shot. Kasper grabs Madeleine's arm and they hide behind a tree.

'Magdalena!'

He's staring fixedly at some leaves. Madeleine had been expecting another dead pilot and is relieved, relieved too that she can't see what Kasper is scared of. Until she looks more closely.

There are pearls of blood on the leaves, scattered here and there at their height. She grabs Kasper's arm, his pale arm, pale face, wide eyes unable to stop staring at the bloodstained leaves.

'What is it? What is it?'

Madeleine knows he is scared as he is speaking in Polish.

'It's him. The monster.'

Not far away they hear the sound of a rifle firing, then firing again quickly. Then some shouts, screams. Like the birds disturbed by the noise, they are flying in their direction. The light seems to be fading to Madeleine when they hear, at once, a crashing and breaking through the undergrowth and, above that, in the air, cries of panic and fear.

Kasper grabs Madeleine and they hide behind a tree. She stumbles over the tree's exposed roots and struggles to find her footing. Planks of splintered wood seem to emerge from the tree – the tree has exploded – exploded into splinters and shrapnel. Madeleine is shaking but then freezes, still. Her mind is consumed by bright light, choking her sight and her motion as if she is being suffocated by smoke...

Kasper moves back to her, hissing at her urgently, then he dares to hold her wrist. He dares to grab her fingers but cannot look at her eyes which have clouded over with... nothingness. Madeleine looks at him, and now Kasper feels unable to move, momentarily, before pulling her to the bushes and the trees.

'What's wrong with you? Are you crazy? It's the monster!' Over his shoulder, on tiptoe, she can see the children of the village running frantically; the two girls last, the boys far ahead of them, stumbling, whipped and lashed by tree branches. And they can hear another sound, in the wake of the children. A sound that disappears. They listen to the sounds decline, picking up everything, no matter how small: a twig falling; the susurrus of the wind scurrying over the leaves; Kasper, coughing. Madeleine feels his palms sheen over with fluid, the pulse that thuds through the fingers. His pulse or hers; she hopes Kasper can't hear her heart slamming against her ribs. Kasper coughs again, and his words begin at a high pitch that normally would have made her laugh.

'We can go – there's no one here.'

And they step out from behind the tree onto the dark path, and in front of them is another boy or what looks like a boy, several metres ahead of them walking towards them, quickly. *He has been waiting for us.*

He stops when he sees them and Madeleine's vision darkens around its edges but she can still distinctly see his pale skin smeared with blood, his skin weirdly light, like milk, and his eyes – his yellow eyes. She swallows and her mouth contracts at the same time. The boy opposite them runs towards them and shouts, a shout neither of them have ever heard; it sounds like a deathly afraid cat or fox. A long piercing squeal. Kasper's grip on her hand tightens but she doesn't feel it, only the shout from Kasper as he moves from frozen stillness to rushing away from the monster. Madeleine, her grip from Kasper's hand whipped apart, is running, running, but she isn't running fast enough. Kasper is ahead of her and then she sees a big black shape emerge quickly from a tree. She stops unsteadily, her breath too big for her body, her lungs too small to inhale the necessary air, her clothes now moist and uncomfortable with cold sweat, rubbing heavily against her back. The black figure hoists Kasper up against the black back of a tree, the thud reverberating like a sack of potatoes; Kasper seems to weigh nothing.

She sees, still stumbling towards them, it is Jan, as she has never seen him before. She doesn't realise it is him at first. His face, nearly hidden by a scarf and hat, all in black, seems crimson with anger, his voice growling at Kasper like an animal, like a monster. Madeleine looks round but the monster has gone. Scared off by Jan. He shouts into Kasper's face and points at Madeleine. She can see Kasper has blanched his eyes, mesmerised by his father, animated by a solid, harsh fury, as if he's a tree come to life to destroy the woodcutter. Kasper's dropped his rifle on the ground and then Jan too flings him to the ground, landing heavily. Madeleine is between them, uncertain who to move towards, uncertain even where is safe to look; she cannot look at Jan. He comes to her, stands close in front of her, although she still cannot look upwards into his face. He takes her gun, examines it, and his hand takes her chin and she sees a quiver in his mouth, the black expression softening, and he asks how she is; did this one put her in danger? She can smell the wood and leather and some other indistinct odours around him, his hands and fingers weave in the air, his presence still lingering in the empty space. She sees his face covered in a beard, black but flecked with grey and white hairs.

'You,' he says to Kasper. Kasper is up on his feet, brushing himself off, and doesn't reply.

'And you,' he says turning back to Madeleine, 'let's go for a walk.' Madeleine falls in beside him and he whispers loudly, loud enough for Kasper to hear, 'Let's see how long he sulks for.' Kasper doesn't reply.

His tone changes: 'There are more and more Germans in this area. They are moving west again. Retreating maybe. And partisans. We – the house – are easy prey.'

She hesitates but then speaks slowly: 'But... there is a monster – he has white skin and yellow eyes...' She looks at

Kasper to confirm this walking nightmare. Kasper remains silent.

They continue walking. If Jan is not alarmed then, Madeleine thinks, they must be safe. He will protect them. As if sensing Madeleine's unease, Jan takes her hand. She feels it rough, but smooth and hard. And warm. She grasps it tightly. As tightly as she can. The undergrowth here comes up to meet them, growing up, Madeleine thinks, as if they are sinking into the forest, like quicksand. There are banks of nettles that brush against her, a deceptively soft caress that gives up its vicious poison, setting her skin on fire. Thick cords of brambles that obstruct the path, at times grabbing Kasper and Madeleine, making them stumble.

The light has almost faded completely now, the canopy above them dark – the dark leaves and the dark sky indistinct, the smoky breaths of ink gushing through water. Neither the nettles nor brambles seem to touch Madeleine as she walks on quickly. Walking at full pace to keep up with Jan, she soon becomes breathless. Not long afterwards they see a house. A house with windows. The light within outlines the window – four lines of light that centre a square of darkness. Jan knocks loudly and walks in. Madeleine and Kasper follow. The house is much darker in the interior.

Jan introduces them to a woman who walks under a beam to the table with a dimly lit oil lamp on it. Madeleine shields herself behind Jan as the woman walks towards them, her eyes looking directly at her – into her. Her arms crossed, her eyes black like an eclipse – black suns. Her hair is wild as if it has been caught in an explosion, beads and threads run up and down, some strands by her head, like veins up and down an arm. She is dressed entirely in black but Madeleine, looking more closely, can see that there are patterns in the black skirt, rococo like the brambles that spiral and striate over the flowers outside. Black but for the red shirt that leaves a triangle of her dark skin, filled by dark gold jewellery that keeps its hand loose round her throat.

She looks at Jan. She says hello to Kasper, who stays close to Jan. Smiling in a way that seems forced, her face cracks and moves as if it is a pressed flower, it seems to Madeleine. It scares Madeleine, as if she knows Kasper's deep, dark secrets – although Madeleine knows he doesn't have any – and she would reveal them if he didn't respond to her satisfaction. He still needs prompting. Jan pushes his shoulder – say hello.

'Hello. We just saw a monster… in the trees.'

She is still smiling, her teeth yellow, her gums brown and black. She turns to face Madeleine. Madeleine sees the little room is dark, only three candles.

'So this is the child of the trees.'

Turning her eyes back to Madeleine, she introduces herself in thick, syrupy French. Madeleine chokes a response.

'You are a lucky child, I hear. Hmm, if you were not so pretty I wonder whether you would have been saved?'

Madeleine can barely make out the French this woman speaks and has to concentrate intently to distinguish the sounds that are distorted and gummed in her throat. She furrows her brow and almost feels like cupping her ear like an old man. Jan looks up from where he is sitting, cleaning his gun, his fingers smeared with grease. The air is fat with its dirty, oily smell.

'Well, here you are. Go make us some tea.' Tereza exhales fully, a cloud, like the locomotive at the front of some long train.

'Sylvester,' she purrs, inclining her head over her left shoulder.

Madeleine's eyes widen and Kasper's jaw slowly drops downwards. The monster emerges from the kitchen, only Madeleine can see it's a boy – or a kind of boy…

'Say hello my darling,' Tereza says. The pig boy holds Tereza tightly and squeaks a word Madeleine presumes is 'hello'. She looks at Kasper who robotically replies with his 'hello'.

This is the monster, a little boy. Madeleine's mind grapples with the fact that Kasper wasn't lying – they did see a monster – but that this is the monster: a deformed boy, his eyes shining golden in the dim light, but he must be the least deformed monster in the world. Then Madeleine realises Tereza's black eyes are targeted on her as she speaks without unfixing her gaze to Jan.

'That's one saved. What does the *Hausfrau* think about it? Of all the orphans in the world you bring her a little French one.'

'We haven't discussed it. There's nothing to discuss. I couldn't very well leave her in the forest.'

The children are dismissed and ordered to make tea. Kasper moves first, quickly, Sylvester trailing him as his shadow from the kitchen. Madeleine follows them into the kitchen, which comes as relief to be away from that woman.

'They're talking about you,' Kasper informs her.

Madeleine ignores him though she is pleased he is with her; she's relieved to be away from the woman. It's brighter in here; she has a task to accomplish and she is away from that woman. In an unfamiliar kitchen, she looks more closely at Sylvester, hoping he will be able to guide her in her task. She looks at his wide, pale face, his small yellow eyes and his awkward smile, which reveals his small tusks on his lower jaw. Under his hat she can see his ears, big, pointed, and she wonders if, down at the small of his back, the ridges of his spine protrude into a little curly corkscrew tail. Sylvester is embarrassed to be scrutinised so closely and turns away, walking back into the other room.

Later, Jan watches them sleep and moves into the other room to see Sylvester curled up tightly next to his mother. She doesn't deserve this suffering. Who does in this world? Apart from those who started the war – Nazis. Those fascists everywhere who rejoice at their victory and abet the destruction of Poland and Europe. But he is drifting into politics, looking at his pipe and looking back at the pale pig boy, his pale, haemophiliac skin covered in bruises and cuts. It is as if she created her child to bear all her sins, all the suffering she has endured – incarnated in the cursed animal boy. Eva would like her. They can both discuss and contest how much it is they have suffered. He thinks how unreasonable Eva is to be jealous and how she hides it beneath scorn for him. How angry Tereza is, too angry, and how she visits the fear she has endured back at those who made her fearful. How he brought her with them into the forest and it turned into her nightmare. That is his responsibility. His fault. She changed, after the attack. Who could blame her?

She is like a wild cat of the woods, dependent on him for her supplies but would rather cut off a hand than thank him for anything. She is at war against the world. Eva endures suffering because she embraces it. She got that from her mother. And to live with her mother – Jan shudders at the brief period that situation endured when they were first married – that is truly to know suffering. To suffer for those women is to prove devotion; the greater the suffering the greater the love for God – that is the only lesson they take from the Bible. Little time for the notion, which he had pointed out numerous times, that Jesus cures the sick and resurrects the dead – does not leave them lingering in pain, does not leave them alone and cold in death. Life does not have to be suffering and pain, or for that matter, the mandatory attendance at church – to engender charity in return. Jan again remembers how futile it all is to argue this point: there is no life eternal – there is only this life. None of us is Christ. Yet Eva is not her mother. He smiles involuntarily at how she took on Madeleine and the smile disappears when he thinks about what could have happened if Tereza had found her.

He wonders if Madeleine would still be alive. It is a miracle. A girl alive in the forest in the midst of all this. The deer that dodges the bullets and outruns the dogs. He wishes Eva would be more realistic about the war; it is proof of God's final abandonment of this earth rather than recognition of its human agency. The war is perhaps the ultimate sign to Tereza, who knows now that life has become what she has always been saying it is: a condition of no forgiveness, no mercy. Perhaps it is the world that has finally caught up with her; maybe she even saw it coming, this new world – to take the suffering and curses handed out by others and spit them back tenfold, ten thousandfold. This is why he does not love Tereza anymore, despite their blood, and why he does love Eva. Even if it is difficult now, more difficult than easy. Even if it is not the same love it was all those years ago. At the parties in the apartment in Warsaw. It seems like another life, the life in the forest his second life, and his son, the silly boy who will be a force to be reckoned with once he realises the depth of his convictions. To be himself. Kasper, his third life; he only wants to stay alive long enough to see his son bloom. Kasper his third life; Madeleine his... what? What is she? Where did she come from? Whose daughter is she? All the time he has spent thinking about her journeys, her destination, has not left him any the wiser. Maybe Tereza will help. Maybe her clairvoyance will unveil the girl's provenance.

'Ach,' he says aloud, his tobacco burned to a cinder. Turning to the other room, he sees Kasper and Madeleine asleep on the mattress, Madeleine with her back to Kasper and Kasper curled up against her back. Silly boy. He shrugs off his braces and pulls off his boots. The girl has no meaning. She is just lost. Maybe he should not ask her to descry the girl's past, scan her hands or read her eyes, make her drink tea and study the leaves. She is fine as she is.

Third Dream

I am on a ship, a small boat maybe. The water around is very dark but there is something in the distance, an unmoving black stillness. I look up into the darkness and slowly the black outlines of trees and mountains take shape in front of the star-studded sky. The boat comes to rest on the sand and I walk up the beach, the stars glittering on the waves. Into the trees. It is silent but there is a rustling behind me and there is a smaller shadow beneath the big shadows of the trees. It is a hunter. Moving closer to me I can see she has long hair and is holding a gun, which she holds up to aim, and I run. There is no shot but a sound that echoes my own running. She is faster than me. I run and run through the trees, stumbling over roots and disregarding the nettles and ferns, but I trip and the sound comes closer and closer to me. I can see her golden eyes shining in the darkness looking at me, and the light that seems to come from a long, silver knife. Her face is marked with strange tattoos and the knife moves to my throat, cold.

Oleander

Madeleine wakes in a panic and inadvertently kicks Kasper awake – 'What are you doing here? Where are we?'

Kasper rubs his leg, up at once, blinking and moving slowly like a tired, uncomprehending dog. Madeleine can see he's breathing heavily, a film of sweat over him.

'What is it?'

They both seem to relax in the presence of the other and Kasper sighs as he falls back onto the bed.

'We're at Tereza's, remember? Have you forgotten everything again?' Kasper's back is towards her.

'No,' Madeleine falls back onto the pillow too. 'No. Not today.' She remembers their hunting expedition and the encounter with the monster – poor pig boy – and his mother.

Later they sit around the table, Madeleine no less nervous than she was yesterday. The woman talks about the *szlachta*, and she spits, which makes Madeleine start, but she sees neither Jan nor Kasper move.

'In the city they're just like the country, they just can't see it. Superstitious fools. Even though they believe in God, their faith does not make them reasonable or fortify them against uncertainty but terrifies them, and they act as if they do not face the true nature of the universe: random chaos, violence and despair. Attack and counterattack. Sounds like history doesn't it?'

She tells Sylvester to make the tea as she rolls another cigarette, her fingertips yellow, her fingernails black.

'Now they say *tylko świnie siedzą w kinie* in the city, but that is just the same as before. In the village they said to me: "Only pigs live in the forest." But now I'm more powerful than those bitches who hexed me and my boy scares the shit out of them day and night, don't you?'

Madeleine and Kasper sit transfixed by fear listening to the woman, as Sylvester squeaks, immune to the terror she inspires in others his age.

'Those pigs in the city got what they deserved, Poland got what it deserved. Treating people like that, now they know how it feels.' She spits. 'Not so clever now, not so talkative now.'

'Enough,' Jan says. 'We must go now.'

'Must not keep her ladyship waiting.'

Jan ignores her.

'Kasper used to have a telescope,' Jan says, settling his look on Sylvester instead, 'back in Warsaw. He said he wanted to discover a planet and name it after himself. I keep telling him to look for another moon instead because it looks like him, his big moon face.'

Sylvester laughs, a high-pitched hiccup laugh that ends in a subdued snorting.

'Wait Jan, please. I promise no more politics, no more Poland. I want to talk to your new daughter.'

She offers her hand to Madeleine, leading her to the table, which is covered in black lace. Or white lace that is very dirty. Madeleine still can't discern things clearly in this house, even in daylight. Madeleine can see her face has a scar across her cheek, leading from the point of her lips to the middle point of her hollow cheek.

'Would you like me to tell you your future? I used to do that back in Warsaw, for the gentlemen,' she says, grasping the brown cigarette paper and the tobacco between thumb and index finger.

'I prefer you tell me my past,' Madeleine says, straightening up in her chair.

'Looking at the stars through a telescope,' Kasper says, not looking up as he speaks, 'is like looking back in time.' A small affirmative noise follows, as everyone looks at him.

Tereza does not appreciate the interruption and Madeleine sees she runs a thin finger along her scar. Jan leans against one of the windows that is blacked out with a rug or other kind of material.

'He's a scientist. Going to build a rocket someday, aren't you?' Jan says, pretending to throw something at Kasper. Kasper ducks. Kasper shrugs.

Turning to Sylvester: 'Did you know CQD means SOS? I've heard one. I can hear them...'

'You need a radio to know when people are about to die, do you...?' Tereza takes Madeleine's hand and Madeleine flinches. Her hand is as cold as she expects; the other one holds an everlasting cigarette between the points of its yellow-brown fingers. Her black eyes are looking into hers, like telescopes, Madeleine thinks, shiny black shields like the backs of beetles. Madeleine looks behind her to see candlesticks of amber until she is ordered to shut her eyes.

'Her mind is like a pool of clear water. I can see nothing except its emptiness.' Tereza closes her eyes and takes Madeleine's hands.

She traces the cold point of her finger down Madeleine's palms and to her embarrassment notices she starts to sweat. 'There is a brightness.' Tereza looks into Madeline's eyes. 'Bright whiteness, like the sun.'

Madeleine looks down and pulls her hand away. Tereza's mouth, the left tip of her lips, pulls upwards as if a string has been pulled and she exhales. 'It's marked on your flesh.'

She stands and walks towards the kitchen, asking if anyone wants tea. Jan replies affirmatively for everyone.

'Watch that one. I've never felt something like that on someone's skin. Except on someone who was about to die.'

'Hush,' Jan hisses, looking into the other room to see if the children had heard and they had; they were all rigid where they sat, their eyes, hers especially, frozen open wide. She sees through the door Tereza run a hand down Jan's face and down his chest and say something in a hushed tone as if speaking into Jan's throat. He catches Tereza's hand, holding it, a hunter's hand, then lets it fall. Tereza pointedly exhales into his face and turns her back on him, slowly, in steps like an actress entering a room, and walks away out of sight. Madeleine doesn't understand what Jan said to Tereza, she has never seen him talk that way before, become angry. He gestures at her and Kasper and they scatter out the door. Madeleine follows Kasper who is making exaggerated gestures of relief at having left and turns round to see Jan striding out. He catches up with them quickly. Madeleine can feel her pace quicken and her heart quicken, and as he adjusts his speed to hers, he takes her hand.

'Do not worry about what she has said. Her anger often disfigures everything she says or does. She thinks her anger is a gift to others, but it blinds her as much as it gives her clairvoyance.'

Madeleine nods and asks the question she knew she had no choice but to ask: 'I'm not going to die am I?'

'No. Not as long as you live here with us. Not as long as I'm alive. Try to forget about what she said. Look around you instead. The world is beautiful. Walk through it with your eyes open and you'll see how beautiful it is. Even this one,' – he throws something Madeleine can't make out, a seed or acorn perhaps, at the back of Kasper's head – 'belongs to this world. Eva and Sylvester too. The world, the forest, is bigger than us, bigger than the war even.'

'The partisans can help us though, can't they? They are good aren't they? They fight the Germans. The Germans invaded your country, this forest.'

'Not all partisans are good. Maybe not all Germans are bad. The partisans, they are choosy in their friends. They are not friends to everyone. Your country...' He breaks off to suddenly gesture a left turn off the path, whistling to Kasper. Kasper doesn't reply.

'Your country is broken in two. It is not always nationality that makes loyalty or common cause. It is not always difference in nationality that means disagreement or fighting. Poland has lost the war – it's over here. Soon either Germany or Bolshevik Russia will lose the war. My war is to keep my family safe. To keep you safe. For as long as necessary.'

They walk back to the house and Eva shoos the children into the kitchen and they can listen to her accusing Jan of being irresponsible.

'How dare you stay away this long with the children? Anything could have happened and I would never have known.'

Jan's attempt to mollify her comes to naught and they can see him, tamping down his pipe, walking towards the outhouse.

'What's in there?' Madeleine asks.

'Nothing. Just the workshop,' Kasper replies, looking at Madeleine as if there is something about her he cannot remember.

For the next few weeks, Kasper was requisitioned to work with Jan. Eva determined to keep control of everyone's movements. Madeleine was assigned to the kitchen and the myriad duties Eva delegated to her. Madeleine felt increasingly at ease with Eva, and they developed a rhythm together, whether washing the clothes, peeling vegetables, making tea or mending clothes and upholstery and whatever else needed mending.

Madeleine feels so much at ease she even ventures some Polish on Eva, who responds, to Madeleine's surprise, candidly without any drama or evidence of a deeply set mood that seems to murmur dangerously beneath her conversations with Jan.

'How long have you been in the forest?' Madeleine asks. And she learns about their life before the forest, before the war, in Warsaw, when Eva was a secretary and Jan worked, much to Madeleine's surprise, in a department within the Interior Ministry responsible for encouraging cultural relations between Poland and other countries, even Germany, a long time ago.

'We had to attend parties, official functions, and they were always full of beautiful women, glamorous, scented. All of them found Jan irresistible. And nobody is ever unaffected by desire, no matter what they say.'

They are carrying the freshly dry sheets up the stairs to the bedroom. Eva does not reveal anything else. Once they have finished making the bed, Eva takes Madeleine's hand and they sit, for the second time, in Eva and Jan's bedroom, brushing Madeleine's hair.

'You have such lovely hair. Shame you cannot take care of things here in the forest.' She sees Madeleine looking at the photograph. Eva, in front of buildings, smiling, so happy she may as well be a different person.

'You see that, those were my friends from the office. It was taken the day Jan proposed to me. He went to see my father. Well.' She puts down the brush abruptly. Washes her hand through Madeleine's thick and heavy tresses.

She says: 'Leave now, go find Kasper. Walk before dinner.'

Madeleine leaves and closes the door on Eva, sitting on the bed. Madeleine walks down the creaking, complaining stairs. The temperature is thickening even as she reaches the kitchen, and outside she comes into the summer's full heat, dust rising from the ground, pollen languidly sifting through currents, up and down and above. She walks through the dry maelstrom to the workshop, the windows latched open. She follows the sound of what sounds like dry snoring but she sees it's Kasper, shirt sleeves rolled up, sweating over a plane, moving up a piece of timber. She looks for Jan but cannot see him in the murk, the sawdust, like snow, waltzing around at the level of their shins. Madeleine has to put her hands over her mouth nevertheless. She gestures to the outside. In the sunlight she sees – and can smell – Kasper's sweat and says: 'Let's go for a walk, by the stream. I don't have any work to do – I'm bored.'

'I need to finish this. It's for a cart, someone in the village.'

'The horse won't miss it. Come on.'

'Why, where do you want to go?'

'Let's go find Sylvester. He must be bored, all alone, with just that woman.'

'His mother.'

'She doesn't seem like anybody's mother.' Madeleine switches to Polish to impress Kasper but also because she wants to practise.

'Fine, I'll get our guns.'

Madeleine is pleased by this, the way Kasper sees them as adults, like partisans, preparing an expedition. They head off through the fields, where Madeleine laughs at Kasper's near constant sneezing and his eyes become red and fluid. She feels guilty almost immediately after, swishing gently through the lilies, bluebells and dandelions, daisies and forget-me-nots. She thinks of Eva.

'Why doesn't your father wear a wedding ring?' Madeleine asks, trying to seem casual by checking her gun. Although she does not know why she said 'your father' rather than 'Jan', which ruins her attempt at being informal.

'I don't know.' Never having thought about it and still not interested now Madeleine's made him consider it.

They walk on, into the cooler heat under the trees. The sunlight lancing through the branches and leaves, strong and thick so it seems as if the beams are golden cables, keeping the earth bound to the sun. Pollen and dust lingers and floats through the golden beams. The forest is buzzing with sounds today, of birds and the noise of twigs and branches marking the activity of every kind of animal, careless to be noisy, motivated and carefree in the summer's slow amber heat.

'Do you remember the way to the house?' Madeleine asks.

'Yes, I can find my way through the forest to anywhere.'

'Eva wears her wedding ring.' Madeleine observes, looking askance at Kasper, expecting more disinterested noises.

Kasper, however, responds: 'If he's captured by Germans, they'll take his ring. They strip prisoners of all valuables before killing them.'

Madeleine's hand moves to the pendant given her by Eva that rests cold/warm against her chest. Her fingers move over the cold glass face of the Madonna. Looking at Kasper's face, Madeleine guesses the look of peeved annoyance on his face means they're lost.

'Are we lost?'

'No.'

'We're just not where I thought we were. Or where the house is. Or should be.' Madeleine isn't worried; let Kasper do the worrying; she is happy ambling through the heat, being occasionally pierced by the sunbeams that sluice through the leaves and branches. She does not recognise this part of the forest. But further on she sees a cluster of silver birch trees and banks of brambles, brambles and nettles that are familiar.

'Let's go this way,' Madeleine says, and proceeds towards the birch trees.

'It's not that way,' says Kasper, but follows her.

They walk gingerly through the nettles and brambles and see the house. Smaller than their house, more compact and darker. Madeleine looks down at the brambles to see a cluster of elegant red-pink flowers trailing to the dark, heavy door of the house. And she hesitates. Before resuming her will. Her questions impatiently buzzing in her head.

Kasper knocks. Too hard, Madeleine thinks.

'We're not coming to arrest her you know.'

She tuts at Kasper who ignores her.

The door opens after what seems like minutes of scraping and clanking behind the thick wood. Tereza stands, still in black, her house dark and partly lit by candles.

'I saw you outside, from miles away. Do you like the Oleander?' Tereza asks, looking to Madeleine. 'Sit down. Sylvester will bring you tea.'

'Is that what they are?'

Kasper looks around, uneasy, curious that Madeleine seems so at ease, so unaffected.

With the dainty tea cup, something Madeleine would not have expected to be in Tereza's possession, she looks up briefly at her before asking: 'What else can you see?'

Tereza sits down and lights a cigarette.

'I mean, can you see...' Madeleine looks sideways at Kasper, 'in time?'

She ignores Kasper's head swinging round towards her in surprise, his unease at being here increasing. Tereza exhales her smoke languorously.

'I can't see anything about you.' Still looking at Kasper. He cannot meet her gaze and looks into his dark cup of tea.

Turning to look at Madeleine: 'It's like looking into black mirror. You're afraid and confused. Your past is lost even to you. It's as if your memories have fused. I don't know how to separate them. Your presence is like a stained-glass window that is not illuminated. You exist but you can't be seen clearly.'

She blows her smoke straight into Madeleine's face, making her blink, and her eyes stream as Kasper's did this morning. But in the back of her throat, although it stings, it tastes sweet somewhere in her mouth, somewhere over her tongue.

'Do you like my son?'

Madeleine doesn't know what to say, unsure as to where her answer will lead Tereza. Just as she is about to respond *yes* –

'You are too clever to even think about lying to me, so don't. We live in an age of monsters. They have taken over the world. Here though, things are different. In the forest all men are pigs and all monsters are kings – the forest shows the truth of things. That's why your being here is intentional. You have survived all this chaos for a reason. The forest will reveal the truth to you.'

Tereza settles back in her chair, looks back towards Sylvester. 'He,' looking back at Madeleine, 'likes you.' Tereza continues: 'And I know because I can see that you know better than to mistreat him or take advantage of him.' Tereza snarls more smoke into Madeleine's face. 'You act against him and you will regret it – you will have to contend with me and no one can protect you from me.'

'We just want to walk with him. We don't want to hurt him...'

'She sent you, didn't she' – she switches her gaze to Kasper who can't return it – 'to steal my boy. That bitch thinks she's the Virgin Mary but despises everyone inside.'

A hot burst of anger flushes in Kasper's stomach.

'Tell her she's failed.'

Madeleine can see something grow in her eyes and backs away towards Kasper.

'No, no one sent us. We're sorry, we won't come back.' Madeleine's carefully articulated Polish is starting to disintegrate in the face of the black heat of paranoia and anger curling around Tereza's mouth. The smoke that clouds her face makes her seem less like a person to Madeleine now and more like some demonic Medusa. Tereza seems to move towards Madeleine, to be before her without having moved.

'Don't lie to me! I can see you, I can see into you. I know what's deep in your heart. I can see it now. You're in love with him, because he rescued you. You stupid little bitch, you can't see he'll never love you. You think you can deceive him, and you want to take my boy so I'm all alone, defenceless. You want the family you've lost and you'll never see again. First my brother, now my son. He loves me!' She sweeps the teacups and pot from the table and they shatter, throwing their dark liquids against the wall.

'And my boy will never leave me.' Tereza growls this last sentence and her last syllables sound nothing like the words that are part of language but the edge of some other form of communication, unrecognisable. Madeleine is up and Kasper stumbles backwards to get hold of Madeleine, but they can't see the door, and Tereza advances towards them, her hands reaching out ahead of her as if struck blind, her black-tipped fingers grasping for Madeleine's chest, and she starts to roll around, melodically, the syllables sound as if she is expressing an agony in her deep being, the speech itself causing unbearable pain. She sings her sounds to a melody while one hand grips the silver talisman around her neck, wrenching it around her neck, trapping the blood in swollen vessels, her eyes fixed on Madeleine, Madeleine transfixed back, hypnotised. Tereza's eyes snap back down to Madeleine, the pupils black. Her eyes signal her words that have sunk back down to the level of rational language.

'You think I don't smell you? I smelled you a mile off. That stink inside you. You think because you've started bleeding like a woman you are a slave to your biology.'

Madeleine stumbles back against the table's edge and, trembling, pulls the knife from her belt. It shakes like a flower in the wind.

She holds it close to her chest.

Tereza smiles, steeples her hands under her chin and asks: 'Too heavy for you, little girl? Where did you get such weapons? Do you think you can defend yourself against me? Think carefully: why do you think I've survived this war, why do you think your new house in the woods is unvisited by soldiers and partisans? I can hypnotise armies, I can camouflage houses, if you kill me with your little knife, you'll all be left defenceless.'

'No. You're... lying.'

Her trance is broken by Sylvester's sudden dash towards Madeleine, and Tereza now moves fluidly and strongly, not like the weak little woman Madeleine has always taken her to be, sclerotic with bitterness and paranoia. Tereza, her hand, fist armoured with rings, swings back to connect with the soft ivory and pale skin of Sylvester's teeth and face as he rushes to save Madeleine. Madeleine sees drops of blood spurt into the air from the contact, like sparks from a log being thrown onto a fire and Tereza's balance is unaffected as if Sylvester has run into a statue. His tight squeal trails backwards as he is hurled back against the wall, arms slapped back, to slump down as if he's nothing but a pile of clothes. Kasper takes advantage of not being in Tereza's line of sight and rushes behind Madeleine and grabs the skin of her dress, pulling her back, chairs brusquely falling onto their sides as they push past. Kasper struggles to unlatch the door, a whole series of locks and beams. One ornate and rusted lock has a whole system of cogs and gears. His hands feel heavy and clumsy in the desperate fumbling to find the lever to discharge the mechanism. Madeleine is still hypnotised, limp and heavy through the ruff of material that flowers through his fist. Kasper turns round and sees Tereza is standing still, her eyes blank and white, her one hand outstretched towards Madeleine, the other still around her neck, and she's intoning more words, sounds Kasper can't make out. Tereza moves towards Madeleine, towards the knife, and she reaches out to run her finger along the knife edge. Madeleine's hand begins to tremble and then her arm begins to shake, and Tereza grasps the dagger more firmly, running the palm of her hand up and down the blade rhythmically to the sound of her words. The dagger is dark with blood, thick crimson lines staining the bright, silvery steel.

'Don't listen!' he suddenly barks out to Madeleine. But he knows what Tereza's doing and he finally dislodges the heavy bolt and frantically throwing the beam out of the way knows he has to get Madeleine away before the curse is completed. Kasper runs out the door, the black rectangle where Tereza's arms span the empty black space looking at Kasper, having to almost carry Madeleine through the banks of nettles into the silver birch trees and, further on, the pines.

She watches for a long time, watches the sliced and uneven spaces between the dark poles of the pine trees, listens for a long time in case she can hear her words start to take possession of Madeleine. Tereza is listening so intently to the breeze ushering in the twilight she does not hear the activity behind her back. And she brings her palm up to her mouth and presses the gash to her mouth, the saliva congealing the blood.

Sylvester feels like he has woken up from a long sleep, sluggish and tired, his nose and mouth sticky with blood and saliva. The interior has darkened, there are no candles lit yet. He can't remember where he is, but slowly, as slowly as the blood still curdles round his mouth, he remembers the actions, his steps, and the fierce backhand of his mother. He stands up shakily, and the words his mother is incanting still prickle in his head. Sylvester doesn't know what they mean. It's a language only she knows but he's seen the effects they have spying on those in the village – those who have deserved it.

But not Madeleine.

He leaves the house by the back door, checking his mother is still out of sight. He thinks of Madeleine, Jan's girl, the one who came looking for him. Someone came to find him. He thinks of Madeleine as he follows their path through the nettles, past the small population of birch trees, their skin, fragile and peeling like his, follows them and starts to run; he must catch Madeleine before his mother's words take effect. Before they worm their way into her flesh, the soft surfaces of her body:

eyes, ears, the hidden parts deep in the coils of her intestines. The other parts, each part that opens to the air. Each one is a way in, each one vulnerable – cursed.

Mandragora Officinarum

Kasper has never sweated so much in his life. The gun bangs against his shoulder blade at each step, Madeleine stumbling along, almost entirely limp. He looks over at her from time to time, wiping the liquid that streams over his brows, her eyes barely open, her mouth hanging open, as if her lower jaw has become much too heavy, and then he stumbles. Then he falls. Madeleine crashes to the cold earth next to him and moans. It can't have hurt that much, he thinks. He gets up, squats over to look at Madeleine, her back coiled against him, her hands crossed over her abdomen. Her moans don't stop and she hunches over the burning core of herself. Kasper fumbles over her back, tries to get a clear view of her face, and she's weak in his hands, no strength in her blushed neck. He sees Madeleine's face. It has turned a deep deep-red; her eyes dotted by petechia, liquid at their edges, blood beginning to gather at her nostrils and at her ears. When Madeleine next moans, her mouth opens, and Kasper places his hands on her cheeks for want of anything else to do.

'Madeleine! Can you hear me?'

Her mouth opens in response, wordlessly, and only a cobweb of blood spurts out, splattering her chin and Kasper's mouth. She can only articulate meaningless phlegm tones in her throat, her teeth spattered with her blood, seeping out of the corners of her mouth. Kasper hears movement in the undergrowth, spins up and around, unthinkingly reaches for his gun, and his reflexes are good, it's ready to fire; he's ready to fire on the figure unless it stops.

It squeals in the twilight, stops and falls to the ground, a shadow without its owner, that of a bird above the earth, all things illuminated by their shadow in front of fire, a flame suddenly extinguished. Kasper runs towards the prone figure to see it's Sylvester, straining his neck to look up to him; Kasper sees his distinctive red cap, worn to hide the pointed tips of his ears. It makes him a moving target.

Kasper doesn't feel there's time to ask what he's doing so he gestures.

'Up! Up! Help me, we have to get Madeleine home.'

Tereza stands with her back to the forest now, looking at the scattered furniture, the empty house. Her black form, upright almost indistinguishable from the twilight seeping in from the forest, her black eyes turning back to the trees, black as the leaves hanging like wet rags from the branches.

Kasper and Sylvester stumble over the roots, Madeleine awkwardly hanging from their arms. She is dimly aware of the trees rushing past her, the scarred breathing of her two porters; the breeze rushing over her slightly helps her breathe. Each breath struggles to find air through the blood that spills round her mouth; the hot wetness covers her face. Her stomach is twisting, as though she wants to vomit but there's no reflex. It's as if there are fists in her stomach clenching ropes and sacks, wrapping up everything within her; all of which is nothing to the pain further down, deep in her belly, as if there are teeth within it, desperately chewing their way through her flesh seeking to be free. Her urge is to push her hands through her skin and rip out the acidic scratching and coiling within.

They struggle and stumble to the house, Sylvester asking Kasper to slow down and squealing occasionally as Madeleine slips from his grasp. Kasper thinks they are going too slow; his heart feels as if it's fluttering as it hits his ribs hard. They rush through the gathering darkness that's thickening between the trees, their branches and roots slipping back into the black tapestry.

Through the darkness they soon breach the trees to see the sky, cloudy, but they also see the soft golden glowing squares in the black silhouette of the house. Kasper sees the light flowing from the windows like the bright tongues of liquid fire; it's just the sweat blurring his vision. Eva and Jan spill out of the house, Kasper afraid of the smack round the head and admonishment, but they ignore him and scarcely notice Sylvester.

Jan snatches Madeleine from Kasper and Sylvester's shaky grip, and Eva pauses briefly, her hand on Kasper's cap.

'Kasper, what happened? Are you hurt?'

Kasper, too breathless to answer, nods, the water on his face and neck white and silvery-gold in the reflected light from the house, an angelic mark in contrast to the blood that stripes Madeleine's face, dripping up the stairs, her clothes becoming saturated with her blood, her red dress. Jan jumps up the steps at a pace, kicks open the door to Madeleine's dark room and hears Eva come in behind him as he lays Madeleine down. Eva puts her hand on Madeleine's forehead, soaked by sweat, and she strokes the damp strands of hair aside.

'Get some hot water and towels, cotton and some aspirin. Hurry.'

She lays her hand on Madeleine's pale forehead again and Madeleine curls up her hands clutching her belly. Jan has lit the candles and brought up an oil lamp, Kasper in his wake. Jan has lit the candles and bought an oil lamp; he barks the ingredients Eva requests at Kasper down the stairs where he and Sylvester are hovering, uncertain as to how they can help.

They both head to the kitchen, Sylvester following Kasper's back, and he is loaded up like a mule with towels and cloths. Kasper sets the kettle to boil. When Eva turns to speak to Jan and asks what it is that has happened to Madeleine, he is no longer there. She watches Madeleine on the bed, much quieter now, but she can see she is mostly unconscious, her eyes shut, the neat line blurred by tears and blood. She takes advantage of everyone's absence to undress Madeleine as far as possible, her dress saturated with blood, and Eva gasps and crosses herself, tears coming to the corners of her own eyes as she sees Madeleine's underclothes are no longer white but deep-red; her inner thighs are streaked by long tentacles of blood that trail beyond her knees to her shins.

Kasper pushes and shouts at Sylvester to move, quickly, quicker, up the stairs. He's being slow on purpose, perhaps because his mother told him to be so. A plot between the two. Madeleine paying for her mistake to trust Sylvester with the blood that covers her now, spreading over the sheets. They stand by the door, mouths open at how pale Madeleine is even in the lamplight.

Eva grabs the towels and water, frantically trying to mop up what she can from Madeleine and her small body, as if a thousand dams within have burst all at once. She orders them back down, mainly to source more supplies – lemon, even some honey from the back of the cupboard, thyme and rosemary – partly to protect Madeleine's modesty. Her sheets are too bloody and heavy to keep over her and she has begun to sweat, seemingly doubling the volume of blood Eva can now see dripping onto the floor, sopping from cloths. She wrings once white cloths into bowls of water, once clear, now blackly polluted.

They return, bringing what Eva has asked for, and for the first time she realises Kasper is with... who, what?

'Who is he?' She demands of her son. 'Is he part of this?' She turns back to Madeleine, mops her brow, cleans her face, ears and eyes.

'He's from, from...' Kasper stammers. Where? 'The forest...'
'Make him wait downstairs.'

Sylvester, eyes downcast, leaves the room and goes to the dark corridor.

'He helped carry her here. He helped me.'

Eva considers this, thinking of Jan. Disappeared – as ever – when she needs answers to her questions. His long walks. And the thought that this was his son, conceived by some deformed forest peasant, struck her like a fist to her stomach; her hand hovered, paralysed, over Madeleine's bloodless face. She could do nothing, hostage to the forest. If only the war hadn't started. She could have left this dark house, the endless trees, taken Kasper back to Warsaw. But a sudden spasm and cough from Madeleine shakes her back from her thoughts; Madeleine's breathing suddenly accelerates, her chest articulating like bellows becomes frantically animated.

Eva turns to Kasper. 'Does he know what this is? Can he help me?'

Kasper shrugs, feeling useless. The first time he's required to help in an emergency and he shrugs. Useless.

'Ask!' Eva almost shrieks as she sets to preparing an infusion for Madeleine, in despair already, knowing that a traditional remedy for influenza and rheumatism will likely have no effect. Madeleine has been cursed.

Jan walks quickly and quietly through the trees – he knows where he is going. Though the night is moonless, he knows where he is going. Though the trees do their best to step onto his path, subtly disguise themselves as one another, he knows the house he is to visit, what is waiting for him there. The night in the forest has its own set of sounds, the occasional vicious shriek of an owl. Bats here and there flit like demonic birds, the normal song of birds corrupted in their small, narrow throats;

their squeaks and echoes ricochet between the trees as little bullets before scattering on the ground – spent ammunition.

It is all Eva can do to keep Madeleine's temperature from igniting her hair, scorching the sheets. At least the flow of blood has stopped. Her hair is soaked with sweat and water and messily spread across her pillow, and her mouth is now a cracked seashell encrusted with dried scarlet blood and mucous. Kasper is downstairs searching for Sylvester in the gloom. He shouts his name.

'Where are you? We need you!'

He lights one of the oil lamps, the matches shaking in his anxious and angry fingers. The lamp burns away the near-smothering darkness but reveals nothing but the silent, useless furniture. Kasper moves outside, hesitant to shout out at night, but, thinking of Madeleine, does so anyway. To no response. He wanders in circles further away from the house, unsettled by his parents. He's not seen them like this since the beginning of the war, since leaving the city. Unsure what to do, how his mother would want him to be of use. Where could he be? How would he ever find Sylvester? He wanders further, past the workshop, around the house, calling out the Slavic name like an animal searching for its lost offspring. He can see the light glowing out from the top bedroom, the room where Madeleine will die. This is the first time he realises this is something that may happen. Maybe something that is already inexorable, which his parents have realised. Maybe that's why his father has disappeared among the dark trees, Sylvester too. His father to enact his grief by slaughtering some animals, Sylvester to, to... cry alone somewhere, mourn the death of his first friend. And then, perhaps, Kasper sees something, by the tree line. A dark shape. An animal – why didn't he bring his gun? He's already stepping back, checking the distance to the small cube of light that he will have to run towards. Failing Madeleine. He knows he should run back to the house, get his gun, but for some reason he stands there, holding the lamp high, knowing this makes him a target – such an easy target. But he knows also it most probably has to be no one else but... Sylvester. Coming out of the trees. He shouts his name and a small strangled squeak comes back to him, and Kasper's relief is such he suddenly chokes and sobs. Some tears appear at the corners of his eyes involuntarily, and he wipes his face clean with his sleeve before Sylvester can see, but his nose has joined in the conspiracy of tears and he is glad Madeleine isn't here to see this, only Sylvester.

As Sylvester comes stumbling up to him, breaking the circumference of lantern light, he can see Kasper's discomfort.

'What's wrong?' His big, golden eyes are wet with concern, curious that someone else should be suffering in the way he thought was reserved for only himself.

'Nothing,' Kasper rebuffs him. 'Where have you been? I have more important things to do than run around looking for you.'

'Digging.' His breaths are still short and rough. Surprisingly deep, Kasper notices.

'What? Madeleine's ill and maybe... why?'

'I know these things my mother does. I've been finding roots. I know the roots that can help Madeleine.'

Kasper does not waste another second and grabs Sylvester's wrist, oblivious to the pain it causes him, to see a bunch of messy, soil-sodden brown vegetables.

'I know where they are because I can smell—'

'Come on!' Kasper cuts him short and, remembering his sensitive skin, releases him but almost pushes Sylvester forwards. 'That way,' pointing to the small level of light plainly visible on a night darkened by smothering clouds blacking out the stars. They rush back to the house, for the second time, Kasper thinks, as he almost pushes Sylvester in front of him, through the door, stumbling up the darkened staircase.

'I've found this.' Kasper bursts into the bright room, not knowing what he has in his hands and desperate to impress his usefulness on his mother. Sylvester, staring at Madeleine in horror, doesn't notice.

Eva, in turn, flinches when she sees Sylvester's bloodied face – once from Tereza's backhand smack, twice from digging desperately by the roots of an elm tree to uncover the mandrake root and by the plane tree to get at the burdock root.

'Well, he did,' Kasper confesses, now that no one is really listening, and his own gaze drifts towards Madeleine, sedated again by Eva after her spasm. Sylvester is still looking at Madeleine, paler even than he, her closed eyes dark bruises above the blurred, bloody mouth, and his own stubbed finger paws go to his face, which he notices for the first time is stinging with pain, the cuts still unclosed to the air. It is how he appears to others. Unnatural, bloody flesh which is too exposed to other people, people who do not think about their bodies except as sources of pain and decay. He and Madeleine are symbols of weak flesh. Normal people shudder, knowing that they too are part of the same species. Only a sharp shout of his name in Eva's voice breaks his reverie.

'What do I do with these?'

Sylvester stares for a bit at the dark, soil-smeared roots. 'Cut them up. Boil them. Add whatever makes for sleep.'

Nocturne

Jan comes to the door of the house. Open. Dark inside. He advances more cautiously. She is so stricken with hatred even he may not be immune. *I am a fly*. Walking along the edge of a spider web. He hears her soft tread behind him.

'Welcome home.'

Tereza lights the candelabrum. Jan keeps hold of his gun, breathing furiously but feels his anger is melting away. He can see Tereza's dark features shine as the candles flare up in front of her.

He pushes her against the wall but he forgets how strong she is. She pulls him back with her, his body crushing against hers, and she doesn't let go, and he is mindful of the gun that marks a hard line down the soft breathing between them.

'Here we are again, Jan. You always come find me.'

'Let me go.'

Jan cannot look at her. The heat and closeness reveals the breaths of the body against his, the column of heat, the moist breath, surprisingly sweet on his beard.

'You are free,' Tereza whispers to his downturned face.

'Just let me go.'

Her free hand strokes the side of his face, moist with sweat. 'But you used to like being so close up against me, to feel my breasts pressing into your ribs.'

'Enough.' Jan cannot look at her. Amazed at her dexterity, his hands are trapped between them. He's thinking hard of Eva, the only other woman the rhythm of whose ribcage he can remember now. Breathing slowly, faster and quicker until they cannot move quickly enough to expel the breaths of pleasure from her mouth.

'Doesn't this remind you of being back at home in Warsaw? You used to like it there.'

Moving her head close, closer, for her tongue to unfurl and dab his cheek lightly. A silver point of wetness, glowing like a star in the evening against his burning skin. Jan can feel her other hand moving, towards his groin, towards the trigger of the rifle. And he can do nothing to stop it. And this wouldn't be the first time he has acquiesced to her. It would be just like every other time.

'What will happen to her? What can I do to stop this?'

'She's been cursed, a curse that acts on her blood. It won't stop until she's dead. Every night at midnight she will suffer occult bleeding for a time until...'

'What will happen?'

'Her heart dissolves.'

'Oh Holy Mother.'

Eva's hands rush up to her crumpling face. It's something Kasper has never seen and he feels embarrassed to see her like this, so frail and afraid. And he knows his father would do the right thing to comfort her but he does not know what it is; he thinks his presence, witnessing her despair, only embarrasses her in turn.

'Mary preserve her. There must be something we can do?'

'I don't know. Only my mother knows.'

'Oh,' Eva sits down heavily on the chair beside the bed. 'Oh God.'

'Usually...' Sylvester continues, seemingly unaware of the effect his words are having on Eva, and Kasper notices an almost complete lack of self-consciousness on Sylvester's part. 'It needs someone else to assume the curse. The curse must be transferred. Do you have any enemies?'

'What?' The tone changes to one Kasper is much more familiar with.

'What are you saying? Enemies? Apart from the entirety and total sum of Germany and Russia, the people who have abandoned God, we have nothing but enemies. Our chief enemy tonight it seems is your mother, boy – whatever you are.'

Eva is back up now, assuming control of herself. Her hands roughly wiping her cheeks clear of tears. She scrutinises the little piglet child, his glowing yellow eyes, rough pink skin, the tapering points of his ears and stubby, conjoined digits on his hands, rendered useful only by the residual presence of stubby thumbs.

'And she is unlikely to want to take this curse back. It is not an item from a shop one can return if unsatisfied. One does not take back an untrained dog into the house after throwing it out. What good are the dirty little roots you say you just found? Are they even helping her?'

Sylvester only realises now that he is a suspect. His voice begins to shake and squeak as he continues, making himself harder to understand: 'No, it is helping her – they stop the bleeding...'

'So you say.' She turns to her son and barks: 'How do we know, how are you even friends?'

Kasper stammers and hesitates. 'It was Madeleine... she went to the house...'

'Ah.' Eva waves her hand and turns her back to them. In sound and gesture she reminds Kasper of his father and he wishes he was here. He nods his head to Sylvester – seeing the tears bud at the corner of his wide coin-coloured eyes – to leave the room. Eva brushes her hand over Madeleine's still unnaturally warm forehead.

Tereza's tongue feels the contours of Jan's lips, circled by the soft hairs of his beard. Tereza's tongue slips under the top lip, searching, blindly, slowly, for the soft flesh nub of his tongue. But it speaks so close to her skin Tereza thinks she absorbs them through her tongue, her lips, rather than hears them.

'Tell me the words...'

She continues to move her hands around his, to dislodge the rifle that is lodged painfully under her right breast; the soft caresses she lays on his hands relaxes them. She knows she will have to tell him her brother is as wilful as she is when he's set on something.

Jan is looking into her eyes, normally slits, now becoming large and wide, like the dilated pupils of a cat. Her hands and their sudden hard pressure on his jawbone and his hand at once finally cause his grip on the rifle to loosen and it falls to the floor, a hard, solid wood sound. Tereza closes her eyes at that moment, afraid it will go off. Relieved, Tereza's hand moves down the side of his abdomen, trailing slowly over his belt.

'Tell me you love me,' she says in a slow susurrus into his lips, still moist with the trace of her tongue, as if she is implanting the words from her tongue to fall into his mouth. She moistens his lips again and his breathing quickens. Jan cannot resist and this shame is arousing in itself. Everyone has a secret. Helping his sister when they were young didn't seem wrong; it seemed normal. He believed her when she said it was normal that every brother and sister did this – *they do what we do, they love like we do.*

'Say you still love me.'

Everything since has been driven by the desire to cleanse this shame. Forcing his sister to come to the forest with them, with the woman she despised. He thought she would be safe in the forest. But she attracted attention. The forest had acted on her in a strange way. Her interest in the esoteric grew beyond astrology and tarot decks and she became convinced of her abilities to control reality and manipulate objects – and people. He had told her to let go of her adolescent fascination with this occult nonsense when he saw her enthusiasm for party tricks had turned into a delusion. Until the day he received news that he had underestimated her. Then he had to act when she was... It was his pleasure, though, to take revenge upon the persecutors she identified in the village. One will never walk again, left alive as a warning; he sits in the corner of the inn, barely coherent through drink. Lucky or not, depending, measured against the punishment of the others who are buried in unmarked graves in the forest without their head or their genitals. The survivor drinks to numb his pain, incontinent from the knife wounds. His pathetic state eventually regained the sympathy of the village and his sister was again ostracised by the peasants. He helped her when Sylvester was born nine months after the rape, conveying supplies despite his wife's suspicions, at home with their own young son. He had never told Eva that his sister had followed them to the forest.

'Do you love me, Jan?'

Unable to resist his sister's sweet tea and smoke-flavoured lips and wild-animal appetite in the small hidden house under the pine trees under the moon, he used to drug her son to sleep so she could make as much noise as she wanted.

'Yes. I love you.' Jan kisses her lips, her mouth soft and wide and warm, if only Eva's...

Tereza's hands move inwards to the warm point of his groin and the thick hard-soft flesh she can feel down by her fingers, her heart beating hard against her brother's. Jan's hand takes Tereza's hand, hard and latticed with thick veins, in his and he moves his hand to her face, cupping it. She feels almost all its hard, hot pressure from temple to chin.

'Now tell me the words, the white chant.'

And Tereza, despite herself, a little glitch, through a broken window in the warm algorithms and pulses of her brain, spills out the words into Jan's mouth, looking up at his blue eyes, like blue oceans, deep and bright.

'Repeat them,' he says, his other hand cradling the other side of her face, the rough strands of her midnight-black hair. Tereza repeats them again, her breathing rushed and hard, both her hands at his groin, moving faster, and she can feel his grip hardening and her own kisses become more fierce, more certain as she knows her desire is engorging his, still, after all this time. Jan pushes her against the wall, his eyes wide, and Tereza gasps in pleasure, her hands beside her, exposing her front to Jan, no barriers, and they move together, unable to keep apart. Jan pulls her away from the wall and she follows him, staying close to his body, and their fingers knot together, not willing to be broken. He brings his other fist to close over the knuckles and polished silver rings and squeezes their bones together, painfully. He feels her other hand rest on his head and grip his hair. The pressure around her fist is too much for her and one of her knees buckles, releasing her grip on his head.

'Let me go,' she whispers.

Jan lets go of her hand in an instant and Tereza rapidly moves back away from him. He looks at her, barely visible now, a black shadow on the wall of this house of shadows. He extinguishes the candles. He hears her hoarse breathing, somewhere, in the darkness. And, repeating the words – words he does not understand; they are just nonsensical syllables – he hums them to the melody of a Chopin nocturne.

He walks out of the house, his gun over his shoulder. This will be his last night walk. He walks back at a fast pace, watching, knowing nothing can be allowed to stop him returning, climbing the stairs to Madeleine's room. He can still hear the sounds of her breathing in his head and so he hums the melody again, and again. Jan sees, through the netting of the tree branches, that the clouds have cleared and the stars sparkle and glitter like electric lights on the boulevards of Warsaw.

Wandering Stars

Kasper and Sylvester have taken up position downstairs, knowing that their presence in the room is an irritation for Eva but not knowing what they should do. It feels disrespectful to Madeleine to go to sleep, although Sylvester's head nods occasionally and jerks back up. For want of anything better to do, Kasper says to Sylvester: 'I'll teach you how to smoke a pipe.' Kasper has Jan's long clay pipe in his hands. Never having smoked it before, but having watched his father intently, he knows the experience as if it were his. He moves to the tobacco tin, bringing a chair to stand on and strains like the neck trunk of a giraffe.

Sylvester watches, increasingly nervous, his palms moist, his mouth dry, wishing he could be upstairs directing Eva as to how to correctly prepare the roots with milk, water and sugar and to make the lotion to apply to Madeleine's heated skin. He doesn't like the look in Kasper's eyes as he advances into the sphere of the oil lamp's dull yellow globe of light; he's seen that look before in other children. He sits down wordlessly, unusually elegant all of a sudden in his movements, sure of his movements. He takes himself for his father. Sylvester thinks, and wishes – another wish, soon he will lose track – Kasper's father were here and, almost despite himself, that he brings his mother back with him.

As Kasper lights up the tamped down bristle of tobacco, the orange sparkles in his face, giving him the aspect of a devil in the corner of a darkened bar, catching the blue-black pearl of his eyes. Sylvester sees the ignition set free plumes of smoke from the pipe, and Kasper puts it in his mouth, his face free of the cheetah marks scattered over his face for an instant as the tobacco flare lights up his face. He exhales the smoke naturally, as if he has just simply switched his element, his lungs absorbing the thick, dark smoke from the pipe rather than the cold blue oxygen from the air. Now, as Sylvester has dreaded, he looks up the dark staircase hoping Eva will appear, but there's only Kasper, still silent, holding the long slender white curve of the pipe. Like Indians, Sylvester thinks, suddenly reassured, they smoked pipes. He'd read that somewhere in a comic strip Jan had left one day.

'This is like Indians,' he squeals excitedly.

Kasper still sits in silence, smoke flowing upwards around him, as if his corporeal temperature has suddenly increased exponentially. The pipe, like a bone, is unexpectedly warm, and he holds it uncertainly, forgetting how Kasper did it, and he has to rest it in the cleft of his hands. He starts to sweat, Kasper still fixedly staring at him. The pipe rests awkwardly and, gripping as tightly as he can, Kasper suddenly leans over and relights the tobacco at the far end and tells Sylvester to put it in his mouth and inhale. Sylvester inhales vigorously and feels as if he's suffocating as a mouthful of thick, sweet smoke rushes into his lungs and he cannot cough enough to get rid of it. He's afraid he might vomit, and above the chaos in his throat and the stinging in his eyes, causing his vision to blur, he can hear Kasper laughing.

'You're not a red Indian.'

He immediately falls quiet as there is a crack in the room. Sylvester feels all his senses have been scorched; someone has entered the room. Jan does not stop to look at them – apart from a burning glance at Kasper that he cannot meet – his head droops to the floor. Kasper takes the pipe from Sylvester and gently pulls him along up the stairs after the quick light steps of Jan have already disappeared into Madeleine's room. They hear Eva's high-pitched surprise and Jan's bass vibrating underneath her quick streaming words, their pitch modulating to their normal, lower frequency.

Jan enters and sees Madeleine, fever breathing in bed and pale as bones. He then smells a thick and acrid combination of sweat and blood, like a boxing ring, of all things, Jan remembers. This memory of his life in Krakow with his friends bursts like the flash of the photographer's bulbs frenzied around the sides of the ring and once burst, fades away, a shivering ghost fading away. Images of the ring, with Eva on one side of him and his colleagues on the other side all becoming animated, all of them invested in the violence. Even Eva, despite herself, forgets her usual reserved restraint and makes a jabbing movement with her own right hand.

'It's burdock and mandrake,' Eva says, and Jan sees she's exhausted too, her head resting heavily on her wrist. Her voice is drowsy, probably caused by the admixture, Jan thinks. He knows this peasant superstition. The roots – taken together as a combining agent – act directly on the endocrine glands and additionally act as an obstruent and have probably stemmed Madeleine's bleeding. It is also a soporific and – when mixed with blood – an aphrodisiac.

'What are these?' His fingers brushing across their bright blue faces; they are soft and soothing to his skin.

'They are forget-me-nots. I gave them to her.' Her voice was quiet and cracked by tiredness.

Jan sits gracelessly at the foot of the bed, suddenly tired, his hand near Madeleine's outstretched, sleeping hand. He watches Eva drift off then sings the soft lyrics of the white words to the melody of the Chopin nocturne into the tight pink curls of Madeleine's ear. He repeats it.

He wakes later in a spasm, seeing Eva blackened by the nearly dying candlelight, the light that is left illuminating Madeleine's pale, bloodless face. The room still has the sweet – too sweet – smell of the root solution. Eva will stay and watch over Madeleine. Ever the martyr, ever ready to suffer her own discomfort. He knows it's not worth the bother to wake her.

Jan walks to a chest in his and Eva's bedroom and retrieves a toy given to Kasper in the city. He takes it and places it beside Madeleine's bed. He finds some candles and cuts them down into suitable sizes to make four shortened candles, and placing them within, lighting them, he watches the heat push the mechanism round and the zoetrope cylinder bathe the room in a deep-blue light illuminating the walls and ceiling with planets, comets and stars in a slow, steady procession. Jan looks back as he leaves the door ajar, at Eva and Madeleine asleep, stars passing over their faces.

As he undresses and falls exhausted onto the bed, he feels ashamed for having judged his sleeping wife too harshly – what would he have preferred, that she be like his sister? Better be devoted to someone else than be devoted to one's own self-pity, one's own pleasure in vengeance. His guilt is assuaged, sinking onto the pillow, by thinking of what he did to his own sister to save Madeleine. His closed eyes cannot shut out the thought, the vicious, blood-hot memory of how much he enjoyed it and, knowing Tereza as he does, how much she would have enjoyed it too. Much harder than all the other times. Scratches and bruises tease the nerves, engorge the heart and thicken the blood. Much harder. Much more pleasurable. He sighs, his eyes open again now, forgetting Tereza, remembering Eva and not thinking where he would be with Tereza if he hadn't met Eva. If she hadn't been introduced by a friend. Shy and quiet. Out of place in the drinking and laughing, and where each word has its shadow, looking for the black and scarlet lines between lips, out of the space lit by lamps and candles.

He saw Eva enter the room with two of the other secretaries. Tereza came up by his side, whispering into his ear that his cigarette was about to lose its ash all over the carpet.

'Who are you looking at?' she asked.

'Oh, nobody.' Tereza laid her hand on his shoulder, which he shrugged off violently, looking at her fiercely.

'Someone's a little tense. This is a party. You should enjoy yourself. Relax.' Tereza said, exhaling languorously. 'Follow my example.'

Her face was pale under the low lights, the chandeliers, her black dress and black choker accentuating her eyes, Jan remembers, glittering at him like opals. Her mouth, her teeth bright against the deep burgundy of her lips, biting her lower lip, in her usual expression of feigned irritation.

'Go to that blonde horse,' she said. 'I'll find mine.'

Jan looked over at the blonde woman, her dress creamwhite, her lips bright holly berry-red against her rose-pink face and snowflake-blue eyes. The blush rising up her neck and to her face, Jan, as a man, didn't quite recognise her – but guessed she might be from the French embassy – stood close to her and took her hand and kissed it. She smiled and her friend looked at her expectantly while the man waited. She smiled and agreed to the man's request to dance. They were dancing to some jazz number – a cacophony about which the ambassador had been instantly dismissive – but whose wife, upon hearing the same cacophony by whomever it was, Duke Ellington, Django Reinhardt or Louis Armstrong, took to it immediately. Hers was the seal of – official – approval that many guests had been waiting for and felt that they could now legitimately move towards the dance floor, only for many of them to then realise that they had little idea of how to dance to this strange music. Jan, instead, walked towards the bar, asked the barman for another vodka and looked again towards the dance floor. The woman caught his gaze and the smile fell slightly – her concentration and poise interrupted. She replied to the man's question given in her ear, but her eyes remained with Jan. On the sofa in the corner he could see Tereza, her hand on a man's knee, his hand tipping his glass into her open mouth. The music finished and Jan put down his empty glass on the bar and walked towards the woman in the cream-white dress.

Early the next morning Jan comes into the bedroom to see Madeleine still sleeping peacefully and looking much less pale, and Eva bustles into the room behind him, carrying towels and a bowl of heated water. She places them by the bed, and Jan sees that she's placed the magic lantern beneath the bed. Jan takes Eva's arms and hands, stops her and holds her close to him. Eva, surprised at first, unresponsive, presses herself to him and he can feel the temperature and pressure of love.

'She will be better now,' Jan says, half in assertion, half in query.

Eva nods. 'Her temperature has fallen. She just needs rest now. I'm going to wash her now and then change the sheets. Go have breakfast.' She rests a hand on his chest and with a brief smile turns to Madeleine.

Fourth Dream

I am in a small boat. The water around is very dark but there is something at either side of the water. It is quiet but for the faint sounds of water brushing against the wood. It is warm and I can let my hand drift in the water, which is not too cold. The sky is dark-blue overhead, but on the far horizon a faint golden glow is illuminating the lower atmospheres. But it is lighter close to me too. I become aware of a movement off to the side of my boat. It is another boat and it is on fire. It is carrying a fire within it, moving towards the light in the sky. The river is widening out, the banks becoming less distinct. The boat on fire drifts past me and then another one off to the other side drifts close to my boat, it too aflame. I sit up, casting off my blanket to get a better view, and there are dozens of boats on fire all heading towards the estuary and the open sea. They make a deep groaning sound as their fires reach high into the morning sky. I follow them towards the fiery light of the dawn.

Territory

A week later and Kasper and Sylvester have been drafted into bringing up the hot water for Madeleine. It's the second morning she's been awake, her colour returned to normal, the iris of her eyes irrigated of the blood that had flooded them. She smiles as they awkwardly place the bowl, spilling a considerable amount, and Kasper *sotto voce* tells Sylvester to shift the towels from where he has laid them. Sylvester, unperturbed, goes over to Madeleine and asks how she's doing.

'I feel much better. Thanks to you.'

Sylvester's pale skin blossoms and he stammers a series of whistles and squeaks until Kasper roughly drags him off. 'Madeleine needs rest, my mother said so.'

'It's fine to stay, and don't touch Sylvester like that,' Madeleine assures them, but her words are lost in their bustle and the slamming of the door.

She enjoys their company; it makes a change from Eva's conscientious but somewhat severe attention and ministrations, the constant serving of red meats, even cold ham for breakfast and lunch, and thick cords and slices of rabbit and occasionally cow and pig for dinner drowning in beetroot and beer sauces. They pray together every evening, where Eva devotedly mouths her fervent devotions and Madeleine watches her, bemused. She has a copy of the Bible she reads before falling asleep, usually after only a few verses, watching the world outside still bathing in the warm summer light that tantalisingly lines the cracks between and around and underneath the shutters and between her eyelids.

Two weeks later Madeleine keenly agrees with Eva's assessment that she is better, her iron levels and weight restored. Eva slightly dampens Madeleine's excitement at the end of confinement by drafting her to laundry duties, and she stays seated on the bed as Madeleine bounds over to the dresser. Madeleine turns round to see Eva setting the sheets, and she leaves her bedroom with an expression of... between disappointment and... of sadness. Expressions which linger in Madeleine's own face, curdled in the clear cold water within the porcelain bowl.

The next morning Madeleine and Sylvester go into Kasper's room. He's still in bed. How dare they come in?

'We're going into the forest. Do you want to come with us?'
'I'm busy.'
'Doing what?'
'Just my things. That I need to do. I don't have time to play in the forest.' Kasper can see the disappointment in Sylvester's eyes. And the suspicion in Madeleine's.

'You have *him*.' Kasper enjoys being condescending to Sylvester in front of Madeleine. Reminding everyone of the hierarchy.

'Fine,' Madeleine says. 'We'll go without you. Do what you want.'

They leave, Madeleine infuriated by him; Sylvester follows in mute incomprehension.

Kasper doesn't see why Sylvester has to join in everything now.

I'm busy.

Listening to the radio. Once he has fixed it.

Madeleine doesn't know why he's acting so strangely. Why wouldn't he want to come into the forest? He always does, if only to show how well he knows it, before getting lost. A half-smile comes to her.

Doing what?

She peers into his room as he comes to the door to limit the scope of her vision. There's nothing except the usual clutter. She's aware of Sylvester standing mutely behind her and doesn't want to push anything into confrontation in front of him. Silly that she should feel so protective of him.

As they leave the house, crossing the fields of flowers under the bright light of the sun and the upper void of the deep cloudless blue sky, she wishes Kasper had come with them. They face the forest better together. They are stronger together.

Kasper watches them go. Thinking of Sylvester's face, downcast as he refused to use his name, a slight nausea comes over him. Hunger. Too much beer last night. But it's neither. As the nausea spreads out, he is uncomfortable in his own skin, cannot look at himself in the small square mirror and cannot stop from thinking about Sylvester and Madeleine. He knows the word is *shame* but has to chop some firewood to stop it forming in his mind, like the spider wings and snake feathers of a black crow splitting out from a red-veined egg.

Madeleine and Sylvester cross the field behind the house, the day already stiflingly hot, heading for the cool shade under the trees. Sylvester is singing the notes of a song that Madeleine likes and, after a moment, she sings the notes too – one note behind Sylvester. Coming under the canopy of the branches they both lift their heads and feel like they can breathe a little deeper. Madeleine likes the slow pace Sylvester is obliged to keep and does not miss having to virtually run as Kasper marches through the trees. They reach a part of the forest near the brook Madeleine recognises and sit on a fallen log. She is curious to see the village but has realised it will be impossible with Sylvester with her. They sit in silence, Sylvester following her lead. So as Madeleine says nothing, neither does Sylvester.

She suggests they get up, having had some water from the canteen, and follow the brook. Madeleine walks upstream away from the village and steps in and out of the quick, almost transparent, water, reflecting the gold light of the sun here and there, its surface lambent with flashing light. Madeleine watches Sylvester skipping in and out of the water and then investigating a large butterfly flitting jaggedly over the cold back of the brook. He ambles back over, sits down next to Madeleine and she gives him some of her bread.

'I'm sorry.'

'What?' Madeleine can hardly understand what Sylvester says, his snout mouth distorting nearly every consonant and vowel as it tumbles out too quickly, with added salivary squeaks and squeals adding further layers of sound that obscure the sense.

She looks at him to see his big yellow eyes, and looking at them sees they are actually a deep-yellow, more like gold, and how nice they are to look at, and she sees flecks of brown peppering his large moist iris. He looks terrified.

'What is it? What's wrong?'

Madeleine puts her hand on his hand, too late, as he flinches and withdraws it. How sensitive is his pale skin.

'I dirtied my shirt, in the stream, mud, dirt.' The golden circles of his eyes sink downwards to the stains on his shirt.

Madeleine smiles and laughs in relief. 'Oh, I thought you had done something very wrong.'

Seeing Madeleine smile and laugh for the first time, Sylvester also smiles. 'You're not angry?'

'No,' Madeleine replies, looking quizzically at him, sideways, 'of course not.' She cannot understand why Sylvester is behaving this way – it's only a bit of mud. She thinks, for the first time in a long time, about the clothes she wore travelling through the forest, before Eva burned them. Of course, it's Tereza, Madeleine realises. And she looks at him again, contentedly making a mess of his bread, noisily eating, noisily breathing.

Sylvester is looking at her. 'Where is your heart?'

Madeleine takes his gummed up little hand and places it above her left breast.

'In the same place as yours.'

'I can hear it. What's inside it? Is that where love comes from?'

'I don't know. It's muscle and blood, and it beats to keep you alive.'

'Is my heart the same as yours?'

'Yes, all hearts are the same.'

'How do you know?'

'I just know, the way everyone's face... or hands—' Madeleine stops. *Every heart is folded over itself – the heart is a wilderness, a dark, wave-tipped sea... a forest – a demarked territory of emptiness on a map.*

'Do you need love to stay alive?'

'I don't know... why are you asking all these questions?'

'My mother would never answer me when I asked her.'

'Yes, you need love to stay alive. Life without love wouldn't be... wouldn't be worth living. Do you miss your mother?' Madeleine asks.

Sylvester looks down, as if, it seems to Madeleine, he has been anticipating this question. And he doesn't reply for a long time. The noise of the stream fills the space between them and around them.

'Yes.'

Madeleine looks away, not expecting this response but considers that it makes sense.

'Do you miss yours?'

She understands why Sylvester took his time replying; how can she miss someone she cannot remember, she has never known?

'I think so. When I see Eva fix Kasper's hair, or she readies you for bed.'

Madeleine does not know whether Sylvester knows of her amnesia. She does not want to bring it up. Her mother, father, siblings? They remind her of her memory loss, the nothingness of all those years before waking up in the forest. She thought she had remembered them when she was suffering her fever, or curse. A song that she woke up with in her head, the first morning she woke up feeling cool, rested. Dry and dehydrated, but without pain. The curse had robbed her of her memory – a black shadow on a black wall. She cannot remember anything after leaving Tereza's house – except she can remember the pain, her hand involuntarily moving to her stomach at the memory.

'I'm sorry she did that to you.'

Madeleine turns to him, puts her hand on his shoulder as delicately as she can. 'It's finished, I'm better now.'

'She must have been angry with me. You are my friends so she attacked you.'

'Sylvester,' Madeleine tries to sound firm, 'it was not your fault. Your mother loves you, it's just she cannot...'

She trails away as Sylvester's eyes fasten to her like his hand in hers.

'Not everyone feels love in the same way.' She hopes this explanation, which she doesn't know how she arrived at, will convince Sylvester and end this conversation. She takes his silence and the unlatching of his gaze as proof of his satisfaction.

'We'll always be friends,' Madeleine tells him.

He looks back at her, pathetically grateful.

'And Kasper? Will he be our friend too?'

'Yes, Kasper too. Remember friendship is different for different people. Don't be sad if he seems angry or impatient.'

'Like this morning?'

'Like this morning.'

Madeleine wishes Kasper were here, despite his pointless mood. She imagines him standing in his room, the sunlight lancing through the window like the lights from cameras as he makes his speech, gesturing to his maps, recounting from his radios the war he is directing and the war he can win.

'Are you finished eating?' Madeleine sees the bread scattered all down Sylvester's shirt and in his lap. He nods.

'Then come with me, let's go find a tree.'

'Why?'

'I'll show you something, something that will make us friends forever.' And Sylvester's hand slides into Madeleine's without hesitation and Madeleine adjusts her pace scanning for a distinctive tree.

'Do trees only grow in the summer?' he asks.

'I don't know,' says Madeleine, never having thought about this. 'I don't think so.'

'The trees are bigger in summer than in winter.'

'They have leaves, it makes them seem bigger.'

They leave the stream as they hear the first drums of thunder. Like giant factories, immense production lines have started to fire up, boiling up the dense and low grey light that begins to filter through the trees.

Madeleine turns round and Sylvester sees for the first time her eyes look black in the shaded half-light under the trees, and by her hand is a flash of white. A knife.

'Where did you get that?' he asks, breathlessly, his mouth swinging ungainly open in a beat of panic within him, snapping open, his eyes bright and wide, straining to see in the gathering darkness.

'Eva gave it to me. She said women need more protection than men. Do you like it?'

'Can I hold it?'

'No. It's mine. Only a woman can handle it.'

'What? That's not true!'

'That's what Eva told me so it must be true. It's only for girls who believe in their own strength. Then the world will look after them.'

'I only want to look at it.'

'Then look at this.'

Madeleine puts the knife, its long silvery blade, like the tongue of some great creature from the Arctic wastes, almost as long as Madeleine's forearm, into the bark as if it were paper, the gouges becoming gummed with the tree's amber sap.

Four scratches: M

'M,' Sylvester dutifully spells out.

Then beneath, some more scratches: et

'Madeleine and...' Madeleine whispers to herself, straining at the effort of digging into the tough bark:

first mark /

and

second mark \

and then, the final mark,

S

Sylvester happily obliges Madeleine by saying his own name in recognition of her work. Madeleine thinks it looks a little jagged; it's difficult to work curves into bark despite the sharpness of the blade. She shows Sylvester how to clear the sap away. He looks at it proudly. Madeleine suggests they leave now and turns in the direction of the house, but Sylvester does not move.

'Are you coming?'

'I want to go this way.'

Madeleine knows where this path heads. She stands still for a minute before taking Sylvester's hand in hers and walking together to Tereza's house. They are within a hundred metres or so, and the trees and brambles prick at Madeleine's memory, tearing little holes of panic and nausea. And when they come closer to the little hut – looking squalid and cold in the daytime, Madeleine thinks – Sylvester starts to run, and she shouts after him that she'll wait here. But she doesn't know if he hears.

Sylvester enters the house gingerly. The darkness and lack of comforts that so discomforts every other guest is familiar to him. The candles are lit on the table and a cigarette is burning on the rim of an ashtray. Tereza moves into the room from the kitchen, the light from which doesn't stray into the main room. Sylvester stops.

'Come here,' Tereza says.

Sylvester ambles over and stops in front of his mother. She puts her arms around him, gently, to avoid bruising his skin.

'She's out there isn't she?' Tereza asks, and can feel Sylvester's nodding against her chest. His arms fold around Tereza's waist, tightly. They stay still for a while.

Madeleine sees Sylvester leave the house. Followed by Tereza. She was not expecting to see her and her grip on her rifle tightens. Her mind feels that it is a clockwork mechanism, slipping one of its gears, the cogwheels sparking against each other, and she begins to lose grip of its rational motion. But Sylvester doesn't seem panicked or distressed, uncertain perhaps, walking slowly and looking over his shoulder. Tereza's arms are folded, a cigarette burning in her right hand as always. And Madeleine starts to tremble as even over this distance and the descending twilight she knows Tereza can see her and is staring right at her. Tereza waves at her and she swallows, awkwardly, coughing. She wills Sylvester to walk faster, walk faster. Hurry.

'Thank God you made it back safely,' Madeleine says, grasping Sylvester's hand. Hating herself for sounding like Eva. Sylvester squeals a little and pulls his arm back.

'Why wouldn't I?' Sylvester asks, in a tone Madeleine has never heard before. He stops and looks back at the house, now a small flicker of light through the trees.

They walk on in silence. They hear a sound behind them and both turn round startled as if caught red-handed, two thieves about to break into the night. Silence. Sylvester's hand grasps Madeleine's. The dark-blue air of twilight makes it difficult to see much clearly. Then, another breaking and cracking sound behind them. Not the sound a boy makes, nor a girl, not even a man. It is the sound of something heavy. Their nervousness contaminates each other. Madeleine grips her knife so that her knuckles are as white as the long, lithe-looking blade. Sylvester, deathly pale, grabs her hand and skirt behind her making it difficult to get her gun, the strap catching on his shoulder. They crowd towards each other, bunching round their tree, as if seeking its protection now they have christened it. Then Madeleine sees – and immediately after – hears another crack, the paw of the animal snapping a branch that is the thickness of their entire body.

She can hear, as if he is far away or speaking through thick layers of material, Sylvester's panicked squealing.

monster

monster

the monster will eat us

And she sees a paw that is connected to a tiger's face, dark like an uncut jewel in the earth through the branches, its fur striped as if it is the avatar of fire, the fire which burns endlessly in its eyes. It stops. It has stopped at the point it can see rather than smell flesh. The tiger seems to have commanded silence in the forest – all the creatures in all the trees have fled, scattered and disappeared. It moves forwards sinuously, one long, thick muscle, rippling to and fro. Like a snake mindlessly undulating forwards, lost in the music of its charmer, the tiger follows the notes of flesh and blood on the breeze.

The tiger sees them, its ears flattening, and Madeleine and Sylvester look straight into its face as it changes, becomes distorted, and they see its lips curl, thick and black, and its teeth, grotesquely large. Its eyes hold them enchanted, cauldrons of molten gold, a black spot swirling, unfixed, somewhere in the centre. Its growl seems to unbalance them, travelling through the ground, and Madeleine, her hands, sweaty and moist, feel like they are dissolving. She breaks free and grasps her gun, Sylvester's hot breath on her hand she has put there to reassure him and stop any unexpected squeals. At the same time she feels all the blood drain from her face, plummeting downwards to her heart, her stomach, and at the same time her heartbeat pounds in her head and she's afraid she'll faint at the pressure behind her eyes. Slowly she moves her hand away as the tiger begins to move with purpose. It can see them, it is beginning to stride, shoulder blades that rise up, fall down. The tiger is beginning to lose its form through the tears in her eyes. The rifle is in front of her.

The bullet speeds out not far above the level of her head so now smoke and the horrible smell of gunpowder discharge envelop them all. The bullet has shredded some of the branches of their tree, bits and twigs of which come tumbling down around them. That second they can see the tiger again, but in a blur of streaked amber the tiger has vanished, leaving nothing but silence.

Madeleine exhales slowly, carefully, as if the tiger will return if it hears their movements again. She moves her arm around Sylvester without stopping to scan the trees; she feels him trembling. After waiting for as long they can, Madeleine starts to breathe more easily, and her grip around the rifle in the one hand and around Sylvester's shoulder with her arm clutching him close to her relaxes.

'Is it gone?' Sylvester whispers. Madeleine has never heard him whisper before and it sounds eerie to her, not like the high-pitched voice that she finds funny, despite herself, with its sudden modulations of pitch, random squeals and squeaks, the bestial knot of flesh that struggles, twisting in his human larynx, to confound meaning and echo the mouth that belonged on the forest floor, sniffing for truffles, down in among the dead wood and filth. But his whisper is without change of tone or animal inflection. It sounds dead, monotone. Madeleine looks down to see his pale face staring out into the trees.

'Don't worry, it's gone… it's gone.'

She squats down sideways to be at his height.

'You're safe, it's gone.'

Sylvester nods enthusiastically as if obeying her statements rather than believing them.

'We're safe now but we have to be careful.'

The thunder sounds again; a warning, Madeleine feels. This sensation is her first memory of the forest, the pilot. She hasn't thought of him for a long time. And the whole force of the tiger suddenly comes back to her and she can't believe it now – a tiger? What's a tiger doing in this forest? They live in India, the silent man-eaters that slide through the trees like their own shadows in the forests… far away. Is it a new weapon? Have they started recruiting tigers into their armies?

She drags Sylvester, uncomplaining, back to the house before the storm starts and drenches them; a warning to stay indoors.

Madeleine thinks: *Is the tiger lost? Where did you come from?*

As they come to the field behind the house, they can see the sky has turned heavily grey and black. Clouds of black and clouds of grey chase and overturn each other, and in the far distance Madeleine can see a split in the sky as lightning shines for a fraction of time and an instant later feels the heavy assault of raindrops on her skin.

'Let's go,' she says, 'before it comes back.'

As before, Madeleine is impressed with the speed Sylvester can generate, a velocity that belies his awkward frame, and has to walk as fast as she can, his hand leading the way. They come back into the house, reassuringly warm and bright, without dark spaces from which tigers can approach. Eva is there in the kitchen, wiping her hands on her apron as they enter.

'There you are. The rain's starting. Be lots of days like this now. It's the season for storms.' She turns back to a boiling, steaming pot.

'They are in the workshop, put your gun in there, I don't like them in this house.'

Madeleine feels as if she is in a trance, unable to speak. Sylvester is tugging at her sleeve.

Eva says without turning round: 'If you're going to stay here then make yourselves useful. Make some tea, dry off.' Then she turns round and sees Madeleine shaking, Sylvester looking at her imploringly. 'What is it?'

'In the forest,' Madeleine begins, 'it was in the forest.'

Sylvester squeals: 'The monster!'

Eva's expression becomes more quizzical, and glancing at the pot, Madeleine doesn't know whether to continue or not.

'It was a... tiger.' Madeleine has to use the French and is tempted to speak the word using a Polish accent but thinks Eva would not be impressed.

'Not a monster,' Madeleine says, looking at Sylvester, 'an animal.'

'It was black,' Sylvester almost shouts.

'What?' Madeleine says, baffled by the boy's inaccuracy.

'Did you shoot it? Is it dead?'

'No, it ran away.'

'It ran away,' Sylvester echoed, 'into the forest.'

'It didn't chase you home?' Eva's patience is at an end, and turning back to the pots, she addresses some herbs. 'Then we shall all sleep safely in our beds tonight.'

They are left standing there, faced with Eva's industry, and they drift upstairs. Sylvester asks if he can sit with Madeleine in her room, and Madeleine says: 'Go away. Now she thinks we're crazy or liars because of you. Go away.' And she pushes open the dark, heavy door and slams it behind her, leaving Sylvester alone in the corridor.

Sylvester has been found a space in the corner of Kasper's room, much to Kasper's annoyance, having been forced to tidy the maps and wires from disintegrated radio sets as well as being tasked with constructing Sylvester's bed, a small cot Jan designed. He sweats with a plane, pushing it along a length of pine. Stops as Jan pats him roughly on the back and heads for the door, his pipe in hand, to watch the rain coming down heavily. Kasper finds his tobacco and rolls his cigarette, his newly acquired habit.

Watching the rain. Madeleine watches the rain pummel her window, her room dark and damp. By the door the rain has unleashed the clotted smell of the earth from the emerald sea of grass and flowers of summer, heads bowing low under the torrent of raindrops.

Madeleine has taken one of the Bibles from downstairs, the French version, after making tea for Eva and herself. She is reassured by the stories in Genesis because they are so familiar, and she hopes they will spark some memory of when she heard them before; in church maybe? In school? At home, with some tea, by a window blurred by rain? As she reads about the expulsion from Eden, Madeleine can see the low black clouds rushing and tumbling over themselves against the higher, thinner grey clouds that seem as high as heaven.

The storm is coming closer. The thunder sounds as if it is throwing around objects in the attic above her. Then, barely a few seconds later, the lightning illuminates the rain around it, momentarily lending a blinding platinum flame to the million pearls streaming onto the trees and onto the house. Madeleine is bored by the stories after Cain and Abel and by the seemingly endless genealogical information of Exodus. Then she reads about the rain. The same rain that's bombarding the windows. The ark and the animals, all of them entering the ark to drift around a drowned planet. There would be two tigers there too, sleeping in a corner of the room reserved for the big cats. The male licking his mate's amber and dark fur. Watched in dim oil light by the listless lion and lioness, ignored by the sleeping lynxes. Madeleine thinks everyone, even those in the Bible – especially those in the Bible – spend some of their time wandering. Lost. She thinks of Sylvester, and for a second hopes he isn't still standing in the corridor, like an abandoned dog waiting for its owner. That would be ridiculous, and just in case, she goes to check, but the corridor is empty and she can hear Eva issuing orders. Madeleine thinks she could have let him in, to sit on the bed in silence and watch the rain; can he read? Maybe she could have read to him? But she is still puzzled by why he thinks the tiger was black. Was it, she thinks, almost as a joke, because he had his eyes closed? The clouds, did they smear the light black for the instant Sylvester looked at the tiger? Was it because he only saw the dark, black spots of its eyes? Did he only see the stripes and not the fawn-coloured fur beneath? Is black the tiger's true colour, the tiger really a black monster underneath the slashes of light fur?

Madeleine forgets all about it when she hears Eva shouting from downstairs, the harsh Polish diminutive of her name. She catches sight of something as she strides to the door. Herself. The mirror. She walks up to it, refreshing her memory with the sight of herself. Madeleine thinks it's easier to miss things than she thinks; how many details are left unobserved? Her face looks tired. Healthy, brown, strong but sad. She walks closer to the mirror, so her face is a mask of blackness to her. Her breath flares up in the glass; she feels its moist heat breathe back onto her skin.

Qui es-tu? Réponds-moi...
Qui suis-je?

'Magdalena!'

The shout explodes from downstairs. Madeleine extinguishes the candles, leaving the room even darker, and shuts the door behind her. At dinner, Sylvester finds his enthusiasm undiminished and tells a surprised Jan and an astonished Kasper about the black tiger. They both look to Madeleine once – almost breathless – Sylvester has finished.

'Is this true?' Jan asks her.

'Yes.'

'Where was it?' Kasper asks her.

'By the stream,' Madeleine replies, unable to look them in the eye, embarrassed by Sylvester's unchecked confession.

'Well, stay away from there.' Madeleine looks up at Jan. 'Both of you.' He quells Sylvester's enthusiasm with his stern, impatient expression.

Afterwards, washing up the dishes, Madeleine is ignoring Kasper's questions.

'So how many heads did it have?'

'I know what I saw. It was a tiger and it was in the forest.'

'So what did Sylvester see then?'

'I don't know.'

'I'll ask him.'

'Leave him alone. He was scared.'

'Did it breathe fire?'

'Shut up.' Then in French: 'Shut up.'

Madeleine leaves the rest of the washing up for Kasper, in a splash of anger.

Once she is upstairs, undressed by candlelight, she throws her dress over the long mirror, blows out the candles and slips between the cool sheets. Sleep nestles up to her quickly as she realises how tired she is after the long day in the forest and the unexpected creatures she and Sylvester found there. Madeleine watches the silvery smoke from the extinguished candles rise and dissipate into the darkness. She hates the phosphorus smell of the candles but watches the glowing orange buds of the wicks slowly flickering out. The smoke seems to play on the inside of her tired eyes, heavy with exhaustion from peering into the forest, only to see what has been watching her until it is nearly too late. The tiger's face appears from the blood-coloured borealis that throbs in the under-sphere of her sleep. But it seems formed of leaves, its fiery eyes floating detached, hovering. The leaves leech their greenness and the whole forest becomes black and white, curling and undulating in the flowing curlicues of smoke. The tiger's face becomes more abstracted until it resembles a Rorschach image: a black-and-white heart exploded, split open and frozen, burning away from the centre by the hot amber fire of the tiger's eyes. The flames illuminate something Madeleine's flickering eyelids cannot quite discern, below the wings of the left ventricle and the right ventricle, a slim band. Studded with bright points of light. A collar. The sight flicks Madeleine's eyes open, staring into the dull darkness. In her memory, where it was not before, she can see the collar on the tiger. Studded with silver spikes. The tiger belongs to someone. Have the zookeepers from Germany and Russia declared war on each other too? Silly idea. She will tell Kasper tomorrow and take him to the tree. Then she will show him. He'll see. He'll see what she can see. In her bed, beneath her eyelids. In the dark kingdom of the black-and-white forest between memory and dreams. As she sleeps.

Crows

The next morning Madeleine is up early, as early as Eva. She can hear her moving down the corridor and bursting into Kasper's room. She presumes Sylvester is already up, ordered off the sofa at whatever time Eva rises to heat the water or start to make tea. Jan can sleep as long as he likes. Smoking in the outhouse till late. Did he still walk out into the forest late at night, Madeleine ponders, throwing open the rough wooden shutters and feeling the heat, and it's so very hot. The sunlight is blinding and the sun's heat scorching as if it is careening towards the earth. A travelling bomb. The frigid water is welcome as she splashes herself all over and doesn't dry herself, letting it cool her skin. She puts on her dress, a light dress for summer that today feels too heavy, and her shoes. She closes the shutters again before she leaves her room.

The corridor is dark and cool as always, and as she walks into Kasper's room, following the bickering Polish sounds she can hear between Kasper and his mother, she sees he's still in bed, only in his underwear. Madeleine has never seen him without his shirt. They both stare at each other for three seconds but which feels like three hours to them both, and they both look away, both blushing, Madeleine retreating to a corner as Kasper wrestles to pull on a shirt.

'Not that shirt.' Eva pulls it off his head, oblivious to the embarrassment of both her son and the girl, blind to their mutual exchange, the blood that now heats both their faces. Kasper desperately grabs at the new shirt proffered by Eva. With Kasper struggling to drag it down over his chest, Eva has only just noticed Madeleine.

'Since you're up, go help Sylvester with the tea and breakfast.'

Madeleine nods and goes downstairs, impatient to speak to Kasper, make him understand. The others eventually come noisily down the stairs, Eva still berating Kasper and Kasper still protesting. She does not dare bring it up while Eva and Sylvester are around. To her relief, Sylvester has been sent out to collect eggs from the hen house.

After their breakfast of tea and eggs and some ham, Madeleine takes away the dishes to the sink with Kasper, who has been sullen since he came downstairs.

'Can you come with me to the forest today?' she asks.

Kasper seems to spark into life. 'What? Why?'

'To show you I wasn't lying.'

Kasper looks away, back at the sink. 'I have to work, and I don't care what you saw.'

'Then let's just go for a walk.'

'Later.'

'Good. When?'

'In the afternoon.'

'It feels like a long time since we've been in the forest together.'

Madeleine leaves him, frustrated at how he's become such hard work recently. Can it really all be because she went for a walk with Sylvester? It's not her fault he's been set to work in the workshop all the time now.

Madeleine is drafted by Eva to prepare lunch and dinner. It is not until late afternoon that she can escape and go see Kasper in the workshop. Jan has him working on Sylvester's bed. It's nearly finished as she can see shaped and sanded parts leaning behind the bench. Madeleine waits by the large open doors that let the heat in, but inside, without any windows, it's dark and cool. Jan sees her and stops what he's doing, starts walking towards her, and Madeleine feels herself blushing. It must just be the heat. Jan stretches and takes some tobacco from a waistcoat hanging by the doors.

'Come to see your friend?'

Madeleine, surprised and embarrassed by her behaviour, can barely look him in the eye.

'You've done enough today,' Jan barks back over his shoulder at Kasper. 'Go play with your friend.' He lights his cigarette. 'How are you, princess?' Jan asks.

Kasper emerges into the light, and Madeleine sees his shirt is blotched with sweat.

Madeleine smiles. 'Very well, thank you. If Kasper's busy I'll come back later.' She's embarrassed still, though this time because of how formal she sounds.

'We'll be back,' he says without looking back. Kasper strides past Madeleine.

'Yes.' Jan exhales a breath-cloud of smoke. 'You will, at twilight. And don't go any further than the stream.'

'Bye,' Madeleine says.

'Goodbye, your majesty,' Jan replies, inclining his head slightly.

As they walk into the cool shade of the trees, Kasper says: 'That's the first time I've seen him smile in days.'

'Why?'

'I don't know.' Kasper kicks some stones. 'Since you had your fever curse he stands by the doors for a long time, just looking at the trees. I don't know what's happening. He doesn't say anything.'

Madeleine is unsettled by this. If Jan is nervous, Kasper is nervous, then it's for a good reason, whatever the reason may be. She looks around at the trees, neutral as ever, and notices with the mildest relief that the forest is noisy today, as it should be, not quiet and still as it was when the tiger was about. They walk on towards the stream in silence.

'This is the tree,' Madeleine announces, when she sees the carvings she inscribed on the tree yesterday.

'What tree?' Not looking up, Kasper slings his rifle off his shoulder and holds it at its middle point in his hand.

'The tree where we saw the tiger yesterday?'

Kasper looks up: 'Oh – the tiger – the monster. How do you know?' He sits down heavily, drinking some water, still unwilling to look at either Madeleine or the tree.

'Because this is the tree Sylvester and I...' she trails off. Will this annoy Kasper further, knowing his initial is not on this tree?

'Oh.'

Madeleine sits down too, not too close to him. She scrutinises his face, still angled downwards. Then he looks up at the two carved initials in the tree's bark.

'Just your initials.'

'Yes,' Madeleine replies despondently. And looking at him, 'But I'll carve yours. Let's do it now.'

'No,' Kasper says, getting up. 'Let's go. I have work I need to do.'

'Already? But... we've only just got here.'

Kasper doesn't reply and starts to walk off. It could still be a joke, Madeleine thinks, but he's been in such moods recently, more like his mother than his father. When she woke up that morning with blood on the sheets, Eva said all women's moods can change at this time because of hormones in the blood, but men... men, they have no excuse, Madeleine remembers Eva saying, with her usual lack of empathy. Why shouldn't men be allowed to have different tempers? But then why is Kasper acting like this? It's infuriating.

'Kasper!' Madeleine shouts at his back, retreating between the trees. She feels like Eva. He turns. 'Let's find another tree, we'll write our—'

At the same time: 'No' – Kasper
'Names' – Madeleine

Madeleine can't quite believe this is happening. She remembers, days, weeks ago, it was Kasper who wanted to take her into the forest, who wouldn't leave her alone; it was his gaze she would catch looking up, looking across.

'Let's go shooting. Let's shoot something,' at a volume she knows he'll be unable to ignore.

To herself: 'I'd like to shoot you.'

Her index finger and thumb become a gun and fire.

'Stupid boy.'

Madeleine squats down, her rifle falling from her shoulder, the barrel striking the side of her knee, but the pain doesn't make her move; she enjoys it. She enjoys mastering it. No such thing as pain if you don't feel it. The same with feelings, she thinks, plucking some grass. Girls. Kasper. Boys. Sylvester. Men. *Tereza*. Women. Poles. Who needs them? Maybe this – all this war – is what they deserve. Tears clot the edges of her eyes as she thinks of the dead pilot. What pain must he have felt? If it is the same for feelings and people, she thinks, then she shouldn't really be crying into the grass. She plucks some blades more fiercely, and this quells her crying. Emotional responses are more difficult to control, clearly. It must just be a question of willpower; willpower she doesn't have. She wipes her cheeks roughly clean of tears and then, something she's never done, spits salty phlegm into the grass. It lands on a tree root and then she stands up.

Is it me?
Did they abandon me like Kasper just did?

Much as it makes her angry, the tears come back, the salt stinging her lachrymal glands, snot choking her throat. She spits again. How satisfying it is. She spits again, again trying to get it further than the first one.

She kicks the next tree root she sees and it's quite painful.

Idiot. Why did you do that?

Madeleine thinks she sees the girl from the mirror between the trees, the bark bathed a soft brown almost caramel colour by the sunlight that seems to shine between the trees as if it is dripping like caramel from the leaves; why is the girl here? Is she lost too now?

'Please find me. I'm lost – save me! Poor little me!' Madeleine shouts at the space where the girl was. The girl disappears. Madeleine snorts in triumph; there's at least one being in the forest she can conquer and inspire fear in. Encouraged by her sudden disappearance, she moves to kick another tree root but sees it's not a root. Something else. An animal. A bird. Madeleine can see something black, smooth made-up lines, smooth and straight. It's looking at her, the crow's black eye, its beak slightly open. Madeleine looks over to see another one, its wings arranged in a different shape, its eye open too but its beak closed. She kneels down to the first one and runs her fingers, gingerly at first but then more slowly and deliberately, to feel the soft sleekness of its wing, so smooth it's difficult to feel she's actually touching it. Looking more closely at it. Madeleine's thighs are beginning to ache so she kneels down, her legs underneath her, and then she sees the dark-red ripped hole in the crow's breast. She looks up, curious as to whether there are any clues as to their demise; there were no gunshots that she heard and she and Kasper were certainly close enough to hear one. Maybe the hole was caused by something else; nothing comes to mind though. Madeleine lies down next to the crow, on her side, placing her hand on its head; the part is still warm.

Did the tiger do this?

Poor birds.

Her hand moves down its soft chest to the ragged hole, and her finger traces the edge, accumulating a layer of blood. Madeleine puts the blood to her cheek, a zigzag down from her zygoma, across her cheek, back to the tip of her mouth and out down her jaw line. The blood feels warm and thick on her skin. With her finger now on her other cheek she pastes one line across her cheekbone and another one underneath, from the point of her lips round her cheek to the hinge of her jawbone. She lets her hand rest on its head. Madeleine closes the crow's eye. Shortly afterwards, her own eyes close and she becomes alive to the whisperings, calls, murmurings and language of the forest and all the animals on the ground and all the birds in the trees.

Kasper walks on. His eyes fixed on the forest floor, thinking of Madeleine, thinking of Madeleine. What did he ever ruminate on before she arrived, he asks himself? Kicking at some ferns. Did the war take up all his time, repairing the radios, circling cities on maps, the routes of passing armies, hoping the pencil lines would stay away from the small 'd' on the map. He imagines his own trail through the forest away from Madeleine. Jan will be furious when he returns without her. His pace slows. She dealt with the tiger yesterday, he thinks, with a bitter smirk – she will be alright. His pace accelerates.

When he arrives home he avoids the workshop and goes straight upstairs; luckily Eva and Sylvester are somewhere else. He enters his room, looking at the empty space in the corner, which will soon be occupied by Sylvester's bed. He sits down on his bed and looks at the telegraph set he so far hasn't been able to make work. He sits down on the floor in the mess of wires straggling from the telegraph and from the battery cell pack. And he cannot think about how to complete the circuit as he looks out the window, beginning to become shaded, the darkness moving like a marine tide falling from the upper troposphere and stratosphere. He lifts himself up slowly, kicking off his shoes, and falls gracelessly onto his bed, fighting against his mind, which keeps a bright light lit against the darkness of sleep, a light that shines in the forest, the forest keeping Madeleine hidden.

Kasper wakes – at a sound – what sound? His mouth dry and gummed with tiredness, sticky with crusted saliva. His head is still heavy and stuffed with sleep. He quickly realises it's Eva's unquiet signal for supper. He glances outside, the sky a deep teal. He swings his legs onto the floor, unsettled by his leaving Madeleine in the forest. Slowly he heads downstairs, certain at what will be an intense inquisition and a further curtailment of his freedoms. He comes into the kitchen to face the stern face of Eva and Jan tending to his pipe and Sylvester rushing around like a flustered waiter in a restaurant. Water more out of the jug than in.

'And where is Magdalena?'

'Upstairs,' Kasper says without thinking.

'Then go get her,' Eva says, not pausing, not desisting from serving some cold meat.

Kasper waits. And he sees his father push himself from the doorjamb, looking at him intently.

'You did come home together didn't you?'

Kasper waits.

The tone of his question stalls Eva in her bustling.

Kasper waits. He knows he must accept this.

Jan puts his pipe down and moves for the door, gathering his coat and gun. Neither of his parents speak to him, and Kasper would almost prefer the usual admonishment and smack round the temple than this silent glowering. When he raises his eyes a fraction he sees that Sylvester has also stopped to look at him, though even this is only because everyone else is doing it, and it makes Kasper blush. Then his father's big hand scrunches up the front of his shirt and half pulls him off the ground and half throws him out the door.

'Get your coat on,' Jan tells him, in a frequency so low Kasper can barely hear him but knows this means his temper is at the edge. Kasper opens the door, waiting for Jan and Eva to stop their urgent discussion, and he looks out into the dark trees under a dark turquoise-teal sky shining without a sun and sees Madeleine. Walking towards the light spilling from the door into the darkness, into the light and into the house. Her face is darker. Everyone looks at her.

'What have you done?' Eva asks.

Kasper does not recognise her, his mouth falling open, as does Sylvester's. They don't recognise the dark, dirty, red-black lines on her face. Madeleine glares back at them all, her gun still strapped over her shoulder. Saying nothing, she moves to walk up stairs.

Jan moves to put his coat back on.

Eva then moves to take her arm.

'What have you done? What's on your face? You look like a heathen savage.'

'Let me go!' Madeleine wrenches her arm free from Eva's hand, using far more force than necessary to break from Eva's weak grip, enjoying too the liberating effect of speaking aggressively in another language.

Eva's hand moves up above her head, ready to strike Madeleine's blood-marked cheek and Madeleine does not move, defying Eva to bring the back of her hand down. Eva's hand is held at the wrist by Jan's; he brings it down slowly and Eva turns her steel-blue gaze onto him and neither one looks away. She shakes her wrist free as Madeleine runs up the stairs into her room and slams the heavy door shut as much as she can. So heavy and solid it doesn't make quite the sound she wants to hear and so, her anger still beating inside her, she flings over the mirror without thinking because she hasn't considered the glass would shatter. The mirror, too, resists; the frame, like the door, too solid and wooden to be seriously perturbed by the physical remonstrations of a teenage savage. Madeleine stands over the mirror. In the semi-darkness, her face, far away from the mirror's surface, is almost dark but she can see the pale glow of her legs before her dress conceals her thighs in shadow. She can make out the dark opals of her eyes, glistening in the darkness, and smears of blood along her face and neck. Madeleine's anger now shocked out of her, she rights the mirror and lights the stubs of the candles. In the soft lambent light of the candles, Madeleine sees the tears running down her crow-blood markings creating dark scarlet lines that streak over her jaw, some of them trickling down her neck in a pleasurable tickle that Madeleine savours. She inhales deeply the thick, heavy smell of blood and salt that quickly reminds her of Tereza's curse, but despite this she inhales deeply the smell of meat and blood, of life and death, beast and human. It is the smell of the forest. Animals and birds and trees and... pilots.

It is my scent.

Madeleine walks over to the porcelain bowl, dips her hands into the tepid water and brings her fingers up to her face, dripping odourless clear liquid to her face and enjoying the sensation of the cold water running down her face, across her breastbone, reaching her chest, freckling the front of her dress. The water becomes dark and clouded with blood.

Drying her face, Madeleine takes one last look at her clean face, her dirty hair in the uprighted mirror, and closes the door behind her. Everyone is still downstairs bustling – apart from Jan – and Kasper is not bustling as such but is carrying out the tasks allotted to him with more vigour than usual. Although they are all busy, Madeleine can see that they're tense. Jan again, a degree lower than the others, and descending the stairs she feels a sudden swell of power; she physically feels herself straighten her back and her head rise, her neck straight.

Madeleine walks down the stairs slowly and she assumes the role of a princess entering the ball, affording all the others their first glimpse of something they all want to be, or want to possess. But her face burns up, hot as any gypsy curse, she thinks. Her skin seems to catch fire as she realises Jan has been watching her too. She is not a princess, not even a woman, just a girl, a deluded girl.

Jan moves away to get a glass while rolling a cigarette. Eva turns to her and tells her to help Sylvester set the table in the dining room. Madeleine wonders briefly why they are eating in there, but is relieved to be out of the kitchen and in the quieter dining room. She can hear the rain tapping against the window and she moves to look out the window and sees how dark it is and how heavy the rain is. As if to confirm her impression, a burst of thunder starts to crackle, building up slowly, unleashing ever-louder bursts of sound. She sees Sylvester in the corner, pale and nervous. Why did they ask him to set the table, strange people? Is it a Polish practical joke? With his piggy hands he can't do it quickly or easily. He has to use both hands to grasp a plate or mug, and cutlery is an impossible process...

'Sit down,' Madeleine says. 'I'll do this.' She proceeds to set the table, bowls and plates assuming their proper places on the large dark table and the deep-red tablecloth. Water jugs and candlesticks. The room is illuminated in a burst of whiteness. Sylvester drops a bowl, which clatters noisily to the floor but does not break. Two or three seconds later, more thunder seems to explode from the clouds directly above the house and the rain gushes down even harder. Once the initial roars of the atmosphere tearing itself apart have subsided, Madeleine can still hear noise. A noise over the thunder and the noise of Sylvester ineffectually trying to place the bowl back on the table.

Before the Devil

Madeleine walks into the kitchen to see them all: Kasper chopping up herbs, rosemary and parsley. Eva and Jan are discussing the weather, the leak in the roof that needs fixing before they are all drowned in their sleep. Jan is rocking back on the chair at the head of the table, a large black boot resting on his knee, his braces dangling by the chair legs, his face clouded by the cigarette smoke.

'I'll send up Kasper.'

Kasper ignores them, hoping it's a joke.

Eva makes a face and goes back to preparing the cold meats.

'He's as good as Jesus was at fixing things rendered from wood.' Kasper doesn't know why his father still baits his mother in this way.

'You watch yourself. Unless you want to start fasting.'

Kasper grips the knife before Jan can reply, tighter than anything he has held before, even the time he held the arm of the dentist's chair in Krakow, when one of his hind teeth was pulled, the gushing stream of ferrous blood coming back into his mouth.

Jan springs up, the chair falling backwards, and rushes for his gun, and Eva screams, short and high as the front door cracks wide and one, two, three, four, five, six men – soldiers – come through the door, guns bristling before them in white-red fists and knuckles like the horns of giant beetles.

One of them holding an automatic machine gun checks Jan's rush for his rifle and pushes his gun up to Jan's face, and Jan backs away, his hands up.

'Stop there. Now back.'

The soldier, damp and dirty, speaks Polish, not fluently, and with an accent. Jan cannot discern their uniforms, black but not SS. This is a small relief. The SS show no mercy, but even other soldiers with codes of honour they so proudly speak of do not apply them to civilians. And not at this stage of a long war. These men, unshaven and eyes dark and bright with exhaustion, look like they have travelled far. German? Ukrainian? Belorussian? They look Polish and might be one of the few Polish units Jan has heard of recruited by the Germans in their war against the Russian Bolsheviks. Traitor souls. They bring a damp, dirty smell with them.

'Back over there, peasant.'

Jan tries German: 'Take whatever you want, we won't stop you or give you any trouble.'

Another soldier, with his German army pistol, the Luger, his jacket undone and showing a mouthful of dirty teeth when he speaks: 'Oh we will, *Mein Herr Banause*. You won't stop us and you won't give us trouble.' The other soldiers chuckle before this man gestures at two of them to search the rest of the house.

One of the soldiers, with a filthy bandage smudged in black-and-red smears which is wrapped around his head concealing his left eye, is looking around amazed. His mouth and his right eye are slack with astonishment. He almost bumps into the officer so entranced is he by the house. He says to himself, as it's barely above a whisper: 'This is it, jackpot, full house.'

The one with his gun aimed at Jan moves closer: 'We're the ones who give trouble.' His officer grins.

'This is it, full house – this is all ours.'

One of them tramps upstairs, noisily in his boots, his rifle carried casually in his hand, and the other heads into the dining room. The leader and the soldier with the machine gun, who's gestured at Eva and Kasper to put their hands on their heads, now talk to Jan who has his hands up at shoulder height.

'Wissen Sie wer wie sind? Wir sind das Übermaß.'

Jan looks at him unwaveringly with no expression.

'Ah, but you speak German? Peasants – live in filth, walk through shit, you ask for pity, how can you when you smell like that? What do you give to the world? The world will be better without you, and it is a world that demands constant sacrifice. And it's we who decide. The *Nachzehrer* visit death on everyone they meet.' The leader turns round to his men. 'Which one looks the tastier?'

'Do as usual,' one of them says. 'Shoot the men and keep the woman to eat.' He smiles to the sound of laughter.

'I think she, the girl, looks best – she gives me a big... appetite. They are all plump, these fucking cowards in the forest, shuffling around like pigs.'

Madeleine can't think about what the soldier's saying as she barely understands it. She feels sick for Sylvester and terrified the soldier will find him there, unsure of whether Sylvester's seen the soldiers and then of his capacity to have hidden somewhere safe.

'Full house.' Spits on the floor.

Then the short soldier at the back, a black scarf around his neck, says: 'Remember that old crazy witch dressed all in black, *brüder*, all the while she was screaming and screeching...'

'She cursed us all,' the officer says, looking at Eva and pushing the heavy table out of his way as he approaches her, as if it were made of paper. 'Did you know that? And now you are cursed.'

'Stupid crazy bitch. We were cursed the day this war started. War is nothing but a heap of bad luck. It's a big pile of shit and we're the ones who have to carry it.'

'But by the end she seemed to enjoy us, though she didn't stop biting. Had to see her off cold before we'd all had our turns.'

'What did she say? *The earth bleeds*. Then this one, our brother with the beard, suggests we crucify her, so when she wakes up... crazy old bitch won't know where she is. But she'll be bleeding for the wolves to come up and sniff her skirts and bite her legs and chew her cunt.'

'No,' the soldier with the gun at his hip says. He says it to himself, staring into nothingness, and so nobody knows whom he is addressing. 'She said: "*the earth burns*".'

Jan keeps Madeleine in his arms and shoves her behind him, the officer seeing this.

'Ah, but daddy here wants her all to himself. Bored of the wife now?'

The soldier with the gun at his hip stares at the ceiling: 'The earth burns.'

'Which one will it be, daddy pig? The woman or the girl first?'

'They look like they'll both be tastier than that lieutenant was,' the leader says, pointing his gun at Madeleine. 'Take her. Take the others outside and put them in the other building.'

'This is all ours.' Spits on the floor.

The soldier with the machine gun pushes it into Jan's chest, pushing him backwards, while the one behind the officer moves to separate Eva from Madeleine.

'We will eat well tonight my brothers—'

Sylvester bursts out from behind the dining room door, and Madeleine, without thinking, breaks from Eva's embrace and rushes after him. In the next few seconds, everybody in the room, except Eva, all at once move at extreme speed to another part of the space, as if their bodies had been aware all along of the unknown vectors on which they propel themselves: one soldier runs after Sylvester and Madeleine as they vanish through the dining room and out of the back door, leaving a chair spinning on one leg for several seconds before it is flung against the wall by the pursuing soldier. Kasper takes the stairs, rushing past the soldiers who are focused on the others, and bounds up the stairs to his room. One of the soldiers, the tallest, follows him. Jan moves the quickest of all and jumps through the air with a knife pulled from his boot onto the soldier nearest to him. The soldier next to him shoots his rifle, still at his hip, as the knife finds and penetrates his comrade's abdomen, severing the thick cords of meat piled up in his intestines. Jan is pushed backwards by the bullet into Eva's arms. Kasper, upstairs, stumbles down the corridor, his body and legs unable to go at the speed he wants, as he hurtles into his room and slams the door shut behind him. His hands are trembling yet he must send an SOS on his radio, to anyone who will listen, anyone with a radio: the Resistance, maybe even the British, but the Germans, the Russians, who could be worse? Desperately tapping out the dashes, dots, dashes --- ooo --- over and over --- ooo --- until one of the militia comes into his room, trampling over his maps and kicking the radio set to the wall where it makes a large dull metallic sound and a million sharper, smaller ones from within. Kasper is pulled up roughly up and over his feet, his feet dangling in mid-air and his throat crushed by the man's hand; he had no idea anyone could be this strong and so free and easy with their strength. They must be able to get anything they want, and Kasper's heart starts to tremble and shake; piss collects at the crotch of his trousers: these men would take whatever they wanted, he realises, as he chokes and a small net of saliva spatters the man's hand. He lets Kasper drop, disgusted. Kasper collapses, coughing wetly at the man's wet, shiny black boots. He receives a kick in his arm, the arm that was supporting him, and he falls onto the floor.

'Stupid peasant, make sure next time that your telegraph is connected to the radio. Otherwise they'll just think you're playing with your little dick.' A hearty laugh follows and then abruptly stops as he remembers there is important business to be getting on with. His mirth vanishes and he spits.

'Get up,' he says, kicking Kasper in the stomach. Kasper could not, of course; his hands were clutching his stomach. The soldier heaves him up by his arm and Kasper has to concentrate on not vomiting.

Madeleine can barely see Sylvester's form, running at a speed of which she didn't think him capable. Fear is running. Confusion in the rain and the thunderheads tumbling down in sound like rock falls from the sky. The lightning burns through the darkness and scorches the earth. Madeleine is drawing closer to Sylvester, but he evaporates in an inferno of white light. The rain when it falls to earth rebounds and flies upwards catching fire, becoming steam in the cauldron the field has become. The ground falls away from her feet. The flowers have each become flares, and the trees in the distance Madeleine can see have become fireworks, flames bursting from the tips of their branches. The raindrops that seem like lances fly upwards with her, splashing onto her skin and become sparks streaming upwards to the dark open skies. Madeleine, from the surface of the earth, can see everything illuminated in the clouds – the rough backs of the rain clouds burnished with white spray like the black backs of whales circling the oceans. The rain soothes her skin that has caught fire in her ascent, her hair a circle of flame like the halo of the Madonna, the corona of heavy artillery. Madeleine is now the source of this light, a bright torch in the night, a tear in the atmosphere, turning rain to superheated steam-white vapour, before the dark earth takes her heavily back into its dark horizon. Quickly, as rapidly as it came, the light disappears, leaving the darkness of the night and sodden waves of flowers. Sylvester runs to Madeleine, through the mud, shouting her name.

The soldier brings Kasper, limp and heavy, back down the stairs to the kitchen, struggling with his weight, and all but throws him down the last few steps. They enter into the shouts of the soldiers and the shouts of Eva. Jan is struggling in her arms, a flower of red on his white shirt. And on the other side of the table and scattered chairs, the soldier is howling in Polish, his fingers wrapped around the knife protruding from his belly. The leader tells him to keep calm. One of the soldiers tries to take Eva, but she shouts and curses him with such fury he retreats. Spitting in his face she scratches his cheek. The soldier with Kasper kicks him aside and helps his comrade wrestle Eva from Jan, but she still won't be still and writhes so much the leader has to step behind her and smash the back of her head with his Luger.

The soldier with the scarf stays still, watching it all eyes wide, and at the sound of feet behind him swerves round to see the doorway full. In all the four years he has been with the different units he has been assigned to officially, and by force of circumstance out in the retreat from Russia, he has seen a lot: entire villagers murdered; the Jews executed wherever they found them hiding or else herded on to the trains like so many animals; men with arms blackened by gangrene up to the elbow; lips eaten away by frostbite; the cooking and feasting upon horses, their flesh barely warm; the cooking and feasting upon men, Italians first, then the Ukrainians and, finally, the Romanians. Choosing bullets. But in all that time he has never seen a tiger. A tiger with a silver spiked collar seemingly barely kept in check by gravity, straining, held by a giant of a man who is just about able to restrain the animal – his two hands grappling with the chain as if it is a vicious, whipping snake. Two dwarves flank the giant, who has a shaved head and tattoos on his scalp and down the side of his face, each holding enormous, elaborate wooden flintlock revolvers. A sword swallower, a bunch of red lace at his throat, in a tight-fitting black suit from the last century, moves lithely holding two rapiers outstretched, meeting, almost touching the throats of two of the soldiers. They keep pouring in – this hallucination – a woman with a ridiculously hairy face in a startlingly blood-red dress and enormous black cleavage shoots her machine gun into the ceiling, her right arm clearly strong enough to handle the percussive recoils. The noise even seems to affect the tiger which retreats back to his master, prowling round the legs of the giant, its ears flattened, its growl like the weight of a tank. The shots usher in more hands with rifles and some with machine guns and knives, some holding the leash of Alsatian dogs that are impatient to bite and chew. They make way for a man dressed in black, rain glistening from the shoulders of his red satin-lined greatcoat, a red shirt underneath his slick coat, a cigar in his gold teeth, a beard round his mouth and a big black gun in his hand. Another darker-skinned man holds an umbrella over their leader's head.

'Officer,' he addresses the man who now has Eva crumpled at his feet and Kasper's hair in his big fist. He slowly releases Kasper who sinks down on his knees to hook his arms around Eva's neck and shoulders.

'What? Who are you...?'

'No matter who we are, *Sir*. You are the ones who are lost. You're in the forest now. Let's see if you can find your way out before the devil catches up with you.'

The officer's eyes widen in recognition of his meaning when the ringmaster's gun recoils and the bullet gouges a hole into the officer's right eye. Kasper idly watches the dead officer's cap fall before the heavy corpse crashes back onto a chair. Kasper sees the body fall as if the film in his eyes has slowed to a flickering, near-frozen speed; the man takes minutes to fall; the cap takes hours to sink slowly to the floor.

Eva wakes to Kasper's wide, tear-blurred eyes looking at her, and the moments prior to her collapse rush back into her mind, and she scrambles to Jan. His eyes open slowly at her warmth that cannot reverse the declining temperature he can feel in every nerve ending.

'Where's the princess?' he asks. Jan put his hand up to her face. 'I'm sorry I couldn't give you the life you wanted. I was too long in the forest.' Eva squeezes his hand. 'I should have been here with you.'

'There is no need.'

She holds Jan's cold head against her chest and feels Kasper against her and moves her arm around his shoulder.

'I'm sorry I was never here.'

'You are here.' Her other side is warm.

The commotion around them is ebbing away; the soldiers have all got their hands on their heads though they continue to spit and shout at the circus folk. Eva's aware of the other soldier's corpse leaning against the kitchen post. She cannot bear to look at him, and she holds Kasper's hand in the lap of her skirts, billowed around her like a flower.

'You are here now.'

The partisans move through the house, pacifying and tying up their prisoners, and discuss among themselves as to who to communicate with: the dying, bloodied man, the tearful woman or the bruised boy. The man with the gold teeth and cigar decides to get the doctor up to the house to see if Jan's last moments can be made less painful, but he seems pretty far gone already, gazing up at Eva like a saint undergoing his martyrdom, his eyes shining strangely. He was speaking before though, speaking words the carnival man can't hear.

Eva holds Jan's head in the skirts of her lap. Tears fall on his face, moistening his beard.

I have to go for my walk...

His hand moves to her face to try and wipe some of the tears that have salted her cheeks and blackened strands of her hair. Eva cannot hold him tightly enough. She would give anything – her own life – to take the bullet from his belly and hold him tight. If she holds him tight enough, maybe that will keep him in this life. Eva's mind plays the scenes back to her. All the splendour of heaven and the soft hand of Christ is nothing to having Jan here. Eva turns to Kasper and tells him – surprised by the calm solidity of her own voice – to go find Madeleine and Sylvester.

Kasper gets up and walks slowly, automatically, through the circus people fanning through the house, tying up the soldiers who shout and push each other. Kasper walks as he does when Eva wakes him too early and every mental function is devoted to putting one foot in front of the other, shivering in the mornings when it's still dark outside, the frost glowing blue, breath in damp white clouds. Outside the rain is still falling, though the thunder and lightning have passed, and Kasper sees Sylvester running towards him, slowing as he sees all the people still circulating around the house and garden. Kasper has never seen him with this expression and Sylvester doesn't say anything, but he is shaking and pulls Kasper by the shirt, with some strength, Kasper realises. He cannot resist and cannot speak either and goes with Sylvester up the hill and down into the meadows of flowers. He takes in the sight of a body, supine on the ground, and even in the darkness Kasper can see it's Madeleine. Her eyes are closed.

'What happened?'

Sylvester doesn't answer, looking at Madeleine and crying. Kasper picks her up, unsteadily, and feels she is hot and almost lets her fall. As he heaves Madeleine up, he almost falls on the muddy ground, and as he stumbles uncertainly closer to the light of the house, Madeleine's features become clearer and the changes wrought upon them become clearer.

Kasper's losing his breath; Madeleine moans. She's alive. Kasper doesn't notice the small army of circus hands leading their prisoners out the back of the house. The light from the house creeps across Madeleine's face, her scorched and smoking clothes, her bleeding, blackened gums and cracked teeth, her blackened fingernails and smouldering hair. Hair which, apart from a few brown strands here and there, is now silver, hair that is matted with the blood streaming from her scalp. He pushes into the house, and some of the women begin to take notice but gasp when they see Madeleine's smoking body. Kasper feels her incredible heat beginning to make his chest feel as if it will catch fire. He thinks what must it be to make the circus freaks be startled by what they see?

'Don't just stand there, help us,' he snarls at them. He pushes his way up the stairs, sweating freely, past the circus hands and their Alsatian dogs descending from securing the first floor and attic, past the doctor, who is accompanied by two or one nurses – Siamese twins, joined at the hip, four hip bones but one pubic bone. Kasper kicks open the door of the closest bedroom – Madeleine's.

The doctor tells two of the circus hands to right the table and to lift Jan upon it.

Kasper sets Madeleine down as gently as he can on her bed, his balance giving way at the last second.

The doctor and the two men all lift Jan onto the table. Eva moves towards him, her hands searching for his hands.

Kasper falls onto Madeleine's stomach, the red-hot flesh.

The doctor cannot find the bullet; he thinks it has probably pierced the appendix – if this man has his – and the gall bladder, and is lodged in the liver, spilling out toxins and deoxygenated blood uncontrollably into the abdomen, spreading infection, triggering septicaemia.

Kasper struggles to maintain his balance and Madeleine starts to writhe fiercely. Some of the women have come up behind Kasper with towels and lamps. Madeleine is upright, her hands over her scorched clothes, unable to touch her blistered,

red-hot skin, and screams so that Kasper falls over, tripping over the carpet in fright. The women freeze, their lights not yet revealing Madeleine and now unwilling to move closer to the screaming darkness.

The doctor hears the scream. He instructs his nurses to clean the wound knowing Jan is minutes away from death. He cannot look at Eva as he runs up the stairs as fast as possible. Madeleine is unconscious. The doctor pushing the women in front of him sees Madeleine's burned face and gasps too; he turns to Kasper.

'What has happened to her?'

Kasper finds he can't speak and stays sitting on the floor, shaking his head.

'The lightning,' Sylvester squeaks from the doorway.

'Christ on the cross, by lightning! And she lives!' To the women: 'Soak those towels in cold water, bring as much cold water as possible up here and be sure to keep bringing it to her.'

The doctor's heart beats fast, spirit revitalised at the prospect of being able to save at least one life tonight. His initial excitement at being able to relate this story over the fire palls as he remembers the other life ebbing away downstairs, the man's blood saturating the wood. He leaves the room to return to the man on the table. The women begin to dab Madeleine's body with cold water and cold cloths. Kasper and Sylvester watch—open-mouthed and blank-faced—the deft locomotion and agility of the Siamese nurses. Then they are ushered out of the room and go downstairs to stand with Eva. They see Jan on the table. The doctor standing opposite Eva. Neither of them say anything. Kasper can't remember a time when the kitchen was lit up like it is tonight. Then a gunshot makes Kasper and Sylvester jump; Sylvester squeals in alarm.

'What...?' Kasper moves towards Eva; neither she nor the doctor move.

Another gunshot and Sylvester jumps a second time. Kasper looks around at the faces of the circus hands, seemingly not hearing anything, and realises this is the end of their dealings with the soldiers. Three more and Kasper clasps tight to his mother, tears coming down his cheeks, crying for the first time without a care as to who sees, once the last gunshot has faded away.

The doctor tells Eva: 'You will need to show us suitable ground for graves. They will... all need to be buried as soon as possible.'

The doctor moves out to the back garden, knowing how sometimes death can be presumed. On the way out, his eyes fall upon Sylvester for the first time.

'My boy,' the doctor wipes the blood from his hands, 'pleased to meet you. My name is Doctor Andrei.'

Empire of Trees

Eva leaves by the back door to show the carnival hands a spot by the tree out of sight from the house where the soldiers can be buried. She watches their corpses unceremoniously bundled by the circus hands towards the trees, their bodies curving with their dead weight to the earth like bows as they are held by their arms and feet. Eva feels no pity but wonders why they give away their lives so freely for nothing. How little meaning there is in death, even for those who die for a cause in the hope that it will flare up like a torch in the dark universe as a sign to others. They cannot know the darkness of the forest is so large it makes their deaths all but invisible and their deaths are as if they had never happened. They, like everyone else in this war, should not have died, but these soldiers – these soldiers – will rot piece by piece in hell just as surely as Jan is dead.

Eva is startled by the ringmaster, who bows deeply, removing his hat, and says: 'My dear woman, allow me to express the most profound condolences for your most grievous loss.'

Eva smiles weakly. She notices two small gold hoops gleaming in his ears. It takes a moment for her to realise that she owes her life – as well as that of the children – to this man and his band.

'Thank you. And thank you Mr... – for saving our lives.'

'Blaze. Mr Cinders Blaze. Owner, proprietor and baptiser of the Cinders Blaze Circus. And it is to my eternal regret and deep sorrow that we did not arrive in time to prevent the death of your dear husband.'

Eva's opinion of the travelling gypsies, not one she dwelled on, was largely formed by her parents' unforgiving standards of those held to be different, outside of social bonds and beyond the love of even God and Christ. Eva can see a dark tiredness around this man's eyes and doesn't know if it is tiredness that gnaws every bone within her, but she can see the deep sorrow and hardness in his eyes. A soldier's face.

'You are carnival? You are of the road?'

'My dear...?'

'Eva.'

'My dear Eva. There were dark times. We are a circus, as you say, from Romania. The war forces new circumstances upon everyone, and thus, like everyone else, we too were forced to adopt a new role. We were entertainers once! But now, now we are partisans – we entertain only the possibility of death!'

Seeing his theatrical explanation is having little effect on Eva, this new widow, he continues in a more subdued and prosaic manner: 'Initially we fought against the Romanian puppet government, the traitor Bulgarian and Polish militia and, of course, the most monstrous force of all, the Nazi Germans. For a long time we were able to operate under the guise of a circus but it was only a matter of time before they linked the sabotage and assassinations that happened in the town we were in to us. Then they marked us and started to hit back and we started losing people. Partisans would join us, but some of them were traitors, in the service of the fascist dogs. Rogue fighters and officers from free Greek and Albanian governments helped us, as far as they were able, then even the British and French began to take an interest.'

He lights Eva's cigarette and she exhales, her head tilted back.

'Not that they were able to find us easily. But we convinced them we were credible and no less effective, and with arms and money we were able to continue the struggle. We claim victory with heavy hearts. It must seem, to you too, that a victory is indistinguishable from defeat.'

'These times are dark still, they cannot get any darker. How can you talk of victory? And your language is all in the past. Why do you pretend this... apocalypse is over?'

'I know. Losses such as yours must make any victory seem strange,' his eyes turn to the sky as if searching for his muse, 'as if we were a scarecrow bent over a field of ashes. Nonetheless we are grateful the struggle is ending.'

'Ending? What are you talking about?'

'The war. The war is...' His eyes meet hers – the tiredness gone for an instant as they widen in a triumphant golden gaze – 'finished.'

Unable to support any more news, anything else the world can throw at her, she nearly falls against him.

'My God. You didn't know?'

'When?'

'Nearly three months ago now. My God – you didn't know? The Germans surrendered in May. The Russians annihilated them. And ground Berlin into dust. With our help of course.' He nearly bows but restrains himself.

Eva rights herself away from Cinders Blaze. She looks away, to the trees, and then walks back inside, walking upstairs among the bustling women into Madeleine's room.

Cinders Blaze motions to the foreman to set up a camp in the back garden and relights his cigar. The trucks rumble up to the front of the house and the horse-drawn caravans follow, the horses tied up and given feed and water.

Eva watches Madeleine asleep on the bed. The sheets seem almost to be giving off steam but Eva can't tell if this is just her tiredness. Red scars are developing on her forehead. She places her hand on her hot skin and kisses her forehead.

'Goodnight Madeleine, I don't know if you are the luckiest or unluckiest girl in the world.'

Eva tells Kasper and Sylvester to go to bed and enters her own bedroom. She strips the sheets from the bed and walks downstairs to the kitchen table where the circus folk are standing around drinking tea and vodka and smoking. Their chatter stops as she descends and they put down their drinks, extinguish their cigarettes and help Eva wrap Jan in the sheets. The doctor comes to Eva to examine the back of her head, and as she sits by the head of the table she lets him clean the cut caused by the officer's gun. She counts the rosary in her hand and tells the circus hands to extinguish all the oil lamps. They do so, and Eva starts to sing lullabies her mother sang to her. Those among the circus folk who know the songs join in and they sing, on and off, until the morning breaks, a few hours later.

The sky glimmers white and golden at the edge of the horizon. Some of the circus hands begin to extinguish the candles and their cigarettes, and six of them each take a position around the table and at a nod from Eva lift Jan's shrouded body onto their shoulders. Kasper and Sylvester are being held by Eva, one of her hands on each of their chests. The bearers move out of the door and through the caravans, past Cinders Blaze, his hat in his hands, up to the hill through the lilacs, foxgloves, daisies, cornflowers, narcissi and forget-me-nots shining bright in anticipation of the sunlight. Eva and the two boys follow them and Cinders and Andrei follow them, succeeded in turn by the company. They reach the bier that was constructed by the hands during the night.

Cinders Blaze turns to Eva as her husband's body is laid down. 'I am sorry we do not travel with a priest. We felt God no longer travelled with us, for a time. Please, say the rites that must be said.'

Eva says nothing, but releasing the boys from her grasp walks to the bier and uncovers Jan's face and takes it in her hands and kisses his mouth, slowly and as long as she might have done when the lips were warm and working with blood and the nerve ends were hot to her touch. She nestles his pipe between the sheets, lays lilies and forget-me-nots on Jan's chest, and Eva covers his face again and walks back to Kasper and Sylvester. Cinders Blaze waits for her nod before the torch-bearing dwarves move to ignite the wood, moving back nimbly as the petrol accelerants lacing the branches run with flames. The flames take hold and burn bright and high, almost translucent in the growing sunlight. The sound of wood burning and cracking cannot conceal the sound of roaring animals that breaks out every so often.

Once the body and wood has been reduced to a small pile of smouldering branches they all slowly process back to the house. Eva goes to the stove to start making tea. Cinders Blaze, the doctor and the bearded woman join Eva at the table, having finally persuaded her to leave the stove and let the circus hands deal with tidying, cleaning and tea making.

Blaze begins, looking at his strong black tea: 'We have been in this area for seven days, trailing this particular unit. We thought there were more of them actually. They are soldiers who are still lost, returning to Germany, returning to Russia, some of them still fighting a war that is finished. Would that we arrived at your house sooner. A few days ago we had to rapidly change our direction of travel because of fires.' The expected question from Eva does not materialise. 'The Russians, we found out, have been setting fire to the forest to flush out the Germans, as the Germans did at the beginning, to push the partisans into the marshes.'

The earth burns.

The first time she has thought about Tereza. Eva smiles, briefly, which surprises them all.

'Mr Blaze, you do own the tiger?'

'Gabriel? Yes. Why?'

'Nothing, he's a beautiful animal.'

They remain silent.

'You must stay for as long as you wish, of course.'

'Thank you, but sadly the war lingers in these woods. There are still bastards like those who came to your house to be put down.'

'Many things linger in this forest. The trees keep things hidden,' Eva says, still looking at the trees. 'Anything my children and I can do to help?'

Blaze and the doctor look at each other. 'There is – permit me – one question I would ask?'

Eva leaves the table, her arms folded under her breasts, walking up the stairs to find Kasper and Sylvester, leaning against the chest of drawers watching the circus women tend to Madeleine's burned skin. Eva beckons to Sylvester, who looks as surprised as if she had raised her shirt, and after Eva almost has to take him by his pointed ear, he follows her out of the door.

Kasper starts to follow them too until Eva says: 'No – stay here. Stay here and watch over Madeleine. I want there to be someone she knows when she wakes.'

Eva and Sylvester go downstairs to the table and the smiles of Cinders Blaze and the woman with the hairy face: 'Hello sweetheart,' she says, though Eva thinks it is almost with a leer.

The woman who introduces herself as Maria moves to stroke Sylvester's pale, pink forehead until Eva intercepts and says: 'His skin is tender and it cannot be touched, even lightly.'

She gestures brusquely to Sylvester to sit, and Blaze begins by leaning over and quickly, before Eva can do anything, pulls a golden coin, so shiny it's as if it has fallen from the sun, from behind Sylvester's ear.

'My boy, come with us and you will receive one of these every month.' He flicks the coin onto the table before Sylvester, where it spins in a blurred golden globe before pirouetting and tottering over to become silent.

'I've never had money before,' Sylvester says, awestruck.

'You've never needed it,' Eva replies for him. 'You do not need to bribe him, what will he do with money? This is not what we discussed – you will be able to take care of him?'

'I was just coming to that,' Blaze said. Grinning to reveal his gold teeth, he asks Sylvester: 'Have you ever wanted to see,' gesturing his arms in a circle, 'the world?' Sylvester's eyes begin to shine.

'Yes.'

'My dear boy,' the doctor began. 'You will see the world and you will see it with us – those who are like you – who understand you.'

'Madeleine and Kasper understand me. They're my friends. We wrote our names on the tree.'

'Of course they are,' the doctor says, 'and they will always be your friends. True friendship is never diminished by distance or absence. But have you ever thought to yourself, my boy, that you are different? Would you like to be the same as everyone else, where everyone is different so that no one is different – with us you will become respected, admired and protected.'

'Will we see the sea?'

'Yes, we will see the oceans, different shores. We may even travel on great ships.'

'It will be a relief to exit this never-ending forest,' Blaze says, addressing the inner lining of coat from where he retrieves a cigar from its glistening silver tin.

'If I may...' Eva leans over to take the cigar, bites the end and, after holding out her hand for a lighter, she settles back exhaling languorously.

Blaze smiles, another cigar for himself in his hand. 'Well, it is a pleasure to meet a woman who appreciates a fine cigar. These beauties are from Azerbaijan, the finest on this continent. Must be a while since you've had a cigar?'

'I find death gives me an appetite for smoking. He used to smoke and I always used to scold him, now he's turned to smoke himself.' Eva's eyes begin to water. 'It's the smoke,' she says. 'You had better leave too before the forest claims you.' She stands and moves to the back door.

The doctor moves to comfort her and takes her hand. 'Your husband has gone to the air of this world. As he was part of the world, he has gone back to it and that means he is not gone.'

'I used to wait for him to come home, listening to the wind in the trees, like sand on paper, and I even began to enjoy waiting for him because the joy each time he came back out of the trees I felt was not of this world.'

Kasper and Sylvester idly walk towards the trees, passing the freshly dug graves embracing the soldiers. Sylvester wants to show Kasper the tiger, but as soon as they pass the first caravan a tall, slim man splits off from the shadows to block their path. He holds his machine gun casually. His skin, like most of the other hands, is a rust-coloured brown and he has three stars tattooed on his neck. Underneath his cap his deep green-blue eyes search them both and settle on Sylvester.

'So it's you,' he says.

They can barely understand him, his Polish is broken and static. They see his eyes are lined underneath by deep crescents of soft purple flesh.

'What are your tattoos?' Kasper asks.

'The number of men I have killed. There is no more room on my shoulder and arm.' He turns to Sylvester: 'Take off your cap.'

Sylvester duly does so, revealing his pointed ears and tight curly knot of blonde hair.

'Aryan pig,' the man says and whistles.

Sylvester looks down, blushing. Several more men emerge from the shadows – all eyes targeted on Sylvester – and they laugh and point in an unfamiliar language. All with something to say.

'He's not a pig,' Kasper almost whispers, 'he's a boy...'

'What?' The man cups his ear, smiling, and his teeth are broken, black and golden. 'What did you say?'

'We want to see the tiger,' Sylvester offers, to a chorus of laughter from the men, another of whom, Kasper sees, has the strap of a machine gun on his shoulder.

'You will. But not now. He's busy.' Another burst of laughter, as if from a machine gun, from behind him punctuates the end of his assertion – 'When he gets hungry.'

His smile drops and jabs the tip of the barrel into Kasper's chest, pushing him backwards.

'The tiger will see you later. Now – go.'

Kasper grabs Sylvester's arm, making Sylvester squeak in discomfort, and they move backwards, away from the men, when they hear a shout and all the men look up to see Maria swiftly approaching. Her perfume washes over Kasper and Sylvester and she smiles at them and tells them to get back to the house. Her eyes are dark-brown, but Sylvester and Kasper are transfixed by her bosom and the stars that appear on it.

'Now,' she orders. And they run back to the house.

Madeleine stirs and moans under the sheet. She opens her eyes and sees the woman. They look at each other and Madeleine says: 'I remember.'

'What?'

'I remember,' Madeleine repeats, 'everything.'

Then she is silent. And stays silent.

The woman leaves the room. She goes downstairs to tell Eva that Madeleine has awoken.

Departure

The next morning, Eva wakes to check Sylvester's packing is going well and quickly, because he does not have many – or indeed any – possessions. She has found as many of Kasper's old clothes as she could and a comb and a copy of the Bible. She helps the circus women cook breakfast and make tea for the company and the hands of the circus. She eats with Kasper and Sylvester, the doctor, Maria and Cinders Blaze as they describe all the personalities in their troupe to Sylvester. Afterwards, she makes a breakfast for Madeleine.

Sitting by her bed, she tells her of Sylvester's decision and tries to convince herself as well as Madeleine that the circus is the best place for him.

'Your hair is beautiful,' Eva says, stroking it.

'I haven't got used to it yet. I look like I'm from another planet,' she says, running her finger down the red scars on her forehead, thinking of Tereza.

'I'm sorry I missed the cremation.'

'You have nothing to apologise for. You were hardly well enough.'

'I didn't see him.' She puts her hands to her face. 'I didn't say goodbye.' And Madeleine sobs into Eva's red dress, her warm breast.

'Godspeed Mr Blaze. May you reach the ocean soon and kill as many soldiers as you can before you get lost in the forest.'

Blaze surveys the tree line. 'We are from Romania where there is no lack of trees, but this forest is – it's... it's different. It seems to go on forever.'

'It's full of monsters.'

'May we avoid them.'

'You will – for a time. Every man, woman and child has their own monster waiting for them. But sometimes their monsters grow impatient.'

Growing unnerved by Eva's metaphysical fatalism, Cinders Blaze motions to his head foreman to order that they expedite final preparations for departure. Eva finishes her cigarette and exhales the cloud of smoke into the hot summer air. She turns back into the house and goes upstairs to where Madeleine is awake, Sylvester and Kasper having brought her tea and bread. Madeleine smiles as Eva walks in and sits on her bed.

Unprompted, she tells Eva: 'My name is Sybille. I was on a train. It was dark and crowded, going to Germany. Leaving Belgium. With my father and mother and sister. We had been on the train for hours and hours. Such a long time. I remember the first explosion. It ripped the carriage open. I saw the night sky and the stars for a second. Then there was a second explosion. And I woke up in the forest.'

'Now you remember. What will you do?'

'I must go home. The war is over.'

Kasper looks out of the window. Eva strokes Sybille's silver hair, her skin back at its normal temperature.

'How will you do that, your home is far away?'

'Come with us, come with the circus,' Sylvester excitedly squeaks.

'No, thank you.' Sybille smiles at him. 'You are going north. I must go west to Belgium.'

'Then you must go to the village first. Mr Blaze tells me the Red Cross have set up a reception area for refugees. From there they will take you to Krakow to be processed.'

'Kasper,' Eva says, 'you will take Madeleine – excuse me, Sybille – to the village.' Kasper, still by the window, nods, his head lowered, and makes an odd noise, followed by some coughs, and strides out of the room hiding his face. They watch him leave and Eva and Sybille look at each other but can't think of exactly what to say to each other about Kasper.

'Is he alright? I mean – the soldiers didn't hurt him?'

'I think he's fine. I hope he will be.' Eva rises. 'You just work on healing. I want you to come down and say goodbye to Sylvester.'

'They're leaving today? So soon?'

'Yes.'

As if to confirm Eva's assertion, they hear some of the circus trucks starting their engines, and some of them start pulling away, through the meadows, over the hill and into the trails that cut into the heart of the forest.

The caravans are beginning to pull away now, the horses sluggish and bad-tempered after a day lazing in the meadows. The caravans that have already departed – thin plumes of grey smoke drifting into the air from their stoves warming up for cooking dinners – make their black silhouettes on the brow of the hill, like ships slowly, slowly dipping into the waves. Sylvester watches them, hypnotised. Cinders Blaze and Maria are talking to Eva, telling her Sylvester will travel with them in their truck initially before he earns his own space in the minor attractions. Now the war is over there will be more opportunity to make people laugh and forget their troubles again.

'It is strange to have to relearn the things for which we are naturally inclined. Yet war is a perversion of our human nature, so in some respects my travelling company are well suited to this great perversion. We have been called far worse than perverts,' Cinders Blaze ruminates almost to the sky itself, holding his cigar.

Eva doesn't smile. 'So has Sylvester. I hope you will not be using that kind of language around him nor introducing such concepts into his mind. He has been through a lot... with his mother.'

'Worry not, my dear,' Cinders Blaze responds, in the breezily condescending and slick way in which his showman routine has infected his daily interactions and which was beginning to grate on Eva. 'For who are perverts but those who have the courage to acknowledge and then transcend those aspects of their selves which make them different. My family's long line of gifted psychics were persecuted under the Transylvanian kings long before the devil Ottomans came to—'

Maria cut him short, registering Eva's darkening looks, telling her this talk of perversion will stop, and at that she gestures Cinders Blaze to leave.

'Is he really psychic?' Eva asks.

As he leaves, Kasper and Sybille come out from the door and Maria offers them all cigarettes. Only Sylvester refuses.

'It is his mother who possesses that gift, or is possessed by that gift – one cannot rightly say which is true. Especially when she is shrieking blindly into the night, in her tattered white dress upright in bed in her purple-walled caravan.'

Sylvester moves closer and closer to Eva, still looking up at the caravans, like lumbering beasts in the sunset, the sky bleeding the last of its light into the long thin gash of the horizon. Layers of light striate the expanses of sky sinking fast over the fat orange-golden disappearing circle of the sun, a bloody eye.

'And so the sun shows its arse to us every night,' Maria says, making all three children giggle, and leaving Eva to exhale directly into her face.

'What did I just say?'

'My apologies,' Maria says, unflinching under Eva's severe stare. 'You must appreciate this war has been difficult for us, as it has for everyone else. Life on the road following some old woman's visions of where the soldiers are hiding in the forest is not easy – it has been far from easy these last five years. You will understand and forgive a little ribald comment.'

Eva is distracted by Sylvester's increasing pressure on her legs; she feels his little head rest on her ribs. She rests her hand on his head and realises he's crying. Sybille moves closer to him as well, putting her hand around his shoulder.

'What's the matter my dear?' Eva asks.

Sylvester's tears shine brightly in the dying sunlight.

'I don't want to... I want to stay with you and Sybille and Kasper.'

Eva crouches down and tells him: 'Think of all that you'll see: the oceans, great cities... You must leave, because how else will you come back and tell Kasper and me all about these great things and fantastic places you've seen?'

Sylvester's face straightens a little. 'I can come back?'

'Yes Sylvester, of course. Kasper will miss you, isn't that right?'

Kasper says: 'I wish I could go with you.' And then twists Sylvester's little cap, 'You'll become famous. Rich and famous...'

Sybille too crouches down and hands him the pendant Eva gave to her, of the Holy Virgin.

'Keep this and think of me. Always keep it with you and that way we'll be travelling together.'

Sylvester opens it and says: 'She looks like you, beautiful and sad.'

'My hair's a little different now, but thank you.'

Eva holds him close. 'Go now. The world is waiting for you Sylvester. Go about it and remember your family here.'

Eva gestures to Maria as Sylvester hugs Sybille for what seems like forever and then awkwardly takes Kasper's hand, and Kasper says nothing even though he seems as though he's about to. They watch as Maria takes him off to the truck, a bright purple and gold sign alongside it – *Cinders Blaze Circus*. Sylvester keeps his eyes locked on them continuously and waves and waves until he is gone.

'Oh God, I hope he survives,' Eva says, without turning to Kasper and Sybille to explain herself. They both remain silent and glumly stare at the horizon. 'Those trucks are like coffins.'

'He'll be back.' Kasper tries to be as reassuring as he is able to be.

And Sybille sees the trees. The trees growing black and blurred in the darkness.

Kasper's hand tentatively presses on his mother's back, and Sybille sees the trees. For the first time they seem to be calling to her, a susurrus of the wind playing over the leaves, and as Sybille sees them, the trees seem to be looking back at her.

The Walk in the Forest

Sybille is lying in bed. The sheets still feel sharp against her skin that is still tender. Her mind is burning with a fever of memory – too much light; her whole life has opened up to her again. Seventeen years fully visible, as if a blindfold had been removed. And she cannot get out of bed to face it. Her family – her mother, father, sister – who spoke the same language as she, who physically resembled her and who christened her – came back to her at the same instant at which they died. Sybille's first memory – as insubstantial as a snow flake – of lying in her crib as her mother looked at her and then left the room, turning out the light. A little mobile hung suspended in darkness; shooting stars and unicorns made of tin. The mobile spins round, shuttering the light off and on until it reveals the source of light behind its blur; the naked light bulb in the train carriage. Her new-old life has disappeared forever.

Looking across the room to the mirror she can see herself in it, wrapped in a sheet, and she also sees, unclearly and distantly in the glass, a family portrait of her mother and father and sister. Her father with his usual stern expression; her mother, temperamental but kind and generous, maybe like Eva had been once; her younger sister, painfully shy, crying all the time, crying as they were loaded onto the train.

When Sybille was fourteen she was cycling along the canal with her in the sunshine. She remembers stealing some make-up – forbidden to her – from her mother's purse and blaming her sister. Their mother lost her temper and slapped her, then felt so guilty she took them both out for ice cream that evening.

Her sister, dead a few days after her fourteenth birthday. She soon fell asleep during the long hours in the dark cargo wagons; how many hours did they travel? They knew some of their neighbours and found them on the same carriage – uncomfortable on the straw across the hard wooden floor – and tried to stay close and keep each other's spirits up under the relentless light of the solitary bulb, her father saying they would all be fine as long as they stayed together. They would simply be put to work, and as long as they kept their heads down and did not attract attention they would be fine and come through it. In the carriage they were talking when they thought the deafening noise and violent motion meant the train had struck something and been derailed. The pails of water in the corner threw their contents over everything.

But as she looks at herself in the mirror she knows her memories belong to someone else; they are not hers anymore. She woke up in the forest. Sybille is dead. Madeleine is dead. The lightning has left marks as a trace of its fierce grasp down and along her body. The vivid crimson of the marks is fading, fading to a colour that reminds Sybille of the crow's blood on her skin. The lightning has gouged its fierce embrace around her neck; the chain and pendant are now permanently etched onto her skin. Her collarbones and her ribs almost form the shape of a great red hand holding her. Or a butcher's diagram.

She drapes a sheet over the mirror and leaves her room, walking slowly and painfully, her clothes rubbing against her skin. Kasper is looking at the bed he was making for Sylvester; his room will never be shared. He doesn't believe Sybille that

Sylvester will be back. He will finish making the bed and sell it to a family in the village.

Eva is sitting in a chair by the back of the house, shaded from the rising sun, smoking her first cigarette of the day. Sybille makes some tea for them both and smokes her first cigarette while Eva has her second.

They both stare at the cloudless blue sky.

Later, Eva, with Kasper's help, makes a lotion for Sybille's skin. To take the heat out of it.

'When will you leave?'

'Today... later today.'

'No point in waiting around.'

Sybille doesn't know what to say. It never occurred to her that she was abandoning Eva, losing three people in such a short time. It never occurred to her that maybe Eva would want her to stay. Sybille tries to think how Jacob or Ruth or Esther would have behaved in this situation. She was always thinking of these names, as if they were real people — Eva seems to think they had been — like they were wandering around in this forest too.

It made her feel a part of this world, part of this world in which they had said 'Yes' to God. She hadn't. Not yet. She said 'Yes' to the Forest. To the trees that had protected her and to her new parents who had found her, sheltered her. Was this what she had been looking for? Was it still somewhere else? How could she ever know? It would help, she considered, if suddenly one of the trees in the forest would burst into flames. That would be a sure sign. But a sign of what?

'Let's go upstairs and see what you can take with you.'

'I want to take a gun,' Sybille says.

'Yes, you can take a gun.'

Eva extinguishes her cigarette underfoot. They both go into the dining room and upstairs.

Later, Sybille walks out into the heavy, hot air and towards the workshop. She peers through the large door into the cool gloom but becomes aware of Kasper sitting down on a stump eating an apple. He gets up and walks past Sybille inside.

'So you're leaving today?'

'Yes.' The closer it gets to leaving and the more she says she is leaving, the more awkward and uncomfortable Sybille feels.

'Do you have to leave?' Kasper puts the apple core, already turning brown, on one of the benches. He doesn't look at her.

'Yes.'

Kasper, almost as dark as a shadow, moves to one of the dark corners and brings back something Sybille can't make out clearly. She sees it's a gun.

'What's that for, Kasper?'

Kasper looks at it for a few seconds and then gives it to Sybille. 'It used to belong to... my father. He wanted you to have it.'

'Thank you.'

'When will you leave?'

'Soon, to be at the village and Red Cross centre by tonight.'

Sybille finds herself unable to look at Kasper's face and instead intently studies the rifle. She walks out back into the sunlight, unable to bear the silence any longer.

She sees something engraved on the wooden part, in her own language: *Not one sparrow is forgotten by God. Even the hairs on your head have all been counted. So do not be afraid. J.*

Walking back into the house she sees Eva preparing some vegetables.

'We can eat before you leave. We can have your favourite – ham and beetroot.'

Sybille can never remember telling Eva that these were ever her favourite foods, either on their own or in an alchemical combination in the superlative Polish cuisine. The thought of staying and eating in silence with the both of them is the last thing Sybille wants to do. She tells Eva she will get her bag from upstairs and that she should be leaving. Eva doesn't say anything, but nods, picks up one plate, and continues to lay out the food on the two remaining plates.

Kasper watches Eva prepare Madeleine some food. He has never thought that she would want to leave. Something else occurs to him.

I will never see you again.

He watches them talk, unaware of Eva asking Sybille what she remembers of her family. Then Eva hands Sybille a parcel of food and another bag of clothes and a hairbrush, a small mirror and toothbrush to take with her. Sybille then sees Kasper looking at them and motions to him to come over. Kasper looks at her, flushed with hatred for a second, before shaking it from his head and moving over to Sybille, unable to say anything as they stand as awkwardly as the day they first met.

'Goodbye, Kasper. Dear Kasper. I will miss you.'

Sybille is unsure whether to take Kasper's hand or kiss him on the cheek or...

'Let me walk with you to the village, at least. I'll walk with you.'

Sybille sees his eyes searching as she never has before. Maybe, once before. Tears come to her eyes as she can remember Kasper picking her up in the field, flowers falling around them. His forceful hug as he bundled her up and her scream scratching furiously in her head, her mouth full of blood, and even the inside of her throat, swollen with heat; her hair was still smouldering, her clothes still raw with fire. Blurry memories of his face come back to her, only as clear as photographs torn into pieces; there is nothing complete to be seen.

'Good luck, Sybille,' Eva says. 'May you find your kin in the town you were born.'

Sybille smiles, as much as she is able to. 'Thank you.'

'Sybille doesn't suit you, I can't get used to it. Goodbye, Madeleine, may the saints watch over you.' Eva embraces her hard, and it seems to be squeezing tears from her.

Sybille understands Eva's wish for Sylvester to leave quickly, before… before preventing him from leaving altogether. They separate. And Sybille moves to go. And she stops. Looking back at Kasper, who's looking at her and who will stay looking at her until the trees close behind her back like the curtains at the end of a play. She tugs the strap of the rifle over her shoulder, fingering the grooves of the inscription Jan made and says goodbye.

She walks into the flowers, into the sunlight. The form of her back soon becomes indistinguishable among the crooked, shielding lines of the trees.

He sees her, a mesh of shadows and angles dressed like him, straps across her chest, her hair tied in a bun at the back, strands falling down the side of her temples, a gun over her left shoulder and the dark blood-red marks on her face.

Sybille walks into the trees, watching them grow larger and taller as she moves closer to them and under them like an embrace. She listens to the trees that sing to her. She follows the stream that flows away from the village and flows like an artery into the heart of the forest. She continues walking through the large tongues of ferns that brush her legs.

The forest feels different now, now's she left the house. The wind whispers through the trees, softly, rustling through her head starting up a melody she can pick up and starts to sing. Where did this song come from? Sybille can't remember hearing any music in the house; she and her sister played the piano in her life at home, but neither of them played this simple piece, like a nocturne. It hums and flows from her memory to her mouth and she sings the melody as the trees pass her by. Behind some of the trees she catches glimpses of her father, his body stretched out, her mother and her sister, their bodies lying as if asleep, arms bending back over roots, pale hands and fingers through the leaves of the ferns. Sybille wishes more than anything that Kasper or Sylvester or even Eva were with her, beside her in the face of what the forest was showing her, the family she has just abandoned. She sinks down, on one knee, tears on her cheeks, falling onto the ferns and onto the roots and leaves. She sits among the bright green fern leaves, not caring where she is or where she is going; the leaves comfort her in their soft embrace, mindful of her newly sensitive skin.

Across a clearing she sees the mirror, the full-length mirror from her old bedroom between two enormous pine trees; they cast the mirror into shade as if its glass is black. Sybille rises and walks towards it and looks into the dark glass. She pulls down her shirt to reveal her collarbones and the delicate brown-red filigree the lightning has inscribed into her skin; it stretches from her neck, wrapping around her ribs, and trails down her right arm. But the darkness reveals another girl, one who looks like her... Madeleine. The girl from the woods. Madeleine. Sybille. She does recognise them, their hair, their skin, their clean clothes. They are nothing; they do not exist anymore. She is the girl from the forest without a name and without a family and she feels each organ, nerve point and artery flash and run with fire and heat as it did that night the lightning took her. The forest, all the trees, the house, the lost pilot – would it all be the same when she was dead? How long had they been waiting for her to pass through?

Shadows walk beside her through the bright green dunes of the ferns that she cannot identify, but they make her feel safe and she is glad that they are there. The girl looks at the trees as they thin out, beyond the stream and up to the village. The first time she has seen more than two buildings close together. More than three people. And she stops. She looks back at the trees and they lean towards her, the wind whispering its invitation through the soft voice of the leaves, the shade cool and sheltering, lit up by the scattered sunlight, like lanterns hanging from the branches, marking the path into the deep heart of the forest, a path she alone knows, a path that would take her back to her own life. Looking back into the village, she glimpses a tattered white sheet with a large red cross crudely daubed upon it, scores of sheets of paper pasted to the outside walls, making the building appear as if some great feathered monster. A large red cross which is where she knows she has to go. But the red cross looks to her like a great cross of blood. A church for the dead. The church door does not tempt her, to sit about with a card with a number on it and wait to be called, tested for tuberculosis and typhus, then sent to a larger room with a higher number on the card in Krakow. Now the moon crawls over the treetops, fat and golden yellow and as bright as a strange nocturnal sun shining its light over her, the sky, like a giant tapestry pointed with stars. Nights they lay looking up, how far were they seeing? If the world shuddered and disappeared all of a sudden, how far would they fall? Throwing a coin down a well and waiting, waiting, waiting for a noise to spiral upwards from darkness below...

I must leave for my walk in the forest.

Eva had told her the partisans had named her the Tiger Girl. The burn marks on her face, from a certain angle, did have the effect of a tiger's stripes, three broad lines cutting diagonally down from her scalp, tapering off towards the cheekbone on the right side of her face. She holds the gun, her fingers tracing the quotation engraved there by Jan. She hears the trees, for the first time in a long time walking quietly by herself, and she is back among the trees.

They can hear something, a sound almost indistinguishable, as one tree is indistinguishable from the next in the twilight. The trees holding the black-blue light from the sky, rendering them invisible, incoherent. The light from the sky that falls down, broken, between the branches, burns with the glow of its own exhaustion, leaving the forest floor cold and dark. They stop on the path and head instinctively to the side, into the protection of the undergrowth and trees. The second time in one afternoon, they are both aware of the distance between themselves, between themselves and the trees. They keep quiet, breathing in shallow breaths so only the very surfaces of their dark meat-black lungs flare with the bright pink light of oxygen. They check the ground for broken branches that might snap completely if stepped on. They don't startle each other; they continuously scan the trees and the place of the dark figure. Madeleine, for the second time, is less certain it's the Germans or bandits or partisans. No matter who or what it might be, she feels ready, even if Kasper isn't. He hears his name and the movement right behind them: Jan.

His face, his rifle, clutched under his upper arm, looking at them: 'What are you doing here? You might be dead now.'

Unsmiling, he says something to Kasper, who looks ashamed, furious, embarrassed, and looks at Madeleine, for the first time, unsmiling, and she can't bear his expression and looks down at the leaves, looks sideways at Kasper.

'Come here.'

Kasper slowly approaches and Madeleine follows, looking constantly between the two of them, like a bird on the ground, across and up. Jan takes Kasper and holds him, says something soft towards his ears and Kasper replies: 'Sorry.'

Jan ruffles his hair, looks up at Madeleine, his familiar and reassuring warmth in his face. He undoes a flask with a dry, popping sound and gives it to Kasper, who drinks down a flush of vodka. He then passes it to Madeleine who recoils from the dry, strong smell that seems to reach into her mouth and grab at her throat. Jan says: 'Drink a bit,' and Madeleine has a sip and finds it tastes of nothing but the smell, but once it's burned its way into her stomach it sparks a warmth within as if an engine has started to run. The warmth spreads outwards from her belly to her chest and up to her head, making her sight more vivid, her hearing more keen. The colours are brighter, the smells of the forest thicker in her nose.

Jan has another drink and then they walk off, Madeleine asking loudly, the vodka having repressed her self-consciousness in Jan's company: 'Where are we going? Home?'

'Yes,' he replies.

Last Dream

I am watching the boats in the late evening. They ride the dark-blue waters like stars. Towards the darkening skies. Small and wooden, wreathed with forget-me-nots and lilacs around a candle. Petals fall from the little wooden vessels at intervals, leaving a stream upon a stream of flowers, their trail. I remember my mother holding my hand in hers. We are with other girls going to the banks of the river and to watch the girls set their little wooden boats down the stream, the candles in them, lighting their path in the twilight. She doesn't want to set a boat down in the water, but the other girls tease her and give her a candle and give me the lighter with which to light it. The boys, older boys out without their mothers, are racing to the bridge, to grasp the tiny wreaths of flowers the boats are transporting. I watch the boats and candles and start to follow them. Eva and her friends laugh and soon she swoops me up and rubs her nose on mine. 'You stay here with me darling, you're never leaving me.' I giggle because my mother's nose tickles but I look back at the boats. I want to follow the boats into the twilight, their candlelit points drifting away, like fireflies hanging in the darkness, the points of light tracing the trails of their departure.

Ultramarine

Kasper wakes from his dream. He lies on his bed, vision unfocused on the ceiling above. He can remember standing by the side of the river with Eva as if it were yesterday, on that midsummer's night years ago. His vision relaxes and the patterns form rivers and coastlines and a vast ocean to the west. It gives way to mountains and they decline to the vast plains of America. Kasper looks up at the tan skin walls of his tepee, tired from fishing in rivers, tired from hunting bison, and wonders if she would ever leave the forest because she has realised the same thing as he has.

He lies in bed, the room already hot in the late summer heat, but as he looks out of his window he sees the sky is overcast and grey; it has been raining overnight. Memories come in such short flashes, like a photograph in time. He gets up and dresses. He tries to remember as far back as he can; can anyone remember that far back? The first day of their life. Once all the goo has been cleaned off and you've taken milk for the first time and slept, slept a long fat sleep. If only his mind were like a telescope, to peer backwards through the darkness of time to that first point of light, of existence, of life. He can remember the first time he saw Madeleine, looking at him, his heart set to beating at once, the blood rushing at once to his skin, to his face. He could only eat his apple faster and faster like an idiot.

His mind keeps swerving away from himself to Madeleine, like a gun which has a skewed aim, consistently shooting off target.

He walks downstairs and, unusually, doesn't see his mother. It is dispiriting how empty and quiet the house is; he wishes he could unwish all those times he wanted to be master of the house, without being told what to do by his parents. Without Madeleine and Sylvester hanging around. Walking outside, he walks into the heat and light and scours the space between the trees in which Madeleine's body vanished. Staring at it until his vision seems to grow dark at the edges and he has to shut his eyes tight. He looks up again not surprised not to see Madeleine there. Now she is gone, he is sleeping better, there is that. Now Jan is gone he has a lot more work to do to fulfil all the orders from the village. Now Sylvester is gone he has no friends left. He sits on the tree stump and absent-mindedly throws some stones into the dust.

The thought that keeps flapping against his mind, like an insect around a lampshade, is not that he will miss her and not that he wasn't there when they needed him to protect them both from the tiger, but that there is nothing left of her; she may as well have never been here. There is nothing left that shows she was ever here. He gets up and, as he moves to go back into the house, he notices some marks on the ground. A deep stain, irregular and faded in the dust; the back of the house has been churned up by the carnival troupe – it must be oil from the trucks. Kasper sees five more by the far wall. They were executed facing the forest. The marks are distorted broken triangles of lines and circles, a visual echo of the noise that Kasper can still hear in his head. Kasper watches the darkness that rises from the forest, and he shuts his eyes tight and tries to look into the darkness, but all he sees is emptiness. Nothing. Her face? The forest is dark. Madeleine was walking in it. And he follows, all at once, urged by something, to keep walking, to follow her. Follow her. He turns back to see the lights of the house, brighter than day it seemed, and for a minute – or is it longer – he doesn't care if he ever went home again. The dreams he has been having have stopped. He remembers the first one was the night before Madeleine arrived.

There is no sign of Eva and so he starts to make tea and to prepare the meal; they are running out of meat, this is the last of it. He will have to go hunting tomorrow. Once it is prepared, he calls out for Eva but there is no response. Kasper walks slowly and heavily up the stairs, knowing the bad mood that Eva always wakes to after sleeping. As he walks along to her room he can hear something and he opens the door, enough to see Eva, her head on the dresser, the chair kicked aside. The collection of objects that stood before the mirror have been swept away, the mirror cracked. Eva doesn't seem to have heard Kasper enter the room. She stands up suddenly, sees Kasper, her face and the colour of her skin obscured by the darkness of the room, the shutters still closed. She goes to the bed and lies down, curled up, facing the wall.

'Are you... going to eat dinner? I've made some?'

No response. Her voice is tired and slow: 'No... you eat. Have a drink. Have some beer.'

'Are you... sad Madeleine has gone?'

'Who?' Eva replies, sluggishly turning to face Kasper. 'She's gone now. Forget her – she was never here. It's just you.'

Eva turns back, Kasper's eyes having trouble discerning her form clearly, but her hair seems to be bunched up on her in a bun, like Madeleine's used to be.

Kasper quietly shuts the door and, after lighting some candles and placing them on the new kitchen table, sets two places and eats his dinner. He has a small glass of beer as well. Kasper takes the food from the uneaten plate, covers it in salt and wraps it in grease paper, placing it in the pantry.

He rolls a cigarette and smokes it by the door, enjoying the coolness of the twilight on his skin, looking at the dismantled old kitchen table leaning by the workshop, remembers how exhausting it was taking an axe to the table his father died upon. He will burn the pieces. There are photographs that show he existed; nothing remains of Sylvester or Madeleine. Looking up at the trees, Kasper knows there is only one thing that will show Madeleine was here. His mother is wrong, she must be wrong; Madeleine was real and she was here. Kasper finishes his cigarettes and goes back inside to do the washing up. Then he goes to bed. In his room the maps and radio and electronic apparatus have been piled in one corner. He falls asleep and doesn't dream.

The next morning, his rifle on his shoulder, Kasper walks through the forest...

The first time since the end of the war, the first time since Madeleine left, the first time since Sylvester left, the first time since my father...

It is quiet and hot and seems unchanged. But the trees seem strangely lifeless. Kasper thinks of the girl and the picture of her by the tree comes to him and his eyes. He nears the place he thinks it must be near. He wipes the sweat from his brow, drinks some water, scanning the trees, and sees it.

Walking towards the tree he sees the M, the S, and, alongside the two letters, a K. He reaches out to feel the grooves of the M and then can't look at it anymore. Kasper squats down by the tree, his rifle falling off his shoulder and with a light sound onto the grass. The trees are all alike but this one is different – this one is ours.

Where are they both now? Does Madeleine have something missing in her that he could not replace and nor could she? Is it the same feeling that sits heavy and black in his chest and throat now she is gone? It feels like sinking into the abyss in the dark centre of the ocean, the other world of sunlight falling away blurred by brine and the small drifting cargo of the sea. Madeleine's question – 'How deep is the forest?' – her bad Polish rendering the question poetic, her voice in his head as if she were there, as real as the tree he is looking at, as the heat bathing his body. She knows as much as he does that the forest is as deep as the ocean. He looks into the trees, endless trees, disappearing in their own multiplicity; the further into the forest he looks, more and more trees appear to conceal the forest's own infinite space, its hollow heart that rises and grows outwards, endlessly, forever, like the endless depth of the blue sky above it. The forest goes on forever. There is no beginning or end to it. And the questions, one, two, three: *Should I have gone with her? Where should I go? Where do I belong?*

The air is still and choked with dust and pollen and silted by silence. The tree will always be here no matter how far she wanders. To her house? In the west? By a canal? Does her mother look like her? Was she in love with a boy back in her own country? Kasper throws the apple core as far as he can; it disappears with a faint rustle behind some trees. How far can things be thrown, he wonders to himself. *I can follow a trail, he thinks, westwards as far as I can go, to Wrocław, Berlin to Hamburg, Amsterdam to London and then Southampton. Westwards – these maps are memorised – following the sun.*

He remembers going with his mother to the stream, before the war, on midsummer's night to set a small boat with a candle and wreath on it, down the river, watching it until it disappeared. He wanted nothing more than to follow the river, to see it empty itself and dissolve into the cold, bright, black sea. The sea is a clear black mirror showing the bright points of stars scattered over its surface, obscuring the horizon. Over the sea, the ship a shadow on the surface, broken black shadows of the sleeping ships on the ocean floor, sunk in time, ships which threw out their signals far into the black night. Like flares of fire from distant, unseen stars...

CQD – SOS – help us. Although we are lost and deep drowned, we will see what you will never see: the shores of night, the ultramarine kingdoms blue and black and green, deep golden rays of sunlight showing us the way down, backwards into time, where there is no sound, only our confederacy of the forgotten.

The ship will move on, avoiding the waves and dodging the lightning before reaching the far shore. The sun is brighter, more generous in its vivid colour and heat. It warms your face as you sleep on my shoulder. We move further west, past the deep green harbours into the new forests, past the trees, far from the tree that bears our initials on it – the one which is ours. Into the land of the sun, the prairies, the flat, battened lands of long grasses. My horse is behind yours, the baby in front of you, its back by your blood-warm belly with your arm holding our daughter. Her face red with the same marks you drew across mine: three stripes.

Kasper

He has no longer been dreaming, but he has no longer been sleeping. Kasper's head is on the table. Exhausted. He cannot stay here, cannot stay here for much longer. Eva stays still on her bed. It is the sun beyond the sky, the stars beyond the night, the sea beyond the mountains. He must start making what is asked of him; there are many orders from the village. They have started to come back to the village. This house is empty – during the day and all through the night. Eva has started to sleep on the floor, wrapped in sheets, facing the wall; her food must be brought to her room and she eats alone. Kasper looks at the maps now pinned to the walls in his room; the borders will be changing again. His radio is still in pieces on the floor, the wires, panels and dials messily positioned as if in a blast pattern. Through his window he can see the sunset. He turns and opens the door, shutting it behind him. He leaves the room and walks downstairs, counting the stairs, the minutes, days and weeks before the house will disappear behind his back, lost between the trees.

> *What will become of the world when you leave? No matter what happens, no trace of now will remain.*
>
> – Rimbaud

Acknowledgements

Grateful thanks go to Asia, Nancy, Richard, and to Melissa.

About the author

Martin Llewellyn was born in London and grew up in Brussels. He currently lives in Canada. This is his first novel.